CYBORG

Kaitlyn O'Connor

Futuristic Romance

New Concepts   Georgia

Cyborg is an original publication of NCP. This work has never before appeared in book form. This work is a novel. Any similarity to actual persons or events is purely coincidental.

New Concepts Publishing
5202 Humphreys Rd.
Lake Park, GA 31636

ISBN 1-58608-696-0
© copyright 2005 Kaitlyn O'Connor
Cover art by Jenny Dixon, © copyright 2005

NCP books are available at special quantity discounts for bulk purchases for sales promotions, premiums, fund raising, or educational use. For details, write, email, or phone New Concepts Publishing, 5202Humphreys Rd., Lake Park, GA 31636, ncp@newconceptspublishing.com, Ph. 229-257-0367, Fax 229-2i9-1097.

First NCP Paperback Printing: 2005

Printed in the United States of America

Other Titles from NCP by Kaitlyn O'Connor:

The Claiming
Below
Guardian of the Storm
When Night Falls (Now in Trade Paperback)
Abiogenesis (Now in Trade Paperback)
Exiled
The Lion's Woman (Now in Trade Paperback)

Chapter One

"I've got a bad feeling about this mission," Johnson VH571 muttered to no one in particular as the ship began to buck upon entering the atmosphere of the planet below them.

Amaryllis VH600's gut clenched reflexively at the comment. She'd been having bad vibes from the moment she and her partner had joined the mission in progress at the TM20 way station. The Company had indicated that the assignment would be a 'piece of cake', but they had a way of understating most of the operations they sent their hunters out on.

This one stank of disaster waiting to happen and she doubted that she and Johnson were the only ones to think so.

To be completely fair, though, there *were* a number of factors that could account for the sense of impending doom that had nothing to do with precognition or even logical assumptions based on previous operations.

She was a seasoned soldier. She'd been on almost a dozen missions, most of them complete successes, but she still had pre-battle jitters every time she participated in a new operation, and this one promised to be something major, unlike any undertaking she'd taken part in before. That was enough to make her uneasy in and of itself.

Beyond that, the story The Company had cooked up reeked of fabrication, and not just because their main objective was to capture one of their own--if possible--and eliminate her if necessary.

Dalia VH570 was one of their best cyborg hunters. It not only didn't make sense that she'd gone rogue and joined 'the enemy'--why would a human join forces with machines?--but, assuming The Company wasn't lying and she had, why the order to capture her if possible? What made her more important than the rogues themselves, important enough to put together three squads of hunters in such a haphazard, poorly planned mission?

Because misery was almost certainly one of the reasons everyone, including her, was so antsy. Discomfort went with the territory. As a soldier, she'd endured her share of it, but she wasn't accustomed to being packed into a vessel designed for eight with sixteen other hunters like a food cube in a package of vacuum sealed rations.

According to The Company, the break in security had been unanticipated, which explained to an extent why they hadn't had a lot of time for preparations. The cyborgs, who'd either captured Dalia, or snatched her from beneath The Company's nose, were traveling in a short range racer and she supposed it only made sense to launch a chase in similar crafts, built for speed rather than distance and capacity.

Contrary to all logic, however, the cyborgs had gone deep space and they'd had, perforce, to follow or risk losing sight of the quarry all together.

The end result had been three days of very little food, water, or sleep and she, for one, was cranky with the lack of all three. With so many of them packed into one small craft, they'd had to rotate use of the two small cabins the ship boasted--which meant she'd had a grand total of twelve hours rest in the last seventy two hours--and almost nothing to eat or drink since they had no idea of how long the rations would have to last.

There was yet another reason for the sense of impending disaster that had nothing to do with the mission, and he was sitting right beside her, but, as always, Amaryllis did her best not to think about her partner, Reese, if she could help it. As long as she didn't think about *why* he could spell disaster for her, she figured she had a better chance of not falling in with the fantasies that could ruin her career and quite possibly lead to a good bit of jail time if the bastards that ran The Company were vindictive enough to pursue it.

She had a feeling they were.

Dismissing those thoughts with an effort, Amaryllis focused on the puzzle of their mission.

The army The Company had built, the hunters, had been tracking and 'decommissioning' rogue cyborgs for years now. As far as she knew, though, there'd never been a concerted assault like the one they currently faced ... which bore the earmarks of an all out war. In general, cyborgs traveled alone, occasionally in pairs. That was the reason she and the other hunters usually worked alone or were sometimes partnered with one or two other hunters, depending on the circumstances--there were a lot of rogues to eliminate and the entire confederation of systems to hide in and she'd spent far more time hunting than battling.

What were the odds, she wondered, that a whole nest of them was about to fall right in their laps?

She didn't buy it, whatever The Company said. The cyborgs might be emotionally unstable due to faulty programming, but there was nothing wrong with their logic circuits. They rarely made mistakes, and certainly not of this magnitude.

The Company, on the other hand, had a bad habit of making stupid mistakes.

Building the cyborgs in the first place was the most notable one. They just couldn't resist playing God. They'd cornered the market with their advances in robotics and robotically enhanced bio-genetic organs, but that only seemed to have whetted their appetite for more glory. The rogues were the first--ever--marriage of robotics and bio-engineering to produce human-like cybernetic organisms--for what true purpose one could only imagine--but they'd succeeded beyond their wildest dreams and failed abysmally at the same time because, like the monster in the classic horror tale, their creation had turned on them. The cyborgs had been so real, so 'life like' that, according to The Company, they'd begun to believe it themselves. Unfortunately, that belief had clashed with their programming and made them dangerously unstable.

The hunter unit, of which she was a member, had been formed after their rebellion and escape to track these dangerous rogue cyborgs down and destroy them.

Why, and for that matter, how, after all this time, had the cyborgs decided to unite and oppose The Company in force when they'd been behaving up until now as one might expect, erratically and irrationally?

And why would Dalia, one of their own, one of their best, have 'turned'?

That part didn't make any sense at all. A few of the hunters seemed just a tad overzealous to her, a little on the fanatical side when it came to the cyborgs. For her part, she couldn't say that she despised them--they were machines, after all--and she thought she was probably typical of most hunters--doing her job, not actually sympathetic to the cyborgs but not particularly rabid either. Sympathy was the key word though, and she didn't see how one of their own could go from hunter to rogue sympathizer at the drop of a hat, particularly not Dalia, who supposedly had.

Even if she accepted that, which she didn't, why would the cyborgs consider Dalia important enough to take such a risk as to land right in The Company's backyard to pick her up? Then, having done something so uncharacteristically stupid, they'd so far forgotten themselves as to be completely unaware of being followed? Leading them back to their stronghold?

The flip side was the possibility that Dalia had been captured by the cyborgs, but that supposition took her no where either since she couldn't come up with a 'why and how' that made any sense.

She considered herself a good soldier, but she didn't like flying blindly into a situation that she didn't understand.

The bucking of the ship finally subsided as they entered the atmosphere and Amaryllis glanced at the soldier beside her, wondering what Reese thought about the situation. Typically, he appeared completely unruffled either by the impending battle or the teeth rattling jolting they'd just been through.

Irritation flitted through her.

It was all very well to be cool under fire, but Reese was just a little too unflappable to suit her. For her part, she'd have felt better about working with him if she'd seen a hint of uneasiness in his cold blue eyes occasionally, a touch of doubt--maybe a little lust when he gave her one of those thorough once overs he was prone to when he thought she wouldn't notice--anything that indicated he wasn't the next thing to a frigging cyborg himself.

Not that she could honestly say she knew him all that well. He wasn't exactly the open, friendly, or chatty type and aside from their current mission, she'd only been partnered with him on two others. Prior to that, her missions had all been solo, but she'd fucked up royally on her last solo mission--almost gotten herself killed--and The Company had decided to pair her with a partner when she had finally recovered enough to take on another assignment.

She resented it. To err was human. It was only to be expected that, occasionally, somebody would fuck up. That didn't mean she needed a baby sitter and she knew damn well that was what Reese was--guard dog--because he'd made certain she saw next to no action since he'd been with her.

She figured they'd saddled him with her because of the credits it had cost the company to rebuild her--not that they were actually footing the bill. The credits were coming out of her salary, but she supposed they meant to see to it that she lived long enough to repay her debt and having a topnotch soldier like Reese to watch her was the best way of getting their use out of her and at the same time making sure she was around long enough.

Regardless, it was still a source of embarrassment and irritation. Probably a quarter of the females in the unit were paired with a male partner, so her situation was by no means unique. It was the fact that she had been deemed competent to work alone before and no longer was that irked her.

It also bothered/embarrassed her that Reese had only to glance in her direction to make her feel uncomfortable in a way she didn't particularly welcome.

She'd been too confused and angry at first to consider the reason for it. Later, she'd put it down to everything except what it really was.

She'd finally been forced to admit, to herself at least, that the fact was that he was a dangerous distraction. She had heart palpitations whenever he looked directly at her-- which, for good or bad, was rare--which put her in far more danger, to her way of thinking, than if she hadn't had a partner at all.

It wasn't the sort of thing she could complain to The Company about, of course. She could well imagine their reaction. 'Yes, I know he's a great soldier, a perfect killing machine and a brilliant strategist, but he's also grade A prime beef and I can't look at him without my brain going to mush and you don't even want to know what it does to me when he touches me, however casually. Do you think you could pair me with somebody that doesn't make me cream in my pants every time I look at him?'

The idea of the expressions such a confession would elicit was almost amusing. Unfortunately, the situation made her feel like a silly schoolgirl in the grips of her first crush, and that didn't amuse her at all.

Shifting uncomfortably, she glanced down at the hand that rested on his thigh only inches from her own. He had big hands, strong, faintly calloused but perfectly groomed, and long fingers that put all sorts of forbidden thoughts into her head. She couldn't look at them without feeling her belly clench and having images flood her mind of those hands skating over her body in a slow caress.

Not that she would allow such a thing even if he'd shown any interest and it hadn't been a court martial offense. To look at her, she didn't think anyone could tell the years she'd spent in reconstructive surgery. The doctors had assured her no one could feel the difference either, but, deep down, she was afraid they could, that if she allowed anyone intimate access to her body they'd 'feel' that she was more mechanical marvel than human. That was one of the reasons she'd never done more than a little experimentation with her sexuality, the other being that she hadn't run into anyone that could banish the image she still carried around of herself from her birth defects. The few times she'd tried to take a lover, she'd been so self-conscious she couldn't even enjoy herself, so what was the point?

The soldier sitting across from her, Johnson, who'd been fidgeting nervously since his initial outburst, broke into her thoughts at that moment.

"I really hate this shit! This is *wrong*," he muttered irritably.

"As bad as I hate to agree with Johnson--this feels more than a little off to me, too," she said under her breath.

Reese slid an assessing glance in her direction and her pulse jumped as his cool blue eyes skated over her.

"Pre-battle nerves," he said succinctly.

Amaryllis glared at him, but it was a wasted effort. He'd gone back to ignoring her.

"It isn't pre-battle jitters," she muttered through gritted teeth. "This feels like a tra…."

An explosion, too close for comfort, cut her off. The craft screamed and bucked as if it had hit a wall, shuddering so hard it felt as if it would disintegrate. Amaryllis' heart slammed into her ribs painfully.

"What the fuck?" Johnson yelped.

"Oh shit!" someone exclaimed.

"Nukes? Are they out of their fucking mind?" Amaryllis exclaimed breathlessly, frantically checking her safety harness.

No one answered, naturally enough, since the question was purely rhetorical. She couldn't see a damn thing and no one had a clue of whether one of their sister ships had launched the nuke or if the Cyborgs were lobbing nukes at them.

"They've thrown up a force field," the captain announced

abruptly, his voice gravelly from the wild jouncing of the ship.

Amaryllis exchanged a look with several of her fellow soldiers. A force field? The long range robo-probes had indicated a crude settlement only--flimsy huts built from vegetation, timber palisade walls. Where the hell had the force field come from?

When they'd set out, she'd thought four squads of hunters would be overkill, but there seemed little doubt now that they'd flown right into a trap--as she'd feared they would. She just hoped she was going to live long enough to say 'I told you so'.

"What the hell …?" the navigator exclaimed suddenly.

The words were scarcely out of his mouth when a strange blue light filled the ship. Something crept along her skin like the touch of an invisible being, lifting the fine hairs on her body. Abruptly, the craft dropped like a stone, leaving her stomach miles behind and then slammed into something so hard it jarred every bone and tissue in her body, detonating an explosion of pain. Time seemed almost to stop, as if holding its breath. The deafening noise of shouts, crumpling metal, wind and explosions vanished.

Curiously the pain dissipated almost as instantaneously as it had erupted and a strange sense of detachment enveloped her. Amaryllis watched as the ship began to disintegrate around them, pieces breaking off and becoming deadly shrapnel that peppered everyone in the compartment. Three shards sliced across her legs, arm and belly in quick succession. Across from her, Johnson let out a yelp that ended in a gurgle as the munitions locker careened into him and then collapsed on top of him, crushing him into a twitching mass of blood and meat. The man next to him disappeared out of a hole that appeared in one side of the craft that hardly seemed large enough to swallow him. Beyond, Amaryllis saw nothing but sky. She stared at it uncomprehendingly, trying to figure out what wasn't 'right' about what her eyes perceived. Why would she see only sky when they'd crashed?

Almost on top of the thought, her stomach clenched, went weightless in freefall.

"Hold on! We're going to crash!" the pilot yelled.

Amaryllis turned to stare at the back of the man's head. Going to? They hadn't already? What had they hit if not the ground?

Something softer than ground, she realized moments later.

She blacked out when the ship slammed into the planet, then bounced and skidded, like a stone being skipped over water. She didn't think it could have been for more than a few moments, however. She woke to the touch of warm fingers against her cheek. Distantly, she heard a deep, rumbling voice she tentatively identified as belonging to Reese, although it sounded oddly rough, urgent with concern. "Amy?"

She frowned. No one had ever called her that but her family. Maybe she'd imagined it? Maybe she was dead and just hadn't figured it out yet? With an effort, she lifted her eyelids. Reese's face swam into view. For once his cool blue eyes didn't seem to see through her. In fact, she thought she saw a good deal of concern, but maybe that was her imagination, too, because it vanished almost instantly, replaced by a purposeful look.

"We'll be overrun in about five seconds. Can you fight, soldier?" he asked sharply.

Amaryllis grunted, but responded automatically to the sharp command and began struggling to get to her feet. Once she'd gained them, she looked around a little dazedly at the others in the group that were trying to form up. Reese shoved a weapon into her hand. She gripped it, reassured by the weight, wondering if it would still function. Staggering drunkenly as she picked her way through the wreckage, she followed Reese and the others who'd managed to collect themselves and were pouring out of a rip in the hull to meet their enemy.

The first sounds of battle reached her before she managed to struggle out of the wrecked craft. She could see very little to begin with beyond Reese's broad back. He glanced back at her. "Stay behind me."

A jolt of surprise went through her at the command. She finally decided, however, that he meant watch his back. Collecting herself with an effort, she checked her weapon and stepped to one side of him. Dazed as she was, she saw almost immediately that they didn't have a chance in hell. Reese was one of only a handful of the squad that seemed virtually unscathed. The rest, like her, were battered, disoriented, or already too injured to fight, and they had stepped into a melee. There was no chance of forming up, of presenting an orderly counterattack. The cyborgs, outnumbering them two to one, waded through them as effortlessly as if they'd been no more than children.

Placing her back to her partner, Amaryllis gritted her teeth and brought her weapon up. She didn't have the chance to discover if the weapon was still functioning. She hadn't even managed to aim when a cyborg struck her arm so hard she lost her grip on the weapon. His next blow was to her chin and her knees buckled.

Blackness swarmed around her again. Dimly, she realized that Reese was standing over her, struggling with three cyborgs, who'd piled on him and were bearing him to the ground.

It wasn't Reese who hauled her to her feet. The grip on her was enough to assure her that it wasn't any of her comrades.

Within a handful of minutes, the battle was lost. The cyborgs surrounded them, relieved them of their weapons and marched them off to a holding area.

Amaryllis was still focusing on putting one foot in front of the other and locking her knees to keep from falling when an explosion nearby announced the arrival of another of their ships. A wave of energy seemed to go through the hunters. Abruptly, the battle was engaged once more as her squad fought their captors in a forlorn effort to reach the other squad on the field.

They didn't make any appreciable headway. Within

moments, their second effort was beat down and they were half dragged, half led to a clearing set aside for captives.

Amaryllis collapsed almost with a sense of relief, too shocked by the crash and their defeat even to feel fear. Mutely, she stared at Reese as he knelt beside her and examined her injuries, which consisted of perhaps a score of gashes on her legs, arms, torso, back and head, none of which seemed particularly life threatening. As if sensing her gaze, he lifted his head and stared at her a long moment.

He was disheveled. The long, ash blond hair generally contained in a queue at the base of his skull fluttered around his square jaw and across his finely chiseled nose and lips.

Regret made Amaryllis' belly clench and she realized for the first time that, contrary to all logic, she felt far more than mere lust for this beautiful man. It would hurt her to her soul to witness his death, to see the light dim in his eyes, to see his great, strong body defiled by violence. She hoped they killed her first. She didn't think she could bear looking on as they destroyed him.

The look in his pale blue eyes as he stared back at her sent her heart tripping over itself.

Almost as if he suddenly realized he'd betrayed more than he'd intended, a shuttered look fell over his features. He shifted away from her. "The wounds look to be superficial … though they should be treated. How's your head?"

She lifted her hand to her throbbing head, realizing only then that, like Reese, she'd lost her helmet. "Feels like hell, but I guess I'll live. Next time, I'll try to remember to fasten the chin strap before we crash."

He smiled grimly and settled on the ground beside her. Amaryllis was tempted to pursue the conversation. As conversations went, this was one of the longest they'd had to date and the most 'personal'. Moreover, she was curious as to whether she'd imagined the significance of the way he'd looked at her.

Not that it mattered now, she supposed, but it would've

been a comfort to know he cared on more than a professional level.

She found, though, that as soon as her adrenaline had ceased pumping through her blood, she'd begun to feel mildly queasy. She wasn't certain if that was due to the knots on her skull or merely the aftermath of shock, but she decided after a few moments that she wasn't really up to attempting to draw Reese out.

In any case, before anything could come to mind, one of the cyborgs guarding them detached himself from the group and addressed the captured hunters.

"You are captives of the cyborg nation. Resistance is futile and will only lead to your death." He paused for several moments. "But you are our brothers--you are as we are--and, in time, when you have come to accept this and understand the crimes against all of us by the humans who created us, you will be given the opportunity to join us and help us to build our own world, our own nation, as free beings."

Stunned, Amaryllis glanced at Reese, wondering if she'd heard correctly. "Brothers? What does he mean by that?"

Reese's expression was grim, but she wasn't certain if that was an indication that she actually *had* heard the cyborg correctly or if it was a reaction to the implication that the cyborgs had every intention of taking their captives with them.

The voices of the other hunters around them joined hers, creating an ominous rumble as they digested the remarks, questioned them, angrily refuted them.

"You mean to brain wash us?" someone shouted above the din of voices.

"We mean to enlighten you!" the cyborg shouted back. "And before you dismiss it, consider this--Why would they send humans against cyborgs when we were designed to be stronger and faster than any natural born human? Logically, they would not. No human could hope to be victorious against beings designed to be physically and mentally superior to them. Why is it that not one among you has a single, living relative--no parents, no brothers, no sisters, no aunts, uncles--no one? The creators gave you your memories. They are not your own. These memories were programmed into you at the time of your creation to prevent the problems that arose among those of us created without a past, with full knowledge of what and who we are."

Amaryllis was on the point of flatly vetoing the suggestion when she noticed that an uncomfortable, thoughtful silence had fallen among her comrades. A sense, almost of drowning, swept over her as she looked around at the other hunters as if seeing them for the first time and finally turned to look at Reese.

She couldn't say that she knew any of them on a very personal level, but of those she did know well enough to have learned something of their background the cyborg's comments struck uncomfortably close to home. She couldn't recall a single one of them that had family. She supposed she'd assumed that that was one of the preferences for their line of work--that all of them were orphans, loners, with no one to distract them from their job, no ties that might interfere at a critical moment.

A coldness followed the sensation of drowning. There was one among them that certainly did not fit that profile, who not only had a wealth of living relatives, but who also had endured a childhood so horrendous not even a mad scientist would consider it mentally healthful to instill such memories.

Her.

Chapter Two

Reese had no living relatives. The two of them hardly exchanged more conversation than was necessary to complete their missions, but Amaryllis had been curious enough about him to do a background check.

It hadn't occurred to her to question his humanity.

She'd always thought he had an almost uncanny control in the face of situations that made even seasoned soldiers flinch, but she'd also admired that cool head under fire, the ability, whatever the situation, to think, and act accordingly. She'd only seen him in action a few times, but she'd admired him from afar long before he'd been assigned as her partner.

She would've been lying to say she didn't think it was a shame the attraction wasn't mutual, but she'd also been relieved at the same time that he was so unaware of her that there was no chance anything could ever get ugly. If it had been entirely left up to her to keep things professional, she wasn't confident she could've managed it, despite the company prohibition, despite her training, despite the drugs they were issued that were supposed to counteract their natural libido and keep their mind on business.

Regardless, she'd considered his coolness pure training-- and a lack of interest in her in particular. He wasn't emotionless. He simply had a better than typical control over the weaknesses that beset other soldiers that weren't as good as he was.

The suspicion had teased at her that he'd become oddly protective of her since they'd begun working together. As many times as she'd assured herself that it was under orders, no more than insurance by The Company to protect their investment, she'd toyed with the notion that, maybe, he wasn't as indifferent to her as she'd at first supposed.

The incident between them on the trip out had seemed to support her wishful thinking.

She'd woken from one of her brief rest periods to find herself virtually nose to nose with Reese on the bunk in one of the cabins, so close she could feel the warmth of his breath caressing her, could feel her body responding to his nearness and his scent.

He wasn't asleep. He was staring at her in a way that had made her belly clench. When his gaze had strayed to her lips and lingered there for a handful of heartbeats, she'd thought that he would kiss her. She'd desperately wanted to feel that hard mouth covering hers, to tear his control from him and feel his heated possession. Instead, after several shuddering heartbeats, he'd seemed to collect himself and had rolled away from her, exerting, once more, his supreme control over himself.

But that presupposed that he was human and capable of feeling human emotion, of experiencing the throes of passion. Maybe what she saw was all there was? Maybe it had only been her imagination playing tricks on her when she'd thought he wanted to kiss her, to make love to her, as badly as she wanted him to, her own desires controlling her mind?

Maybe he was nothing more than a machine, incapable even of curiosity?

"You believe them?"

It wasn't a question, not really. Amaryllis' gaze skidded away from making eye contact even as she glanced toward him. "They seem to believe it--unless they've evolved to the point that they're capable of lying. But then The Company has assured us they aren't capable of evolving, that it's only faulty programming that makes them behave as they do."

He merely grunted. The sound could've indicated agreement, disgust--any number of things. It seemed like a purely human reaction, but Amaryllis felt as if she'd been drugged, as if she was caught up in some sort of bizarre hallucination.

She refused to allow herself to dwell on the fact that she was, quite possibly, the only human on this world, surrounded by cyborgs who despised the race that had created them. To allow it would be to allow terror to seep through her veins like a corrosive acid and the one thing she was certain of was that she couldn't afford to fall apart. Her chances of survival might be slim anyway, but she had no desire to let go of a slim chance for none at all.

It was almost a relief when the cyborgs began to move among them. The fact that they singled out the injured seemed to indicate they had meant what they'd said. Extermination would not be immediately forthcoming.

It would've been more of a relief if Amaryllis hadn't feared the treatment itself would expose her. She'd been debating the matter and what her chances were for some moments when a shadow fell across her. Her heart seized immediately, as if a fist had closed around it. "I'm fine," she said without looking up, her teeth clenched to keep them from chattering with reaction.

"You are injured."

"Not seriously."

"I've checked her myself. She has superficial wounds only."

Both surprise and relief flickered through Amaryllis at Reese's unexpected championship. It was short lived. Even as she glanced toward him, she sensed the cyborg kneeling on her other side to examine her more closely. Her tongue clove to the roof of her mouth when she glanced toward him.

He was as dark as Reese was fair, and somewhat slighter of build, but his face was so similar they might have been cast from the same mold--so to speak. Nausea swam through her as the thread of doubt she'd been nursing vanished. If they weren't brothers--and she knew they couldn't be--then they'd certainly been developed from the same gene donor cocktail. She jumped when the cyborg tucked a finger beneath her chin and tilted her head, examining her closely.

After a moment, the cyborg's gaze moved from her to Reese. "She has head injuries. It can not hurt to have her examined."

Reese's hard mouth tightened into a thin, uncompromising line. "She has displayed no symptoms suggesting serious damage. She is cut and battered, but sound enough to need no treatment."

The cyborg's lips tightened in response to the challenge in Reese's words. Abruptly, he rose to his full height, pulling Amaryllis to her feet. "Nevertheless, she will be examined."

Reese stood, his manner challenging.

A battle seemed imminent. Moreover, they were attracting attention Amaryllis didn't care for. "I'll go," she put in quickly. It wasn't as if she was going to be able to avoid it at this point. She could only try, once she was there, to convince them she needed no internal examination--and hope for the best if they insisted upon it.

She'd never considered that the day might come when she would be grateful for the birth defects that had required so much reconstruction to make her 'whole'. Now she mentally calculated her chances of survival because of it as actually fair.

The planet her parents had been terra farming had, unknown to everyone except, perhaps, The Company, been regularly bombarded by radiation that had proven disastrous to developing fetuses. There was the unsaid accusation that the colonists had had no business breeding naturally anyway, but they'd certainly paid for it. Most of the pregnancies had ended in miscarriage. The few, like herself, who'd been born alive had been armless and legless, among other even more horrible deformities. She'd almost reached puberty before her parents had managed to save enough credits for corrective surgery. Fortunately, she hadn't grown a great deal or she might have had to endure even more. As it was, the cybernetic arms and legs she'd been fitted with had had to be replaced twice to keep them in proportion to her body's growth. Internally, her skeletal structure had had to be reinforced--an excruciatingly painful process--with metals to support the weight of her robotic limbs and a chip had had to be implanted in her brain to enable her to control them.

Her internal organs were her own, except for the biological replacement organs for those that had failed her, but then she knew that the cyborgs also had bio-engineered organs.

As far as she could see, all she really had to worry about was her reproductive organs which the cyborgs, naturally enough, would not have been given, and the chip in her brain, which would not match the internal CPU the cyborgs had.

Both men--both cyborgs--looked down at her with nearly identical expressions of surprise, irritation and, faintly, amusement.

Reese shook his head ever so slightly. "It isn't necessary."

Amaryllis had the unnerving feeling that the comment and the look in his eyes were a warning. Had he done a background check on her, as well? Was it possible that he *knew* that she was human? "But it is inevitable," she responded. "We're captives, outnumbered, with no means of escape. I see no choice but to do as our captors demand."

To her relief, Reese desisted, bowing to the inevitable as she had.

The cyborg did not release her. She wasn't certain whether the hand on her arm was for support, or to establish his control, but it nixed the budding hope that she might have the chance to make a break for it before she was discovered. "I can walk unassisted," she said coldly.

He ignored the comment.

Angry and frightened, Amaryllis focused her attention on keeping step with him for several moments. She was a trained soldier, however, and despite her fear, she began to assess her situation almost unconsciously.

The planet they found themselves on had little to recommend it beyond breathable air--the cyborgs required that as well as she did since they were not mere machines, but biological hybrids, and human biology required air, water, sustenance.

Almost as if on cue, her stomach growled. She wasn't unduly self-conscious. Her life had not allowed for a great deal of modesty or privacy and if she'd ever been squeamish about such things it had been leached from her through the years that had brought her to her current situation. Years of undergoing medical treatment and surgery to correct her birth defects and being poked, prodded and dissected by doctors, nurses and orderlies, followed by the years of training and work in her chosen field--the militia--had not allowed for self-consciousness in very many areas.

She somehow doubted, however, that cyborgs actually experienced hunger pangs that vocalized.

She had no doubt that he'd heard it, though, for he glanced at her sharply.

"What is this place?" she asked, more to distract him than because she had any real interest in it. "Not the cyborg stronghold as we'd supposed, I guess?"

"No."

She wasn't surprised that he seemed disinclined to chat, but it irritated her that he was so resistant to her efforts to distract him. "A trap, then?"

"Yes."

Amaryllis studied the crude huts that made up the 'village' the cyborgs had built to complete their illusion. Most of the 'props' were in shambles now, and she hadn't had a view of the compound before, or during, the attack, but from what she could see she wondered why their leaders had fallen for it at all. The carelessness of the construction should have been a dead giveaway in her book, but then they'd always had the tendency to have their head up their asses where the cyborgs were concerned. The company had *really* underestimated them this time. "Why not simply kill us?"

The cyborg lifted one dark brow. Finally, he shrugged, as if he wasn't in total agreement with the decision that had been made but had accepted it. "We are the same. We wanted you to join us in building our own world ... free from persecution by humans. Contrary to what the company has led you to believe, we have no desire to subjugate mankind. We only wish to live our lives as we choose."

Amaryllis' throat went dry. She debated for several moments, wondering whether it would seem less suspicious if she refused to accept their insistence that both hunter and hunted were cyborg, or if it was even safe to claim her humanity under the circumstances. She finally decided that she just wasn't comfortable insisting that she was not cyborg when she had no idea what the consequences might be to the discovery that she actually wasn't. "Why?"

He stopped, tilting his head slightly. A slow smile curled his lips. Amusement gleamed in his dark eyes and something indefinable curled in her belly in response. "We had few women."

Amaryllis' knees went weak at the wealth of implications in that one, simple statement. A heated blush suffused her cheeks as her mind instantly leapt to what use the cyborgs might have for women.

It was absurd, of course. The cyborgs were imitations of human life, but imitation was a key word. They had been programmed to mimic human behavior and even some emotions, but they only appeared to experience emotion. They didn't actually feel as human beings did, and they could not experience desire--or anything else for that matter.

She didn't particularly care for the trend of her thoughts anyway. He was a design of sheer perfection, a gorgeous machine, but he *was* a machine. Thinking of desire and this replica of a human being in the same context was nearly as insane as lusting over a toaster.

She finally decided that it was shock and confusion. She'd been lusting over Reese from the moment he was assigned to work with her--from the moment she'd first set eyes on him, to be truthful. She'd believed Reese was as human as she was--which was now up for debate and only added to her confusion--but there was no excuse for transferring those feelings to this cyborg, however much he reminded her of Reese. "Uh. I don't think I follow."

He lifted his dark brows, and then frowned, as if working through an internal debate. Or perhaps it wasn't that at all. Maybe he was only waiting for the noise of the arrival to subside before he spoke again, for the sound of an arriving craft caught their attention at that moment. They watched as a huge, deep space trawler settled slowly to the ground a short distance away, its engines kicking up a cloud of debris. Once it had settled and the engines were killed, a gang plank was lowered and the cyborgs leading or carrying the injured began to move toward it.

"It is not enough to simply form a world for ourselves. We need purpose, a future. We want mates--offspring."

Amaryllis blinked several times, rapidly, as a new wave of shock washed over her. "Offspring?"

"Families."

Amaryllis felt her jaw go slack with stunned surprise. "But you ... I mean, if we're cyborgs, we can't ... couldn't ... uh ... wouldn't be able to reproduce," she said a little weakly, trying to shove the implications to the back of her mind. The inner voice refused to be silenced, however.

Never, in her wildest imaginings would she have considered what the true purpose of this mission appeared to be--not the utter defeat of the hunters that had been dogging them for years, but the capture of--mates for the purpose of colonization.

Chapter Three

The ship the cyborg led Amaryllis into was a modified commercial freighter. Under the circumstances, one wouldn't expect luxury. It was as well she hadn't, for the ship looked more like some medieval dungeon than a passenger craft, even of the lowest order.

Amaryllis' tension built as it slowly, but inevitably, sank in upon her that nothing short of a suicidal attempt would win her more than a few moments of freedom. Even the sliver of a chance vanished as the cyborg forced her up the gangway and into the freighter, towing her along one dimly lit, dank passageway after another until at last they reached a large cabin that had been converted into a sickbay. It was already beginning to fill with the injured and the medics attending them. After leading her to a gurney, the cyborg ordered her to undress and climb onto it.

As stunned as she was by everything else that had happened, Amaryllis felt still another jolt. "*You're* going to examine me?"

He eyed her speculatively. "You would prefer another?" he responded coolly.

"I'd prefer a medic," Amaryllis said tartly.

"I have the programming needed."

There didn't seem much she could say to that. She didn't know why she didn't want him in particular to examine her. It shouldn't have mattered one way or another.

It did, though.

Despite the fact that it occurred to her that she was really far better off to have a cyborg *not* completely programmed in medicine to examine her, she wasn't at all keen on having him touch her.

She reminded herself, again, that she had no choice in the matter. She was a trained soldier. She knew when the odds were stacked against her and resistance was futile. After a moment, she removed her uniform, climbed onto the gurney and lay back, staring up at the lights on the ceiling, her teeth gritted to prevent them from chattering with reaction, trying her level best to empty her mind of any thoughts at all.

"I am called Dante."

She didn't care what fucking name he'd been given. In fact, she didn't want to know anything that would make it any more difficult for her to remember what he was. She preferred to simply think of him as 'the cyborg', a machine.

When she glanced at him, she saw that he was holding a scanner. Her heart slammed into her ribcage and she swallowed audibly. It looked pretty antiquated, but she had a bad feeling it was functional enough to give her away.

Her mind instantly began to flutter frantically in search of possibilities--and came upon one dead end after another. Short of leaping from the gurney and fighting her way to the door, fighting her way out of the ship and across a field swarming with cyborgs, there seemed no escape. She was a realist. Whatever advantage her cybernetic limbs gave her, it wasn't nearly enough to overcome those kind of odds.

"What name are you known by?"

"Amanda Rios." Brain malfunction. The moment the words were out of her mouth Amaryllis wondered if the head injury--or pure fear--had taken her wits completely. She'd been designated Amaryllis VH600 from the time she'd joined the militia. What had prompted her to regress to the childhood name her family had given her? Watching her life flash before her eyes? No one--except backwards terra farmers--even used such names anymore. The population in the 'civilized' universe had reached such proportions that it only made sense to use the codes issued by the government.

It was too much to hope he wouldn't notice the slip.

He went still. "Rios?"

Amaryllis could've bitten her tongue off. Try though she might, however, she couldn't think of any way to retrieve the blunder that she thought would be the least bit believable. She should have simply given him her military designation.

That's what came of allowing oneself to become distracted with useless speculation. And it *was* useless. There was no escape and no way to avoid detection. She could only hope he wouldn't be able to decipher the differences he found once he got the readouts from the scanner.

"It's a nickname," she added lamely, amending, "Cpl. Amaryllis VH600."

His expression was unreadable, but she didn't think for a moment that he'd swallowed her story. Regardless, he seemed disinclined to pursue the matter. Instead, he activated the scanner.

Amaryllis swallowed audibly as he slowly moved it over her.

When he'd finished, he stood perfectly still, analyzing the readout, his face carefully expressionless. After several moments, he moved away from her. She tensed, uncertain of what to expect. Had he seen that her brain implant was merely a control device rather than a fully operational CPU? Had he detected the organs she had that no cyborg would have been given? That her skeletal structure was titanium clad calcium, rather than pure titanium?

Her mind supplied her with a half dozen attack and counterattack scenarios while she waited tensely to see what he would do next, resisting the temptation to simply take matters into her own hands and launch the first assault.

What were the odds that he hadn't detected the fact that she was human, not cyborg?

Was he still assimilating the differences and trying to decide what they meant?

She jumped when he returned once more with an extractor.

"I must remove your locators."

Amaryllis stared at him blankly for several moments, trying to shift gears. "Locators?" she echoed.

"There are two. One here," he said, touching her hip and sending a strange bolt of electricity through her. "The other is at the base of your skull."

The remark was enough to jolt her back into real time. "Two?" she repeated, frowning while she slowly considered the possibilities. "One is a decoy?"

He stared at her a long moment and finally seemed to shrug. "Both are operational."

"I don't understand. I knew about one. Why would they imbed two different locators?"

He frowned as he placed a hand on her hip, drawing the flesh taut with his fingers as he aimed the laser he held in his other hand. Amaryllis gulped, bracing herself as the full ramifications of her deception assailed her. He wasn't going to use anything to deaden the area.

If she were cyborg, she would be able to shut down the nerve endings in that area and close herself off from the pain.

"They expect us to behave as humans."

"What?"

"The Company. Strange, don't you think, that they maintain that we are no more than machines, and yet they behave with the expectation that we will react as a human would. Finding one locator, we would look no further."

It was a good point, but one Amaryllis wasn't terribly interested in at the moment.

Some of the tension left her as he moved away from her again. When he returned, he smoothed a gel substance over the area he would incise. The gel was cold. Amaryllis felt her nipples puckering in reaction.

The movement caught his gaze.

There was nothing remotely detached, or mechanical, in his eyes. His reaction was surprising, to say the least.

Her own reaction to the look in his eyes was almost as stunning. Heat surged through her. Her mouth went dry. She was still trying to gather enough moisture to swallow when he seemed to become aware of his surroundings once more. Briefly, their gazes met. Something flickered in his eyes and then vanished.

He'd opened her hip with the laser before she recovered enough to tense against the expectation of pain. There was no pain, however, and she realized he'd deadened the area after all.

Her heart thudded painfully in her chest as that sank in.

He proceeded to remove the locator and destroy it, however, as if nothing was amiss. When he'd closed the wound, he directed her to turn over. She did so reluctantly, wondering if he would strike while her back was turned.

His hand felt warm as it skated over her back, brushing her hair from her neck. She tensed, trying to ignore the tingles of warmth that spread through her. Again, he rubbed the cold gel into her skin. The smell of burning flesh stung at her nostrils as he made the incision and extracted the second locator. She made an abortive attempt to rise when she realized he'd closed the wound. He placed a hand on her back, silently commanding her to remain as she was. Reluctantly, she desisted.

Discomfort assailed her as he ministered to her wounds. It was not the discomfort of pain, however. She would almost have welcomed that as something to focus on at this point, for, lying face down on the gurney, her other senses sharpened and she was more acutely conscious of the strength and warmth of his hands, and the surprising gentleness of his touch even than before. Desperate to close her mind to the effect he was having on her senses, Amaryllis squeezed her eyes shut, only to discover that that made things even worse. Something tightened and fluttered in her belly, spreading warmth throughout her body. Her heart rate kicked up a few notches so that it was a struggle to try to regulate her breathing to anything even approaching normal.

He had to have noticed her distress.

She saw, once he'd finished and told her to sit up, that he was no more unfazed than she was. As unfamiliar as she was with the look of desire in a man's eyes, as certain as she was that cyborgs would know nothing about human passion, what she saw when she finally nerved herself to meet his gaze was as unmistakable as her own erratic heartbeat and instantly recognizable because it reflected her own needs.

With an effort, she redirected her thoughts as he finished his examination, trying to decide whether he'd realized she was human and, if so, what the possible repercussions might be.

It was difficult, to say the least, with him standing so close, with the touch of his hands on her thighs as he examined the wounds there.

"Why do they call you Rios?"

Amaryllis gaped at him, mentally kicking herself. Shit! Why hadn't she considered when she manufactured the lie that she might have to explain it?

She managed a credible shrug of unconcern. "My family is--uh--were terra farmers on a world that used their family names since it was too under populated to create a problem. Or, at least, that's the memories I was given, according to what that other cyborg said. But I guess it's because Rios is--or was--such a commonplace name and I am--pretty average."

His dark gaze swept over her in a leisurely appraisal that seemed to miss nothing. She thought she'd become immune to self-consciousness about her nudity, but blood was pounding in her cheeks by the time he met her gaze once more. "They lied."

She blinked. "What?"

"You are small, not average, in stature and build."

The comment angered her. The cyborgs were superior specimens, so she supposed she could see why he might consider her less than perfect, but she figured she was fairly average for a human--alright a little less than that, but then she'd had medical problems that had probably contributed to stunted growth.

"Your features are exotic, not common--your body far better than average. You are a beautiful, desirable woman and there is nothing at all common about that, even in this age of genetic manipulation in the search for perfection."

Amaryllis wouldn't have thought it possible to blush any harder, but she did. She stared at him speechlessly. She decided, finally, that it was just as well. The more she said, the deeper the hole she seemed to dig for herself.

She couldn't think straight, and she no longer had the comfort of thinking it was purely shock or even fear.

He'd analyzed her and expressed an opinion, she realized finally. Cyborgs weren't supposed to have them. She could understand the comment about her not being average. As hard as she tried to delude herself into thinking of herself as average or typical, she never had been and she had the emotional scars to prove it from the taunts and teasing she'd received from the other children as she was growing up. She liked to think she appeared, on the outside at least, fairly average now--because being average was much, much better than standing out from the crowd if standing out meant being a target for revulsion, criticism, or amusement.

It would never have occurred to her to consider herself more than passable, however, and she couldn't help but wonder what Dante saw that made him perceive her as 'beautiful'.

And how would a machine perceive such a thing anyway?

Trying to wade through her confusion made her head ache even worse than it had been.

"You should locate the pain centers and switch them off until the nanos have mended the organic cells."

The comment caught Amaryllis by surprise. She was within a hair's breadth of snapping that she would if she had that ability when she thought better of it. Instead, she merely slipped from the table and bent to gather her uniform up as he stepped back, giving her the signal that he was through with her.

He clasped a hand over hers, stilling her movements. "You are hunter no more and you will not wear that uniform any longer. Come. While you shower, I will find clothing to fit you."

Amaryllis was instantly torn at the mention of a shower and fresh clothing. However, she'd been in worse condition, on missions, and had to endure it for days. It wouldn't kill her to wait, and being around this particular cyborg might be the death of her. She needed to put as much distance between herself and the cyborgs as possible, not chum with them. "Actually," she said when he'd pulled her torn uniform from her fingers and tossed it to the floor, "I'd as soon dress now."

He caught her arm just above the elbow and tugged, leading her past the other gurneys toward the door they'd entered. "You will not get the chance until tomorrow if you do not go now."

"Fine. Just give me my uniform back. I'll wait for the others."

"You are afraid?"

The question was asked without inflection. Amaryllis thought, perhaps, it was the complete lack of inflection that put her on guard. "Should I be?"

"No."

Amaryllis ground her teeth. She'd fallen right into that one. She cast around in her mind trying to think of an objection he might heed. He'd bandaged a couple of her more serious wounds, but it seemed doubtful the ship was equipped with anything but particle showers--she hadn't seen a real, honest to god, wonderfully primitive, water shower since she'd left the colony--which wouldn't present a problem.

It wouldn't really have been a problem even if he was talking about a water shower. She had scratches and slightly deeper scratches, only a few cuts had even warranted sealing. She might have suspected his motives for bandaging her at all except that the only thing that came to mind as a possibility was a desire to keep her longer and she couldn't imagine why he would want to.

"Maybe you're the one who should be wary," she said finally, when they'd reached the corridor once more.

He glanced down at her questioningly.

"I *am* a hunter."

"I don't doubt your skills, but you are without weapons."

"I don't need them."

He sent her a look of amusement. "Against a male cyborg, who is fully aware of your training?"

He had a point. Even her cybernetics didn't make her stronger than a male and he had the advantage of a good deal of reach and weight besides. The only way a female hunter could bring down a male cyborg toe to toe was to outwit them, or catch them off guard. She doubted, under the circumstances, that she could manage either.

She fell silent. They passed, after a time, through a large room filled with supplies. Dante released her long enough to select a number of articles, which he placed in her arms, and then led her out once more and down a short passageway.

It was immediately apparent when he led her into the next room that the showers were indeed of the primitive variety. Amaryllis was so surprised, so caught up in nostalgia, that she merely stood stock still as Dante took the supplies from her, settled them on a bench and removed the bandages.

After explaining how the showers were operated, he took up a position near the door.

She studied him in silence for several moments, but she wasn't the least surprised that she would not have any privacy. "You could guard me from outside the door just as well," she pointed out coolly.

"I could, but I won't."

Her lips tightened. Finally, she moved to the bench and found what she needed.

There was heated water. Within moments of submerging herself in it, Amaryllis had almost completely dismissed the cyborg, Dante, from her mind. Those who'd grown up on Earth and Earth's well established colonies seemed revolted by the very thought of having water on their skin, but she'd known nothing else until she'd left her own world. She knew that the particle baths were not only more hygienic but almost as importantly, they conserved a precious resource, but she found them very unsatisfactory.

This was almost pure heaven and brought memories of her family crowding into her mind.

She hadn't actually seen her parents but once since she'd decided on a career as a soldier. Her parents had been horrified by her choice and she had been so reluctant to face their disapproval that she'd pretty much cut herself off from them.

She supposed she could see their point. They'd scrimped and saved for years just to earn the credits needed to make her 'normal'. They loved her, and she knew they'd done it out of love, but there was also the unspoken and unacknowledged obligation of debt--that they considered she couldn't possibly appreciate their sacrifice properly if she was willing to risk throwing it away by her choice of career.

Maybe that had played a part in her choice. Maybe, deep down, there'd been some resentment on her part toward her parents. The decision had been far more complicated than that, however.

A large part of it had been because she wanted to show everyone that had ever looked at her with pity, revulsion, or fear that she was just as normal as anyone--better even because her cybernetics allowed her to do things they could never do. Some of it had been sheer desperation to escape the world and people that had represented as much misery to her as love, and some a desperation to fully live life, if she had to do it on the edge, because she'd missed out on so much of life when she had been confined by the limitations of her defective body.

Some of it had been anger, and the need to find a release for her pent up frustrations.

She'd hated the reproach in her family's eyes, though, and except for that one, uncomfortable trip home on leave, she'd avoided them.

She wished now that she hadn't. She might never see them again and she wanted them to know that her choice had been a celebration of the gift they'd given her, not a reproach for the birth defects and the hell she'd been through because of them. She wanted them to know that she didn't blame them for something they could not have prevented short of not conceiving her at all.

"Enough!"

The sharp command jerked Amaryllis out of her abstraction and back to the present. "What?" she asked blankly, trying to think how long she'd been in the shower. It didn't seem to her that she could possibly have used that much water, but then she had no idea what sort of rationing they had.

Dante, she saw uneasily, had strode across the room toward her and was standing no more than two feet from her now, an angry scowl on his face.

Amaryllis' lips tightened in irritation. If he'd given her a specific length of time, she would have complied. His anger seemed unfair, to say the least, when he hadn't indicted anything of the kind.

Sloughing the residual water from her hair and skin, she shut the shower off and moved past him toward the bench. Lifting the length of cloth she decided must be for drying, she quickly dried herself and then studied the garments he'd selected for her. A wry smiled curled her lips when she lifted them to study them. There wasn't much to the garments ... only enough to cover her breasts and genitals.

She'd seen such garments plenty of times, of course, but she'd never worn anything like it. Soldiers wore garments designed to protect them as much as possible from injury. They had no concern for current styles and they worked in less than favorable conditions anyway. This was the sort of thing women of leisure wore, not working women--unless they made their living on their back.

Shrugging mentally, she slipped the garments on. She was still the next thing to naked when she'd dressed, but for the first time in her life, she actually felt a sense of her femininity. She felt--pretty.

The look on Dante's face when she turned to face him at

last was only marginally better than before.

"I underestimated you."

Amaryllis blinked at him in surprise. "What?"

"You are not above using your femininity as a weapon. They taught you to seduce and destroy, did they not?"

Her jaw went slack with surprise for about two seconds before a wealth of conflicting emotions flooded her. Anger took the upper hand and she spoke before she considered the consequences. "You're a cyborg. Why in the hell would I bother trying to seduce you?"

His eyes narrowed. His face grew taut with suppressed anger. "I feel everything any other spawn of humanity feels," he said through clenched teeth.

"How would you know?" Amaryllis shot back at him, still too angry to consider the foolhardiness of provoking her captor.

An expression of frustration flickered across his features. Abruptly, he caught her, jerking her fully against his length. "If you are so certain I do not, prove it--human."

Chapter Four

A coldness washed over Amaryllis. "You said I wasn't human, that all the hunters were cyborgs--just as you are," she said stiffly.

"*I* did not. It was Kiran who spoke, but I suppose we all look alike to you humans."

He knew. Amaryllis suddenly realized that with perfect clarity, knew she should have realized it immediately and would have if she hadn't been in such a state of turmoil. What had been his purpose in bringing her here, then? Why hadn't he simply denounced her, dragged her before whoever was leading this band of rogues? Or simply slain her on the spot? He didn't need privacy to kill her. He would only have had to announce that she was human and no one would have even questioned his actions.

When she remained locked in shocked silence, he shifted his grip on her, freeing one arm. His hand settled lightly on the bare skin of her waist, then skimmed upward, settling just beneath one breast.

Amaryllis swallowed with an effort, fighting a surge of panic, and something else she didn't even want to think about. She wasn't helpless. She'd been well trained. Unarmed, she might stand little chance against him, but she still had her wits and her strength.

Her wits had deserted her, though, and taken her strength with it.

She felt dwarfed by his size and the sensations that evoked wasn't just fear.

With an effort, she gathered moisture into her dry mouth. "If you believe that I'm human, not cyborg, then why did you bring me here?"

He frowned. After a moment, some of the tension seemed to leave him. His grip loosened fractionally, not enough to allow her to escape, but sufficiently that she could drag a deep breath into her laboring lungs. To her surprise, a faint flush colored his skin.

"Perhaps so that you would consider me favorably."

The tone was almost flippant, seeming to belie the suggestion, but his body language said otherwise, and she realized with a touch of surprise that he was telling the truth, that the bath had been in the nature of an offering. Courtship? He'd said they were looking for mates, but then she had been so acutely aware that she was the only one among them that was human, and therefore not compatible, that it simply hadn't occurred to her that he would decide he wanted her and she wondered if that was the reason he'd singled her out in the field to begin with. "I don't … look upon you as an enemy," she lied. She would've been willing to suggest something far warmer except that she didn't think for a moment he would believe her.

His lips tightened into a thin line. "No?" He tilted his head, studying her appraisingly. "Because you consider that I am no more than a machine and a machine can not be an enemy? It is merely a thing."

She couldn't think of a response to that that wouldn't just piss him off more. At the moment, she definitely didn't--couldn't--think of him as a machine. The body pressed so closely to her own felt as real as any other man, but far better than anything she'd ever touched, and her body certainly didn't know the difference.

After a moment, when she didn't deny the accusation, he slipped his hands along her arms, tugging them behind her back and manacling both slender wrists in one of his large hands. He pulled her closer, dipping his head toward the crook of her shoulder and breathing deeply. "But I smell the perfume of your flesh and it sends pleasure through me." He slid his free hand in an exploratory caress up one arm and cupped her face. "I feel the softness of your skin and it begs the touch of my mouth and tongue so that I can bring your essence inside of me and savor it."

He rocked against her so that she could feel his lower

body pressing into her belly, feel the hard erection that told her he wasn't lacking in any of the parts that made him a male. "I want to bury myself so deeply inside of you that you can not think, can only feel ... so that you know I am no machine, but a living entity ... just as you are."

Amaryllis swallowed with an effort, trying to fight the pounding of her heart. Her lips tingled with the nearness of his mouth to hers. She could feel his heat.

She realized suddenly that she wanted to feel his lips on hers. She wanted to ignore every protest screaming at the back of her mind and yield to the promise his heat offered. It took more strength than she would ever have thought possible to deny the desire welling inside of her.

With an effort, she lifted her gaze to meet his. "Why would it matter to you--what I think?" *How* could it matter? Unless The Company had lied to them--which wouldn't be a great surprise considering their penchant for it--and there was far more to their creation than they wanted credit for.

Frustration clouded his features. After a moment, he relaxed his hold on her, stepped away.

"You should ... leave me here," she said a little desperately. "You know I don't belong. If you take me, they will discover, eventually, as you did, that I'm human."

He shook his head slightly, but she wasn't certain what the denial was--a refusal to release her or a refusal to believe that she would be exposed for what she really was. He had to know that the longer she stayed, the greater the chance that someone else would figure it out.

"I would not leave you if I could. When we leave this place, all trace of our presence will be removed."

There *was* no hope of escape then. She could either take her chances with the cyborgs, or have no possibility of survival at all.

"What will they do with me when they discover?"

He frowned, apparently considering, and finally shook his head. "It will be better not to know."

He grasped her arm then and pulled her from the facilities, walking her quickly down one passageway after another.

As they progressed deeper into the ship, they nearly ran afoul of other groups of cyborgs, striding purposefully about the ship as they went about preparations for departure. Each time, he pulled her into a cabin off the main passageway before they were seen, leaving her in no doubt that he had something in mind that didn't include turning her over to her captors. They came at last to a narrow corridor and turned down it. Doors opened off of it more regularly than any of the others and Amaryllis realized that this area must contain smaller cabins for the cyborg crew. About a quarter of the way down, he pushed a door open and thrust her inside, following her.

"You will be safe here ... for now."

Amaryllis looked around the small cabin curiously, but she knew it must be the cabin that had been assigned to him. Beyond a narrow bunk barely wide enough for one and a locker, the room contained little else.

"Facilities there," he said, pointing to a narrow door on the back side of the cabin. "But this is shared by four cabins and only safe for you to use between shift changes." When he'd explained the rotation, he moved toward the cabin door once more, but hesitated once he'd reached it.

"Give me your word that you will not leave the cabin."

"Where would I go?" Amaryllis hedged.

His expression tightened. He shook his head slightly. "This is a dangerous game, Amaryllis."

"Survival isn't my idea of a game," she retorted.

He studied her thoughtfully for several moments and finally left the door, advancing upon her. Surprised, Amaryllis backed away. She'd forgotten the bunk. The backs of her knees caught the edge of the frame. Her knees buckled. Before she could recover her balance, he was upon her, pinning her to the bunk. A brief struggle ensued for possession of her hands, but she was in no position to find the leverage she needed to escape. In moments, he'd subdued her struggles.

Shifting, he caught both her wrists in one hand, and then ripped the silky skirting from her garment, securing her wrists together with it. The sheer fabric was soft but chafed her wrists as she twisted her hands, trying to pull free, and she quickly discovered that it was far stronger than she would've thought.

When he'd finished binding her wrists together, he pushed her arms above her head and secured the binding to the head of the bunk. After tugging on it a couple of times to assure himself that she was secure, he rolled off of her and moved to the door once more.

"Asshole!" Amaryllis snarled at him as he reached it.

He hesitated and turned his head to glare at her. "I realize that you are handicapped by your human weaknesses, but you may wish to consider the consequences of making your presence known."

Amaryllis gaped in outrage.

He'd called her stupid and weak! He thought she was inferior because she was human! "Bigot!" she muttered furiously. "It's better than being a fucking machine!"

It was obvious from his expression that her shaft had struck home with a precision equal to his. For several moments he looked so furious that fear tickled at the base of her spine. Finally, he merely pulled the door open and departed, locking the door behind him.

A combination of relief and uneasiness washed through her when she heard the sound of the lock.

He was right. She *was* stupid or she wouldn't have allowed her temper to overrule her head. Whatever else the company had told them about the cyborgs that might or might not be true, there was no doubt that they were unpredictable. Insulting the one cyborg who knew her dangerous secret was probably one of the least intelligent things she'd ever done.

She struggled with the bonds for a time but found that the more she tugged and pulled the tighter the knots became. After resting for a few moments, she began trying to move herself into a position where she could use her teeth to loosen the knots. An earnest effort failed to produce any results, however, and she subsided to rest again and consider her options.

Regardless of what he'd said, she thought she would prefer to take her chances on the planet than with the cyborgs. Whatever they had in mind to use to erase their presence here, she didn't believe they would destroy the entire planet even if they'd had the weapons to do so, and she was willing to stake her life that they didn't. If she could only free herself and escape the ship undetected, then cross the clearing to the wooded area beyond, she could hide herself until The Company sent ships to discover what had become of the mission.

That was a lot of ifs, particularly when he'd removed her locator--both locators. Mentally, she called up an image of what she'd seen before and since capture, both of the compound and the ship. The compound had been no more than crude wooden huts, but the entire area was surrounded by a wooden palisade built from the trees cut to clear the compound. That constituted a very large area to navigate undetected, ending with a wall that would be difficult, to say the least, to scale.

More immediately, there was the problem of getting loose and finding her way out of the ship. She didn't think it had been locked down yet. The cabin where Dante had imprisoned her seemed to be a good distance from the workings of the ship, but she'd been hearing occasional movements that she thought must mean they were still preparing for departure.

The thought had scarcely entered her mind when she heard footsteps directly outside in the corridor. She held her breath, wondering if Dante were returning. The steps passed the cabin door, however, halting close by. In a few moments, she heard movement in the cabin adjoining the one where she was and then in the facilities. Her heart leapt in her throat and she craned to stare at the door Dante had told her led to the facilities.

There was no lock on it … which explained why he'd decided it was necessary to tie her even though he'd locked the outer door.

She lay perfectly still, hardly daring to breathe until she heard the cyborg leave once more.

When the last of his footsteps faded along the corridor, she studied her situation and began trying to work out a contortion that would bring her teeth within range of the bindings. She'd broken a sweat by the time she managed it. Every muscle and joint in her body was screaming at the unaccustomed strain. Ignoring the pain, she began gnawing at the knots.

She'd begun to think she was beginning to make some headway when she became aware of a vibration communicating itself through the hull, the frame of the bed and the mattress. She stopped, gasping for breath, hoping against hope that she'd imagined it and that it was nothing more than muscle fatigue.

It wasn't muscle fatigue. The vibration rapidly became more and more pronounced. A whine joined it. Within a few moments the entire cabin around her was quaking as if it would disintegrate any moment.

They were taking off.

Mindlessly, she began tugging at the knots again.

A heaviness settled over her, pressing against her harder and harder until she could scarcely breathe. Abruptly, the heaviness vanished. She began to float upward. She'd levitated perhaps two inches from the bed when the artificial gravity kicked in and she hit the mattress once more.

She lay gasping for breath, staring at the shaking hull above her head while the vibrations slowed and finally subsided altogether.

They'd taken off.

She'd lost her only chance of escape.

Chapter Five

Amaryllis wasn't certain how much time passed while she lay on the bunk, too shocked and dismayed even to think beyond the litany that kept running through her mind that she'd lost any chance of escape. After a while, her training kicked in and a calm settled over her.

She couldn't escape, at least not until the cyborgs reached their final destination. Once there, she could assess the situation again. They had ships. She might have a chance of stealing one and escaping. If not, she might have a chance of stowing away on an outbound vessel and escaping from it once it reached deep space.

There was no point in even trying to come up with options, however, now, when she had no idea of what she would be up against. What she needed to do was to try to assess her current situation and figure out a way to survive.

Dante was the only one who knew that she was human.

If she killed him, there would be no one to give her away.

She cringed inside at the thought and struggled to banish her revulsion. She'd destroyed dozens of cyborgs. There was no reason to be squeamish about it now, particularly when this one represented a serious threat to her.

What would be the repercussions of doing so, however? Would he be missed? If so, would they immediately suspect that there was a human on board? Or would they think it was one of their own?

She shook that problem off. She could face that when the time came. The problem was she had no weapons and no idea if she could find one. She didn't have much hope of overcoming him in hand to hand unless she could take him off guard.

And what were the chances of that now that she'd shown her hand?

Not good, she decided, but she could do nothing but wait anyway. Maybe, over time, she could lull his suspicions?

Maybe the key to doing so was already in her hands?

He'd hidden her. There had to be risk involved in doing that, and yet he'd gone to great lengths already to keep any of the others from discovering what he had.

Why?

The only possibility that presented itself was that he'd taken the notion that he wanted her for himself.

She dismissed it. It seemed too farfetched a theory. It kept teasing at her mind, though, little snatches of memory feeding it.

He hadn't saved the readings of the scan. She'd been too unnerved at the time to realize it, but she remembered now that he'd studied the read out and then shut the device off without saving the readings to memory ... except in his own memory.

He'd been angry after he'd taken her to the showers, accusing. She'd been too surprised and angry herself by his strange behavior to figure out exactly what he'd been accusing her of, but it occurred to her after a while that he'd implied that she was trying to use her training against him ... the art of deadly seduction.

She'd never tried that particular method of overcoming a cyborg. She'd thought the entire idea ludicrous if these things were, as The Company claimed, merely defective machines. A woman might seduce a man and overcome him while he was distracted, but a machine? Anyway, she didn't feel confident enough in her femininity to consider seduction a realistic possibility for her. It seemed more likely that any attempt would be ignored, or worse, a source of amusement.

She was so deep in thought, she hardly registered the sound of approaching footsteps until they halted outside the cabin door. The sound of the keys being depressed jerked her from her abstraction, however. She held her breath, staring at the door as it opened.

Dante stepped through and closed the door behind him.

Moving to the bunk, he settled beside her and began tugging at the restraint. His lips tightened into a thin line when he saw the results of her efforts to free herself.

Pain shot through her arms as the feeling began to return when he'd untied her. Carefully, he lowered her arms, examining her wrists. She would've jerked free except that she had no use of her arms at the moment.

It was just as well, she realized, mentally kicking herself.

She was supposed to be trying to lull him into a false sense of security.

Her wrists, she saw as he examined them, were raw and bruised from her efforts to free herself. "That was...." He hesitated as he met her gaze. "An exercise in futility."

"I didn't know that until I tried though," she retorted tightly.

"You should have deduced that I had tied a knot adequate to hold you."

"But then I'm not a cyborg."

He said nothing for several moments. "No, you're not."

Amaryllis reigned in her temper with an effort.

When she said nothing more, he returned his attention to her wrists. "You have done more damage than I had thought possible. You skin is ... delicate. Will this repair itself without aid of medicines?"

"In time."

"How much time?"

"How would I know that?"

He looked both surprised by her comment and irritated. "You do not have nanos?"

"For infection and internal, life threatening injuries, yes."

To her relief, he released her hands at last, settling them on her thighs. "I did not intend to cause you injury, but to protect you from...."

When he didn't finish, Amaryllis asked, "Your fellow cyborgs?"

"Yourself. To keep you from taking foolhardy chances."

Amaryllis gave him a look. "If you have such a low opinion of humans, why are you ... doing this?"

He studied her a long moment and finally shrugged, rising from the bunk. "I must return to my duties before I am missed. I will bring food for you when I return."

When he'd gone, Amaryllis moved to the door of the facilities. After listening to make certain no one was about, she went in, took care of her needs and rushed back to the cabin. She would've liked to soothe her hurts with cool water, but she didn't dare linger too long in the facilities.

She'd had worse and endured.

The burning subsided in her wrists after a while. Exhausted from the pain of her injuries and the shocks she'd endured one after another since their craft had crashed, too wary even to consider leaving the cabin and, despite everything, bored beyond belief, Amaryllis finally curled up on the cot and allowed sleep to overtake her. She woke when the sound of the key lock being punched alerted her to imminent company.

As much as she hated to admit it, relief flooded her when she saw that it was Dante.

As promised, he brought food for her--enough for several days from the bounty of it. There was no place to sit except the floor or the bunk. She chose the bunk, folding her legs and bracing her back against the bulkhead. Dante settled beside her at the other end of the bunk, watching her.

"Have you eaten?"

"Yes. This is for you."

She was starving, but discomfited by his attention. "Where are we going?" she asked finally, more to distract him than because she expected him to answer.

He hesitated. "We discovered a world well beyond the human colonies."

"In unexplored space?" she asked, surprised.

"Not now."

Amaryllis frowned thoughtfully. "The Company was certain the cyborg stronghold was near the outer rim."

"They were wrong. Does that surprise you?"

"Not particularly. They're wrong more often than not. That's what comes from having a superiority complex."

Amusement entered his eyes. "You think we are guilty of the same."

It wasn't a question. Amaryllis shrugged.

"We were created with all the advantages of human beings and none of the disadvantages."

"You think so?"

That effectively silenced him for several moments. "I am as human as you are. Why do you consider me a machine and yourself ... human?"

He couldn't have said anything more certain to cut her to the quick than that. Amaryllis lost her appetite. Ignoring the question, she very carefully covered the food and looked around for someplace to put it.

"You are finished?"

"Yeah."

Dante frowned. "You have hardly eaten any. No wonder you are so tiny."

Amaryllis glared at him.

Something flickered in his eyes. After a moment, he took the food from her wordlessly, rose from the bunk and placed the containers in his locker.

She was staring at the floor when he returned to the bunk. She studiously ignored him as he stood over her, eyeing her curiously.

Finally, he settled on the bunk beside her. "You are offended."

"You are so fucking observant."

His brows rose. "Why were you reconstructed with bionics? Were you injured in duty?"

"I don't want to talk about it," Amaryllis snarled.

"You have no data banks," he observed pensively.

"No shit." Thank *God* he couldn't access her memories!

"The gutter language does not become you."

"Does it bother you?"

"Yes."

"Well, I don't give a fuck," Amaryllis snapped. "I *feel* like using it."

"Why?"

"Why don't you just go … recharge or something?"

His face tightened with anger. "I derive energy from food, the same as you."

"Really?" Amaryllis said sarcastically. "I had no idea we had so much in common."

"I don't particularly care for the sarcasm either," he said tightly.

"Too fucking bad."

He caught her jaw in one hand, forcing her to look at him. She made an aborted attempt to pull free, but realized fairly quickly that she couldn't. Instead, she glared at him coldly. He studied her in angry silence for several moments before his expression softened. "I wounded you."

Surprise at his perception flickered through her. "You wish," she said derisively, but not nearly as convincingly as she would've liked.

"You are wrong. I do not wish it at all," he said. "And I think we have much more in common that you are willing to admit."

"Wrong. We have nothing in common," Amaryllis said tightly, feeling her anger rise once more as it occurred to her to wonder if he meant to bring up her bionics again.

"You may hate me for what I am, but you are not … indifferent to me."

The comment took the wind out of her sails. "What?"

Releasing her jaw, he trailed his fingers lightly down her throat, across her collar bone and down between her breasts. Amaryllis' breath caught in her chest as he traced a light circle around each trembling globe. Even through the cloth, his finger felt like a firebrand. Her nipples puckered, stood erect, begging for his touch.

Her reaction embarrassed and infuriated her. Before she thought better of it, she swung at him. As if he'd anticipated her retaliation, he caught her wrist mid-air, pushing her back against the bunk and pinning her with the weight of his body. His eyes gleamed as he stared down at her. "I am cyborg, no more than a machine. Surely you are not offended by my touch?"

Amaryllis swallowed with an effort.

After holding her gaze for several long moments, his gaze slid downward, settling on her breasts, heaving now with her efforts to drag in a decent breath of air. With deliberation, he leaned down, covering the tip of one breast with his mouth. Heat, like fire, instantly flowed through her, clouding her mind. She tensed, tried to block her mind to the pleasure that immediately assailed her. Her heart began to thunder in her ears so frantically that she could hear nothing but its drumming and the rush of air as it sawed almost painfully in and out of her laboring lungs.

She might have been completely naked for all the difference the thin fabric made.

She was sorry she wasn't.

She wanted to feel the moist heat of his mouth on her skin.

As if he'd read her mind, he nudged the fabric aside and covered her nipple with his mouth, sucking, teasing the sensitive tip with his tongue. She gasped as a fresh rush of mind sundering sensation boiled through her. Her belly clenched almost painfully. Her femininity quaked, gathering heat and moisture.

With an effort, she summoned her defenses, closed her mind against the maddening stimulus, certain that he would stop if she could convince him she found no pleasure in his touch.

He seemed to sense her battle. Instead of accepting the lie she tried to tell with her body, instead of teasing her and then releasing her, he continued to suckle and torment her nipple until her shaky defenses crumbled, until she was drunk with the euphoria of pleasure, her mind chaotic, and she became so weak she felt as if she would black out.

It wasn't until all resistance was leached from her and she went limp that he ceased to torment her. It took several moments to gather the strength to lift her eyelids when he released her at last and lifted his head to look at her once more. She couldn't even manage a look of reproach, certainly not one of indifference.

Apparently satisfied with what he saw, he rolled off of her and lay down on the bunk on his side, tugging at her until he'd tucked her back against his chest. "Rest now."

It took several moments for that to sink in to her heat fogged brain. Rest? Amaryllis thought, abruptly outraged. Her whole body was on fire!

How could he do … *that* and then just fucking stop?

As irritated as she was, Amaryllis only tensed, yielding without any more protest than a slight resistance. She'd had time to cool, if only slightly, and time to remember, belatedly, that she was supposed to be lulling him into a false sense of security, supposed to be trying to seduce *him* so that she could overcome him.

She stank at this.

It didn't take a mental giant to see that she was in far more danger of being seduced than he was.

She also had a bad feeling that the longer it took to accomplish such a mission, the less likely it was that she'd be able to go through with it. Machine or not, he had personality. It might be as maddening as it was appealing, but it wasn't something that she could feel indifference about.

It was one thing, she realized, to target an unknown entity, trust that it was no more than a runaway machine, and blow it to bits. It was quite another to cozy up to one who looked, and felt, and acted like a human being and commit an act that would feel like cold blooded murder.

She was fairly certain she wasn't going to be able to go through with it.

Why couldn't he have been like he was supposed to be? Cold. Mechanical. Unfeeling. Why couldn't he have been insane?

Damn him anyway! How could he have seen through what she'd been so carefully hiding from herself? She wasn't going to be able lie to herself, or to him, that she was immune to him.

Maybe it was merely a psychological reaction to being taken captive? She'd never been captured before. She'd had training for it, but no scenario had been anything like this. The expectation had been that she would be tortured-- with pain, not pleasure.

Maybe she hadn't properly assessed the situation to start with? Maybe killing him was not only not necessary to her own survival, but entirely the opposite? Contributing to her downfall?

"It would be easier to avoid broaching a painful topic if I knew what it was."

Despite her distraction, it didn't take her two seconds to realize he was harping on their earlier disagreement. Amaryllis gritted her teeth. "Jeez! Could you just drop it? It doesn't matter."

"If it didn't, you wouldn't be angry."

She tensed, considering rolling from the bunk and stalking across the room to put some distance between them. His arm tightened as if he knew exactly what was running through her mind. She relapsed, fuming.

He fell silent. She didn't know if he was sleeping or not, but his hold didn't loosen and she found she couldn't maintain either her anger or her tension. Slowly but surely it seeped away. The desire he'd aroused in her didn't.

He was warm. He breathed. His body was hard, but in the sense of well honed muscle and tissue, not cold metal.

He felt good.

He felt damned good.

He's a machine! She mentally screamed at herself.

Why the hell had they made them so real? Stupid, conceited, megalomaniacs! What was it about humans and their preoccupation with perfection anyway? Why create something so perfect it was better than the real thing? Because they liked to think they could do a better job than nature? Hell, that wasn't all that damned hard! Look at her! A freak of nature if there ever was one. She should never have been born at all, much less survived outside her mother's womb.

She should be glad he'd pushed that particular button and summoned her personal demons. It was enough to remind her to keep her distance in every way possible.

If she could just keep reminding herself of that, she might get through this.

Chapter Six

Amaryllis didn't know whether to be relieved or sorry that Dante hadn't pursued the matter. On one level, she harbored a good deal of regret. She couldn't recall ever having been so quickly, or thoroughly, aroused that she'd become lost in it. She was sorry it had ended without the promised fulfillment, especially since the incident seemed to have left her body in a ready state that showed no signs of going away and only added to the tension she was already feeling about her situation.

On another level, she realized that she'd been spared a step that she would never have been able to retrieve. If Dante had possessed her, given her the pleasure his touch promised, she feared she would've been addicted to his touch in a way that she would never be able to free herself from.

She didn't want to be tied to him in any way. She couldn't afford to be. Her life might well depend upon escape and she couldn't afford to be torn by conflicting desires.

The cyborgs, if they discovered she was not one of them, would almost certainly perceive her as a threat to their plans, whatever those were. They might decide to simply keep her, in which case she would never be allowed to see her family again. Or they might decide that it would be better all around to kill her.

One thing about the situation plagued her.

Why had he decided to help her? Why hadn't he simply turned her over when he realized that she was human?

She would've felt better if she'd known that.

She would've felt even better if she could've put some distance between the two of them.

Her situation didn't truly allow that. She managed distance of a sort, though, by refusing thereafter to share the bunk with Dante. She slept when he was gone. When he returned to the cabin, she occupied herself with her thoughts or her workouts. There wasn't a great deal that she could do for hours on end, confined to the one, small cabin, but it was sparsely furnished.

She needed to keep fit. More than that, she needed something to work off her excess energy. It was far better to exhaust her body in staying fit than to simply stare at the walls and allow her imagination to take her places she didn't want to go.

Dante didn't try to interfere, or even try to converse with her after that first night. If he hadn't been a cyborg, she would have been inclined to think he was brooding over the fact that she so assiduously avoided any sort of physical contact with him. He often watched her instead of sleeping. She made it a point never to look directly at him, but she could feel his gaze.

If he hadn't been a cyborg, she might have been inclined to think that the 'lesson' he'd given her to show her that he was well aware that she found him attractive, whatever her prejudices, had backfired and caught him, too.

That would require an admission on her part that she wasn't ready to concede, however.

He behaved very much like a human, but she knew he'd been programmed to do so. Even the sexual aspects of his behavior, although it had taken her by surprise, didn't really change anything. For all she knew, he might have been designed to be a pleasure droid. Most of the cyborgs had been designed as soldiers. Before she'd met Dante, she'd thought they all were, but that didn't mean that they were. She could've been wrong.

She had an uneasy feeling that she hadn't been, but she resolutely refused to acknowledge it. She tried very hard not to think about it at all, but with indifferent success. She'd experienced an awakening on that first night they spent together. Each time she felt his brooding gaze upon her, it was like a touch and her body warmed and images rose in her mind that made her body vibrate with anticipation. Each time she failed to keep her own gaze from straying to him, she felt heat begin to rise inside of her, felt her pulse begin to beat a little faster.

After weeks in space, confined in so small an area, she'd almost begun to hope she would be discovered. She supposed that accounted for her carelessness.

Or perhaps it was only that Dante had made her so aware of her femininity that she'd become preoccupied with the distant ache that found no surcease.

She'd stayed far longer beneath the pounding water of the shower than she should have, caressing her own aching body with her soapy hands until the discomfort grew to be too much to bear. For someone who'd spent most of her life trying to divorce herself from her body, it seemed doubly difficult to find this new awareness of it that she couldn't chase away no matter how hard she tried. Finally, she'd turned to washing her hair. She'd just rinsed the soap from it when she finally sensed a presence nearby.

Her heart leapt into her throat as the realization sank in that she'd been vaguely aware of the sensation of being watched even before she'd begun to wash her hair, too preoccupied with the ache between her legs and the uncomfortable tenderness of her breasts to consciously acknowledge it, but aware in some distant corner of her mind.

Her instincts had atrophied from boredom and disuse.

She had to force her frantic mind to function, consciously call her training to her aid.

She'd alerted him, however, by the sudden tension of her body. Even as she swung into action, he countered her strike, slamming her into the back wall of the stall. For all that, the collision was carefully controlled and didn't even knock the breath from her. Amaryllis blinked the water from her eyes and looked up at the man pinning her to the cold metal wall.

"Dante!" she gasped, torn between relief and dawning anger.

He was furious. That much was instantly obvious. "That

was either unbelievably careless ... or calculating," he ground out.

Right up until the very moment he spat the accusation at her, Amaryllis had carefully avoided the fact that she had dallied in the shower because she knew Dante would be returning soon. She'd convinced herself that she would be in and out before he returned, but she'd made no attempt to hurry.

She'd wanted to bait him.

She wasn't certain why, but her transparency embarrassed her and because it did, it also angered her. "I don't have an internal clock like you do!" she snapped.

The reminder angered him far more than she'd expected it to. Grasping her hand, he guided it to the crotch of his uniform, molding her palm over his heated erection. It was huge, rock hard, and throbbed at her touch like a live thing. Amaryllis' eyes widened. Her heart faltered, then began to race. Heat curled low in her belly. Her mouth went dry and the breath froze in her lungs.

"Does that feel to you as if I feel nothing?" he ground out. "If I were no more than a cold, unfeeling machine, do you think desire would torment me every time I look at you?"

She licked her lips nervously, tried to gather moisture into her mouth. "You were probably designed as a pleasure droid," she said a little shakily.

Several emotions chased across his features before they hardened once more with anger. "I was designed to kill ... but I can give pleasure, as well. Do you want me to pleasure you?"

Under the circumstances, no. She wasn't about to ask for it! But she needed it, she realized, desperately.

To her relief, he didn't wait for a yeah or nay. When she hesitated, he lifted her against the wall, pinned her there with his body and pressed open mouthed kisses along her throat and shoulder, licking the moisture from her skin and leaving fire in the wake of his touch. She gasped as he invaded her senses, shuddered as his mouth moved hungrily across her flesh and settled over one erect, throbbing nipple. Her mind and body melted as the fire of desire engulfed her. Weakly, she wrapped her arms and legs around him, clinging as he moved against her, caressed her with his mouth and tongue, scorched her skin with the heat and touch of his hands as they moved restlessly along her body, exploring her, giving pleasure that left her dizzy and disoriented.

Her body quickened. Moisture gathered in her sex. The walls of that nether throat trembled with want, quaked in supplication of his possession.

Tightening her grip on him, she arched against him.

He seemed to know what she needed. Shifting, he aligned their bodies so that her cleft enveloped his shaft. The fabric that separated them chafed her as he pressed against her, frustrated her, but she moved eagerly against him as keen pleasure stabbed through her from the rough caress of his cock against her clit, along her cleft. It teased her as much as it pleased her, fed her desire, frustrated her body's attempts to reach culmination.

When he lifted his head at last and gazed into her eyes, she saw her own tumultuous desire reflected there, saw that his need matched her own. She lifted her lips, brushed them along the hard ridge of his jaw.

He drew in a ragged breath, tipped his head to brush his lips along the sensitive surface of her own.

Fire poured into her, anticipation like acid in her veins. Her mouth watered to taste him, tingled with the need to feel the rough caress of his tongue.

When he pulled back suddenly, lifting his head in alertness, Amaryllis felt a stab of both surprise and disappointment. Then she heard the sound, as well.

Fear smothered the flames of desire so abruptly it made her dizzy, faintly nauseous.

Rigid now with the possibility of danger, Dante allowed her to slide slowly down until her feet touched the floor. There was warning in his eyes as he jerked his head in the direction of his cabin, but it wasn't necessary. As shaky as she was, Amaryllis fled for the door on tiptoe the moment

Dante released her. Shutting off the shower, he followed her out.

Neither of them said anything as they dried off quickly and quietly.

Dante's uniform was dripping wet. It clung to every beautiful inch of his well honed body. As much as she would've liked to watch him undress, to see the body she'd only imagined thus far, Amaryllis was also embarrassed by her lack of control and the dangerously stupid error in judgment that had almost gotten them caught. She turned her back to him, pulling her own garments on jerkily as he peeled the wet suit from his body and tossed it aside.

Behind her, she heard the rustle of cloth as he quickly dried his body, heard him step to the locker and remove a change of clothing. She didn't dare look at him, afraid of what she might see in his eyes.

Instead, shivering with reaction, she settled weakly on the floor across from him once she'd dressed, listening to the movements in the cabin adjoining Dante's.

After a time, they heard the door to the corridor open and close again, and then footsteps that diminished into the distance.

Amaryllis licked her dried lips. "What would happen if we were caught?" she whispered.

Dante looked at her for a long moment. "Cyborg or not, that's not something I'm particularly anxious to discover," he said finally.

Chapter Seven

Amaryllis gaped at him, realizing for the first time that she was playing Russian roulette with his life, not just her own.

It made her feel ten times worse.

There was no point in trying to resurrect the wall she'd built over the years to enable her to do her job and still sleep at night. Dante might have been created in a lab, but he was no 'mere' machine.

The truth, as hard as it was to accept, was that he was probably no more machine than she was. She'd been born to parents, but so defective fully half her body was robotic. Defective internal organs had been replaced with healthy bio-engineered organs that had only become hers after they'd been transplanted into her body.

She was as self-righteous and bigoted as any other member of her kind.

She knew now why The Company was so hot to destroy the cyborgs. They were trying to cover their asses, not protect mankind from machines. They didn't want it to be discovered that they'd so far forgotten themselves as to create life when the morality laws forbade such tampering.

"I'm sorry," she said, finally nerving herself to meet his gaze. "That was ... unforgivably stupid and careless of me."

She knew the moment the words were out of her mouth that he'd misinterpreted them.

"Already regretting it?" he asked coldly.

"Yes, but not the way you're thinking."

"I don't think. I collate. I'm sure you haven't forgotten that. You make certain to point it out every time I come near you."

"Stop it! I'm trying to apologize. I know, now, that I was

wrong."

His lips tightened. "I failed to perform as expected? You do realize your revulsion of cyborgs creates a problem. Next time, close your eyes. Maybe you'll be able to pretend I'm human, not a machine."

Amaryllis felt her temper spark to life. "I know you're not just a machine," she said tightly.

"You discovered something?"

"Damn it, Dante! You could at least give me a chance."

He shook his head. "I already did. My life might mean nothing to you, but I'm fond of it."

"He wasn't supposed to be there, damn it! How was I to know he'd show up?"

His eyes narrowed. "He wasn't supposed to be in his own cabin?"

"Not at this time … he never has been before."

"But you were expecting me?"

Amaryllis blushed. "Yes."

"The shower was a nice touch. You could have disposed of me and it would've looked like an accident."

Amaryllis gaped at him. "You can't be serious!"

"That wasn't the plan?"

"No!"

"What was the plan, then?"

The blush that had barely died, rose once more. "I didn't really have one."

"The human capacity for half truths, complete lies, and malicious subterfuge never fails to amaze me. You did not decide, when you saw that I wanted you, to wait until I was half crazed with need and dangle the promise in front of me? It was not your plan to use my weakness to dispose of me, to rid yourself of the only one aboard this ship that is aware that you are human?"

Horror washed through Amaryllis that he'd so completely understood her original plans. In point of fact, she'd forgotten them in the time since. Having him recite them back to her as if by rote brought them crashing back into her memory, however, and she could not prevent the guilt that showed on her face.

No wonder he hadn't touched her since! No wonder he'd avoided her as assiduously as she'd avoided contact with him.

"I didn't know you then," she said a little weakly.

"You do not know me now," he said tightly.

A shaft of fear stabbed through her. "What do you mean by that?"

"I mean, if you are so determined to reveal your presence, I see no reason to risk my freedom, and perhaps my life, to preserve yours. I could turn you in now and claim that I found you hiding in the ship."

He was angry and, she thought with a touch of surprise, it was as much because he was hurt as from sheer sexual frustration. He'd said that he wanted her--that was why he'd taken the risk of protecting her--but all that she'd done from the moment they'd met was to throw his origins in his face.

She couldn't reason with him, though. She'd done a hell of a good job convincing him that she held him in contempt, couldn't see him as anything but a cyborg. He wasn't going to listen to any attempt to explain that she really didn't feel that way, probably never had.

She couldn't resist the temptation to try, though.

"I wasn't trying to get caught and I wasn't trying to seduce you to hurt you. I … wanted you."

Something flickered in his eyes, but vanished so quickly she might only have imagined it. "Unfortunately, as much as I would like to accommodate your needs, I do not trust you."

Amaryllis was still staring at him in shocked dismay when he left the cabin, locking the door behind him.

When he'd gone, she moved to the bunk and sank down on it weakly, too distressed, at first, to think about much beyond her humiliating rejection.

He didn't come back. Days passed with no sign of him at all.

She finally realized that Dante had taken a page from her

book. He returned to the cabin when he knew she would be sleeping to get the things he needed.

She spent the first few days jumping at every sound, expecting a contingent of guards to arrive and seize her. She couldn't maintain that sort of fear, however, and finally decided that the threat had been an idle one.

Maybe, if she did as she'd been told, he wouldn't turn her in.

Or maybe it was some sort of punishment he'd devised? Maybe he just wanted her to agonize over when she'd be taken?

Chapter Eight

Amaryllis had combed every square inch of the cabin she shared with Dante and even ventured into the other cabins that adjoined his in search of a weapon or anything that could be used as a weapon. She'd come up empty handed. Either the cyborgs simply weren't taking any chances of a weapon falling into the hands of the hunters, their leader didn't altogether trust his men, or the ship had been a prisoner hauler when they'd taken it and had already been stripped of anything even resembling a weapon.

With no weapon, she wasn't going to be able to put up much resistance when/if they came for her. In truth, just how much difference would it make?

She wanted to live, but what were the chances of it?

Would it be best to fight to the death and take as many with her as she could, comforting herself with the thought that her life had cost them? Or would that only insure her death when they might have no intention of taking her life otherwise?

She still hadn't decided what she would do when she heard the sound she'd been dreading; footsteps in the corridor that halted outside Dante's cabin door; the musical notes that signaled the code being keyed into the lock.

She never consciously decided what she would do. Her training simply kicked in and she acted.

She realized even as she launched herself at him that it was Dante. Doubt went through her like an electric current, distracting her, but he was on duty. He'd never come to the cabin during his watch and he should not be here now … unless, as he'd threatened, he meant to turn her in.

The moment of doubt, the slight hesitancy, cost her.

He blocked the flying kick aimed at his head, sending her spinning out of control. Her momentum slammed her against the bulkhead. Before she could thrust herself away and launch another attack, he slammed against her, pinning her against the cold steel.

"'Ware! Else all will know you are here!" he growled next to her ear.

Gritting her teeth, Amaryllis struggled to push herself away from the wall. He caught her shoulders, turning her to face him and pinning her back to the wall.

"It is I, Dante!"

Amaryllis stared up at him warily. "Why are you here … now, if you didn't come to turn me in?"

To her surprise a faint wash of color entered his cheeks. He loosened his hold on her slightly, swallowed convulsively. "Because…." He hesitated for so long that she thought he would say no more. "Because I could not stay away. This hunger gnaws at me until I think I will lose my mind. Or maybe I already have. I can think of no logical reason for the things I have done since I met you or the way that I feel." He paused, swallowing audibly. "If you say you still want me … I do not care anymore if it is a lie."

Warmth suffused Amaryllis, but only a part of it was the desire she'd been trying so hard to deny. His face was haggard, as if he'd found little rest, and his words bespoke of far more than physical need. He needed more than to possess her body. He needed to feel acceptance. Briefly, desire warred with wariness, but there was no contest really. She lifted her hand, caressing his hard cheek. "It wouldn't be a lie."

It seemed to take several moments for that comment to sink in. When it did, he surged toward her, crushing her body between his own and the unyielding wall behind her. Capturing her face in his hands, he tilted her head back, seeking her mouth with his own, his hunger evident in the fierceness of his possession. A wave of dizziness crashed over her the moment his lips covered hers, melding, clinging, pressuring her to part her lips and allow him intimate access to her body. Fire followed in its wake as she parted her lips for him and felt the faintly rough texture of his tongue as it plunged inside her mouth and raked across her own. His essence filled her, consumed her mind like a fiery intoxicant that allowed little room for thought.

Doubt flickered briefly through her mind--her own demons, the knowledge that he was cyborg and her enemy. Pleasure banished the doubts far from consciousness as every nerve ending in her body came alive, pelting her with the pleasurable sensations of his heat and the feel of his body, the strength and pliancy of his muscles, the texture of his skin against her own. His hands moved over her body as his tongue danced along hers, coaxing, caressing, consuming her life force until she felt weak, giddy, hungry.

He snapped the thin supports of her garments so that not even that thin barrier separated her from his touch. Liquid fire gushed through her as he cupped a breast in either hand, massaging them, plucking at her tender nipples. Her insides liquefied, became molten. Her breath froze in her lungs.

Abruptly, he broke the kiss, caught her beneath her arms, pushing her up the wall. Mindlessly, she twined her arms around his shoulders, buried her face against his neck and wrapped her legs around his waist to hold herself upright. His cock, swollen, heated, nudged along her cleft, sending hard shafts of pleasure through her that made her gasp for breath as it rubbed against her exposed clit.

He caught her hair, tugging on it, tilting her head back to expose her throat, and sucked a burning trail of kisses along it, rotating his hips rhythmically against her cleft as he did so and making her mindless with need. Tension wound inside of her as the pleasure escalated almost beyond bearing, tightened. Her body clenched in time to the pressure. Abruptly the pleasure reached a point of extremity where it could no longer be contained. Blackness swirled around her as it burst, making her body quake endlessly with release.

She collapsed weakly against him, scarcely aware of her surroundings as he carried her to the bunk and lowered her onto it. With an effort, she opened her eyes to look at him as he stepped away from her.

Doubt swarmed through her when she saw that he was still fully clothed, his face harsh with his own needs. He hadn't sought to assuage the desire he'd claimed he felt for her and could not contain, hadn't possessed her body with his own, hadn't even removed his own clothing. Chaotic thoughts flickered through her mind. Before she could voice them, he worked the fastenings of his uniform loose from neck to groin, exposing a sprinkling of dark hair in the center of his chest that formed a thin trail downward to the nest from which his cock sprang. With hands that shook noticeably, he stripped his uniform from his body.

She shouldn't have been surprised by the sheer perfection of his body, but she was … and fascinated at the same time. Mesmerized by the play of muscles beneath his silken skin, Amaryllis didn't even think to protest as Dante grasped her legs, parted them and settled against her, wedging his hips between her parted thighs. An aftershock of pleasure went through her as she felt his cock settle along her moist cleft, nudging against her still throbbing clit.

He absorbed her gasp of pleasure as he covered her mouth once more in a kiss that neared desperation. The dying embers of her release leapt to life, threatening to consume her. She was breathless and already drunk with passion when he tore his lips from hers and moved downward, lathing her flesh with his tongue, nipping at her skin with the edge of his teeth and sending stinging nettles of delight through her.

A hoarse cry scraped along her throat as he covered the trembling tip of one breast with his mouth, nudging it with his tongue. The hunger of his kisses threatened to send her over the edge once more, brought her perilously close as he divided his attention between her breasts, teasing first one and then the other until she thought she would black out.

She was mindless with need by the time he ceased to tease her breasts and dragged kisses along her belly. The heat of his breath against her clit was her first inkling of his goal and his intentions. Her protest died on her lips as his mouth covered her and she felt the rough caress of his tongue against her clit. The air left her lungs. Molten fire poured through her veins. Something between a gasp and a hoarse cry escaped her as her body seized with ecstasy, hovered for so many moments she thought she would die, and then exploded with the force of a neutron bomb, mushrooming outward in a wave of fire.

She was barely conscious when he rose above her, settled his weight on one arm and guided his cock into the mouth of her passage. The rounded head of his cock felt enormous, sparking a flash of doubt that penetrated her semi-consciousness. Her flesh, quaking still in the aftermath of her climax, resisted his possession.

He pulled slightly away and thrust again, eased along her channel by the moisture gathered there. Amaryllis gasped, opening her eyes wide as she felt him stretching her, felt her muscles clenching around him.

He watched her face as he claimed her inch by excruciating inch, retreating and then pressing forward again each time she thought she could take no more, could feel the muscles of her passage burning from the resistance to his intrusion. She'd begun to fear he would rend her in two when she felt his hips grinding against her, felt the head of his cock nudge her womb. A mixture of relief and pleasure filled her. As he withdrew once more, she lifted her hands, skated them along his arms to his neck and locked them behind his head. Pulling herself upward, she moved her lips along his hard, bulging pecs, nipped them with her teeth.

A shudder went through him. She gasped as he surged deeply inside of her again, burying his cock to the hilt, grinding his hips against her briefly and then withdrawing as slowly as he'd entered her. When he thrust again, she lifted her hips to meet him, sucking a love bite on the side of his neck. Groaning, he collapsed against her, thrusting and withdrawing in a slow, measured rhythm that drew heat from her once more, made her body burgeon rapidly toward release again.

She clutched him tightly, moving in concert, urging him to move faster, plunge deeper. He paused, drew in several ragged breaths and abruptly increased the tempo of his thrusts, plunging harder and faster with each thrust until Amaryllis could feel herself slipping up the bunk with the force of his possession. She dug her heels into the mattress, met his escalating assault with gratification as his hard thrusts sent her spiraling out of control.

Her culmination was so shattering it dragged a ragged cry from her despite her efforts to restrain it. The clenching muscles of her passage around his hard length sent him over the edge, as well. He let out a hoarse groan and covered her mouth with his, shuddering as waves of ecstasy rolled over him.

Amaryllis went perfectly limp, exhausted with repletion, listening to her heart thundering in her ears. A fine sheen of sweat dampened them, made their skin cling as they struggled to catch their breath. Finally, Dante settled a shoulder and hip beside her, scooped her into his arms and rolled so that she was draped bonelessly atop his chest.

Nothing, Amaryllis realized with a dawning sense of amazement, had ever felt so right before in her life as this moment did. Her entire body sparked and throbbed with the dying echoes of the ecstasy he'd given her, and yet she was even more aware of the chest rising and falling beneath her cheek, the warmth of his skin. It should have felt foreign to her, alien. Instead, it seemed almost as comfortingly familiar as her own body--more so, because she'd never really felt that comfortable with her own body.

"I have to go," he said after several moments, his voice still sounding gravelly.

Surprise jolted through her. She lifted her head to look up at him. "Now?"

His face was impassive. "I should not have come at all."

An odd sense of uneasiness began to work its way through Amaryllis as he slipped out from under her, leaving her in sole possession of the bunk. As she watched, totally confused, he snatched his uniform from the floor and quickly pulled it on. Dozens of questions crowded into her mind, but she couldn't seem to voice any of them.

He'd wanted her.

He'd had her.

He was done?

Anger sparked to life at that thought. The next one tamped it. What had she expected? They would fuck like a couple of bunnies and then he'd profess undying love? She wasn't that naïve--that antiquated in her thoughts--was she?

And he was a frigging machine, for God's sake!

He paused at the door and turned to study her for so long that she thought he might say something. When he left without a word, she was even more confused. She was still trying to figure out how she felt, beyond stunned and confused, when she heard the retreating thread of his boots stop suddenly and then the sound of distant voices.

She couldn't make out what was being said. Abruptly, the conversation ceased. The sound of many feet, coming in her direction, followed.

They didn't pass the door. They halted outside. Amaryllis had just leapt from the bunk when the door flew open. Within seconds, the room was filled with cyborgs.

Chapter Nine

Reese stood at the forefront, wearing the uniform of the cyborgs. His gaze swept her from head to foot. "Leave us," he said without turning.

After the briefest of hesitations, the cyborg guards behind him backed from the room and closed the door behind them.

Amaryllis was too stunned even to think. He looked like Reese. He sounded like Reese. But was it her partner?

"Reese?"

Something flickered in his eyes. "Get dressed."

Unconsciously, Amaryllis glanced toward the garments Dante had left in a ruined pile on the floor. When she looked at Reese again, she saw that his gaze had followed hers. Before she could think of anything to say, he strode to the clothing and lifted it to inspect it. His head whipped toward her, his gaze capturing hers. "He forced you?"

Amaryllis blushed to the roots of her hair. Not unless climbing all over someone and moaning 'fuck me' constituted force. There was something in his expression, however, that told her that wasn't something he wanted to hear.

He saw the answer in her eyes. His face hardened.

Amaryllis took a step back when he straightened and surged toward her, catching her upper arms in a painful grip. "Bathe," he said through gritted teeth, thrusting her in the direction of the facilities.

She merely gaped at him when he released her and moved to the door. Opening it, he spoke to the men outside.

Belatedly, it occurred to Amaryllis that the facilities might be her only hope of escape and it still took an effort to force herself to move. Reese, or the cyborg who looked like Reese, caught the door before she could close it, following her inside.

"There is no where to run to, Amy."

The comment stopped her in her tracks although she wasn't even certain by that time if there was even any point in trying to escape. It also added considerably to her confusion. No one called her Amy except her family. She'd thought she'd imagined it before when Reese had called her Amy. Maybe she had. The plain fact of the matter was that no one, including Reese, should even know her real name, much less the name her family had called her. She was fairly certain she didn't want to ask him how he knew, though. "I don't … understand … any of this."

"You do. You just don't want to," he responded coolly, taking up a position by the door.

Reluctantly, Amaryllis moved to the shower and turned it on. She felt as if she was living the bizarre reality of a nightmare. The man watching her so coldly looked and sounded like Reese, her partner, the man she'd had secret fantasies about from the time he'd joined the hunters, even before he'd become her partner. "You're not … you aren't…."

He lifted a brow. "The same man who worked beside you for the past eighteen months? I am."

"You're a … cyborg?"

His lips flattened into a thin line. "I would say that we are the same, but we both know that isn't true, don't we? You were born of woman, born with a soul. While I … I was cooked up in The Company labs."

A wave of dizziness washed over Amaryllis. "They said we were all the same," she said through lips that felt strangely stiff and uncooperative.

This couldn't be happening.

He couldn't know that. No one had access to that information except The Company.

Unless Dante had told them?

Nausea followed that thought.

He *had* turned her in. He'd come to her, fucked her six ways from Sunday, and then fucked her over.

Christ! She was *such* a fucking moron!

And she'd been feeling all maudlin over the fact that Dante hadn't even made an attempt to convince her that there was affection involved in the act.

The sense of betrayal was almost more than she could handle on top of the shock of discovering that Reese was one of the cyborgs ... not a hunter/maybe cyborg as the others were, the people she still thought of as people. A cyborg.

Like Dante.

And, like Dante, he had betrayed her trust ... except that she'd given her trust to Reese unquestioningly. She'd admired him. He'd been an intergalactic ranger--they'd been told he had come to them from the rangers--and she'd thought he was one of the finest soldiers ever to live--thought of him almost like a ...god.

A chill went through her despite the warmth of the water. With a shaking hand, she shut it off and sloughed the water from her body. Reese tossed her the linen from the bed that she'd been wrapped in when the cyborgs had burst into the cabin. She managed to catch it and wrap it around her although a good portion of it dragged through the water that still puddled at her feet.

She didn't look at Reese as she headed for the door.

He barred her passage as she reached the opening, bracing his arm against the door frame. "I give you my word I will not betray you."

Amaryllis glanced up at him and then fixed her stony gaze on the floor. "You already did."

His lips tightened. "I was sent to infiltrate the ranks of the hunters."

There didn't seem to be much she could say to that. He was a soldier. He'd followed orders. God alone knew what those orders had included, but she was fairly certain she didn't want to know.

He wouldn't let her pass, however. She didn't know what he wanted from her, but it was obvious her silence wasn't it. "It doesn't matter now."

He caught her chin, forcing her to look at him.

"It matters."

She frowned, confused by the intensity of his gaze. "Why?"

Catching her shoulders, he dragged her up against his chest and covered her mouth with his own, kissing her deeply, hungrily. Too stunned even to consider resisting, he'd invaded her senses with the bold stroke of his tongue, his heat, his scent, his taste, flooding her body with the drug of desire, and annihilated any chance for thought even before Amaryllis realized what was happening. Heat curled in her belly. Her bones turned to putty. The only thought that flitted through her mind was the half formed one that she'd known Reese's kiss would be devastating. She staggered when he released her almost as unexpectedly as he'd seized her. "Think about it."

Think about it? Amaryllis thought blankly. As *if* she could think at all! Feeling very much as if she'd been blindsided, she followed Reese back into the cabin. A fresh stack of garments had been placed on the bunk. She moved toward them when Reese indicated she should put them on, but she was so shaken she couldn't make heads or tails of the pieces at first. Finally, she managed to dress herself.

"Where are you taking me?" she asked when Reese grasped her arm and escorted her toward the door.

"The barracks."

Amaryllis glanced at him sharply. Not a cell? Or maybe 'barracks' was merely a polite euphemism for prison?

She *was* a prisoner. A four man--make that cyborg--escort constituted an arrest in her book.

She discovered when he had escorted her through the ship that the barracks in question had been set aside for the females. She didn't know whether to be relieved or alarmed that they were being segregated by sex, but she discovered very quickly that it *was* a cell, regardless of what Reese had called it. As soon as she'd stepped inside, the door was locked.

Still, it was a relief just to be free of the overwhelming

presence of four enormous cyborg soldiers and the barracks at least had the feel of a barracks, not a jail cell.

She felt less relieved once she'd surveyed the room. Naturally enough the majority of the bunks had already been claimed. It was obviously a sleep period, for the room had been dimmed and the bunks were occupied, but the commotion at the door had roused most of them and she could feel dozens of pairs of curious eyes on her. Stiffening her spine, she moved down the aisle between the two rows, searching for an empty bunk.

"Cyborg whore!" one of the women muttered.

Amaryllis stiffened and glanced toward the sound of the voice. She couldn't recall her name, but she recognized the woman--a fanatic if there'd ever lived one. Half the hunters referred to her as Psycho.

To Amaryllis' relief, she saw the woman had been chained to her bunk. She didn't currently feel up to defending herself from attack.

Deciding to simply ignore the remark, she moved on, wondering what the chances were that her secret would remain a secret. Reese's comment seemed to indicate that Dante hadn't betrayed that much, at any rate, but she doubted it would be long before everyone knew regardless.

She'd never made any attempt to socialize with her fellow hunters. It wasn't encouraged, and, in any case, she'd never really learned how to interact socially with others, never having had much opportunity for it growing up. On the other hand, she hadn't exactly tried to keep her background secret either. She kept images of her family in her locker and it wasn't inconceivable that those had been seen by at least some of the other hunters.

And that was just the sort of juicy tidbit people liked to share when they were bored and couldn't think of anything else to talk about.

Apparently, her whereabouts since take off *wasn't* a secret and Psycho's nasty remark was only a prelude to what she could expect to have to endure.

She selected one of the last bunks for her own, in the

corner near the far bulkhead, not so much because she was trying to hide--although she wished she could--but because, strategically, it would be easier to defend if she came under attack.

She should've been used to being the pariah. She'd been 'the freak' growing up and the reputation of the hunters was such that civilians generally gave them a wide berth and, of course, the hunters themselves were encouraged to be loners.

Now, however, she didn't even have the comfort of knowing she was among her fellow soldiers.

She was human, the only human in the barracks, the only human on a ship loaded with cyborgs and bound for a planet inhabited and ruled by them.

She was pretty sure she knew what it felt like to be the only guppy in a tank full of sharks.

Chapter Ten

Amaryllis' internal clock, attuned to her uneasiness about her surroundings, woke her periodically. She'd considered staying awake, but she had to sleep sometime or she wouldn't be able to defend herself even if she was attacked and since the only alternative was sleeping while everyone else was awake and that seemed far more dangerous she composed herself and slept with one eye open and one ear cocked for trouble.

Under the circumstances, she was surprised she got any rest at all, but the past weeks had worn at her, frayed her nerves and exhausted her both physically and emotionally.

The events of the night before had wrecked what little composure she had left.

She didn't want to think about Dante.

It was like having a sore tooth. She couldn't resist touching it, but the moment she did excruciating pain replaced the dull throbbing ache that was her constant companion.

She didn't want to think about Reese either, but it was as difficult to block him from her thoughts as Dante. Consciously dismissing them from her mind and refusing to think about them by focusing on something else did very little good. Erotic dreams of both Reese and Dante tormented her nights.

Nearly a week passed before she saw Reese again and by that time she'd arrived at some fairly unpalatable conclusions.

Despite the company's claims about the cyborgs, these were beings. Strictly speaking, they might not be human beings, but she thought that was debatable--they certainly weren't the spawn of alien DNA. As far as she could see the only thing that made her any different from them at all was the fact that she'd been conceived 'naturally'. Physically, they had no greater ratio of mechanics to biological material than she did. Mentally--except for being well above average intellectually--their thought processes didn't seem to differ a great deal, and emotionally--they were capable of pretty much the entire range of nasty human traits.

Psycho might've been the only one to vocalize her feelings about Amaryllis fraternizing with the 'enemy', but since pretty much everyone else treated her like the invisible woman she had a fairly clear idea of what their feelings were on the matter. And being tried and convicted by one's peers on nothing more substantial than a rumor was certainly a very human situation.

When she added to that the fact that both Reese and Dante had betrayed her, she had to admit the differences between human and cyborg were blurred to near indistinguishable.

For a solid week after she'd been placed with the other female hunters, they were confined almost exclusively to the barracks, even taking their meals there and it dawned on her after a while that nothing had changed a great deal from her previous situation, except that now she was surrounded by people who ignored her. The only break in the monotony was when they were lined up and taken to the facilities for showering.

Excitement rolled through the barracks when they discovered the following week that they would be allowed to leave the barracks during wake period to mingle in the rec room. Any break in the monotony was welcome, but Amaryllis didn't see what there was to get so excited about. When they reached the rec room, though, she saw that the male hunters had been allowed access to the rec room, as well.

After weeks of confinement, she supposed it was only natural that everyone would feel as if they'd been released from prison. It wasn't much of a release in her book. Guards still watched them from windows in the deck above them. Guards escorted them to and from the barracks. Once they reached the rec room, they couldn't leave until they were escorted out again, under guard.

Dalia, the huntress who'd supposedly gone 'rogue', remained with the group of hunters, as much a prisoner as the rest of them. Despite the fact that their bunks were on opposite ends of the barracks, Amaryllis had caught several glimpses of her in the past week, along with the rumors that Dalia was a plant, there to spy on them and report everything they said and did to the cyborgs.

Amaryllis didn't know whether to believe it or not. There didn't seem to be much point to it when the cyborgs could as easily survey them and collect intelligence through electronic means, but she wasn't the least surprised that the rumors persisted. It was just the sort of thing that 'people' did when they were bored and/or scared--search for a target to take out their frustrations on. Unlike her, however, Dalia was neither 'invisible' nor ostracized.

Mentally, Amaryllis conceded that that was most likely because Dalia was the best of the best and there probably wasn't one among them, the males included, who didn't suffer just a tiny bit of hero worship where she was concerned.

Regardless, as tired as she was of having nothing but her own thoughts for company, of being alone even in a crowded room, she knew better than to attempt to change the situation. Any overtures on her part would almost certainly be resoundingly snubbed, and she thought she might as well spare her pride at least.

To Amaryllis' surprise, she discovered on the third day that either the hunters hadn't heard the rumors the huntresses were speculating on, or they simply didn't care, or the rumors intrigued them rather than repelled them. One of the hunters, Cain, who'd actually been her recruiting officer, approached her. She eyed him warily, wondering if he'd merely come to see if he could discover any juicy tidbits to pass along to the others pertaining to the rumor that she'd taken a cyborg lover.

They were bound to be getting bored with what they had

and had managed to invent by this time.

"I didn't realize until the other day that you were among the captured."

Amaryllis felt a blush rising in her cheeks in spite of everything she could do, but, even if he was alluding to the rumors about her, she wasn't going to acknowledge it. "My partner and I were close enough we were called in to take part in the mission."

He looked uncomfortable for several moments and she thought he was going to leave again. "Do you think there's any truth to what they told us?" He asked after a moment, and then shrugged. "I suppose anything's possible, but it's hard to accept that nothing I think I remember was real."

Amaryllis relaxed fractionally, realizing he wasn't referring to her time with Dante. She wasn't a great deal more comfortable with the conversation he'd chosen, however. "I don't know, but it's hard to argue with their logic," she responded. "No matter how well trained, it seems unlikely a human would be a match for a cyborg in strength, speed, or agility." The comment prompted a line of thought that hadn't occurred to her before and she frowned. "But if it's true, it makes me wonder what The Company had in mind for us when we'd finished cleaning up for them. I'd assumed we would be reassigned to security, but…."

Cain studied her assessingly for several moments. "Actually, it's fairly clear what they had in mind."

Amaryllis looked at him in surprise. "You must know something I don't."

"I must … but then I'd assumed we all had the second, 'mystery' locator."

Amaryllis nodded, but she was more puzzled, not less so. "The tech found two on me, too. Which was almost as curious as the fact that I don't even remember them planting that second one."

"That second one--the one none of us knew about--was a termination chip."

Amaryllis felt her jaw go slack with stunned surprise.

"You don't mean … you can't mean…."

He smiled faintly, but the amusement didn't reach his eyes. "I do mean exactly that. When we'd finished, they would've had no further use for us, and I have to assume they figured it would be too risky to leave any of us 'in service' … unless they had something against me in particular."

"You're positive?"

"Did I take their word for it, you mean?" he asked, jerking his head fractionally in the direction of the cyborgs that were watching from above. "I don't trust anyone that much. No. I checked it myself."

A wave of nausea washed through her. Anger followed it. "This is … outrageous! Who the hell died and made them God!"

He shrugged. "The government. They've been dipping deeper and deeper into big business' pockets. It was only a matter of time before power shifted. The government wields very little control over anything any longer.

"The situation with the cyborgs threatened to become far too big for a cover up, however. If word got out, terror would follow and mass hysteria is beyond anyone's control. I feel sure the government and The Company were in agreement that it would be far better to sweep it under the rug as quickly as possible than to risk having a public outcry widespread enough to threaten toppling them from power. The Company depends upon having their puppets in place. Then, too, hysteria is contagious. There's no saying but what knowledge of what they had done wouldn't cause rioting, which in turn could cause a great deal of damage to the property and profits of The Company."

Amaryllis realized he was probably right, but it didn't make her any less angry. "In other words, we really don't have anywhere else to go, whether we want to stay or not?"

Cain released a sigh that was tinged with exasperation. "I don't precisely relish the thought of becoming a colonist, but fortunately, I learn fast," he added with a trace of amusement, referring to the ease with which he could assimilate additional programming. "I feel confident that I could find a niche for myself that would satisfy me. And I have to admit there are certain incentives that appeal."

Recalling her life as the child of a colonist, Amaryllis wasn't sure she could agree with him, but then her own experiences, she had to admit, had been tainted by her situation. She supposed she'd never given much thought to what she would be when she retired from active service in the militia. Maybe she hadn't expected to live to retire?

A death wish?

She didn't think so. She thought it was more a matter of never having had any expectations of having a life like her parents had had. Who would want a freak as a companion, after all? And since that was the only life she was intimately acquainted with she either hadn't wanted to imagine spending the end of her days alone or she just hadn't been able to envision it, having come from a large, loving family.

"Such as?" she asked finally.

"The family units they will need to build a society. I hadn't given much thought to what I would do if I lived to retire from active duty, but now that I have been retired from company service, the idea of a companion and children holds a good deal of appeal."

Amaryllis blinked at him in surprise. "But … cyborgs can't…."

He shrugged. "Dalia is pregnant … proof that the cyborgs are evolving into a unique species."

"Or that Dalia is actually human," Amaryllis pointed out dryly.

"And yet it was you who pointed out that no human would have the speed, strength, or agility to best a cyborg. If that is true then Dalia, who has had more kills than any other, would certainly fit that criteria. Besides, Reuel claims the child as his own."

Amaryllis' eyes widened at his mention of the most feared, and sought after, cyborg of all. "Reuel?" she whispered in a voice threaded with awe.

He shrugged. "I don't know what the likelihood is that we will find we have all evolved the ability to procreate, but it certainly isn't impossible if it has already happened once."

"Making plans already?"

Amaryllis and Cain both turned to look at the huntress who'd joined them.

Cain's lips flattened into a thin line of irritation. "Merely discussing possibilities. You know my partner, Violet?"

In pretty much the same sense that she knew all of the hunters. She recognized both the name and the face. "We didn't train together," Amaryllis said non-committally.

Violet divided a look between Cain and Amaryllis and smiled thinly, then fixed Amaryllis with a significant look and jerked her head in the direction of the observation booth above them. "I just thought you might be interested to know that the dark twin has been released from the brig at last."

Amaryllis' heart skipped a beat as she instinctively glanced in the direction that Violet had indicated. Dante was standing at the front of the observation booth. Beside him stood Reese. Her heart did a back flip when she saw that both were looking directly at her. Disconcerted, Amaryllis looked away again quickly, trying without success to keep the blood from rushing into her cheeks.

Violet, she saw, was smiling like the cat that ate the canary.

When she glanced at Cain, she saw that he was still studying the two in the observation booth.

He didn't look particularly pleased.

She didn't especially want to ask, but she couldn't seem to resist. "What makes you think he's been in the brig?"

Violet shrugged. "It's what we heard … that one of the cyborgs had been caught harboring a huntress and was confined to the brig. Then, low and behold, you appeared in the barracks. Naturally, I assumed…."

As badly as Amaryllis wanted to wipe that smile off of Violet's face by knocking her head clean off her shoulders she didn't particularly want to end up in the brig herself. Besides, her thoughts were chaotic. She'd assumed that Dante had betrayed her, but it seemed less likely that he had if he'd been thrown in the brig for hiding her.

Did that rule out the possibility altogether, though?

She thought it might, but then she also thought there was a strong possibility that she wanted to believe he hadn't used her and then callously turned her in … which meant she should distrust her reasoning since it was obviously tainted with emotionalism.

She absolutely didn't want to consider what sort of emotionalism might be involved. Moreover, she couldn't help but notice that both Cain and Violet were watching her with interest.

"Why did you call him the dark twin?" she asked, more because she was trying to turn the conversation to something less uncomfortable than because she had much interest.

"His brother, Reese, is fair," Violet pointed out dryly.

A jolt went through Amaryllis. "Brother? They're cyborgs."

Violet chuckled. "And? Look at the two of them. Except for their coloring, they look like twins--which means they have to share at least one parent gene donor. Besides, I partnered with Reese. Don't tell me you partnered with Reese a year and a half and he never mentioned his twin brother, Dante?"

Chapter Eleven

Amaryllis reddened, but she saw she didn't have to say anything at all. Violet had read the answer in her expression.

She wanted nothing so much as to escape the inquisition, and the smug look on Violet's face, but there was no escaping the rec room until the cyborgs allowed them to leave.

She glanced at Cain, wondering if he'd set her up for Violet.

His expression was carefully neutral, but anger flickered in his hazel green eyes. "Is there a point to this, Violet?"

Violet shrugged. "I suppose you could say I was just testing the wind."

Cain's brows rose. "For what?"

She divided a malicious glance between Amaryllis and Cain and finally shrugged, and Amaryllis realized abruptly that jealousy was driving her. "As you were telling Amaryllis earlier, we'll be allowed to choose companions once we arrive at the colony. I was just curious to know what her interest was in Dante and Reese."

Amaryllis glanced from Violet to Cain and back again, restraining the temptation to glance toward Reese and Dante. She had the feeling, though, that Violet was more interested in Cain than either Reese or Dante.

Or, perhaps, she liked the looks of all three and didn't want competition until she'd decided which she would choose?

It must be nice to have that kind of confidence, however misguided it seemed to be.

With an effort, she pasted a smile on her lips. "Go for it. I really don't have any plans to stay."

It didn't take the smug smile on Violet's face to assure her she'd just left herself wide open. She knew the moment the words were out of her mouth that she'd allowed her chaotic emotions to overrule her wisdom--if she could claim any and she was beginning to think she no longer did if she ever had.

"You're leaving us?" Violet asked, pleased. "Exactly how do you plan to do that?"

"I hadn't made any plans," Amaryllis said tightly, if not with complete truth. "However, they have said we are not going to be prisoners, and that implies that we'll have the right to choose to stay or to go. I'm just thinking I'd rather take my chances with my…." She stumbled to a halt, horrified that she'd almost said 'my own kind'. "Company," she finished lamely.

Violet laughed. "Your company?"

"Give it a rest, Violet," Cain said tightly.

Violet glared at him. "The crash screwed up her logic circuits." Her eyes narrowed. "You really ought to consider whether it's a good idea to hang around her or not. The cyborgs are likely to take any escape attempts very badly."

Amaryllis watched Violet as she stalked off. When she glanced at Cain, she saw that he was studying her retreating form, as well. "She's probably right."

"Only in the sense that she managed to trick you in to voicing dangerous thoughts … or at least what appear to be dangerous thoughts." He turned to study her for a long moment. "She's likely to report the conversation … assuming they didn't hear it already, which they probably did."

"You think?" Amaryllis asked dryly. "I wasn't referring to my … logic circuits," she said after a brief hesitation. "I meant, the hanging around me thing."

"You aren't considering anything, are you?"

Amaryllis gave him a look. "If I had been, I wouldn't have mentioned it. I *was* talking about after we land. They did say we'd be given the option of joining their colony."

"They didn't say what the alternative was," Cain pointed out.

Amaryllis glanced at him sharply. "You think it's do or die?"

He shrugged. "I don't trust The Company ... never did. That doesn't mean I do trust them. And, strategically speaking, it wouldn't be safe to let any of us go when we could head straight back to The Company and tell them how to find the cyborg home base."

Amaryllis shook her head. "We've entered uncharted space ... uncharted by humans, at any rate. They removed the locators and destroyed them. Setting aside the fact that we now know The Company's plans for us and only a complete moron would even consider going back to The Company, the cyborgs could leave us anywhere in the known universe without any worry whatsoever that The Company could track them down. There's no reason for them to terminate us, unless they just want to, and if they did, they've had plenty of opportunity to do that."

He shrugged. "I guess we'll find out whether we can trust them or not."

* * * *

"We need to talk."

The voice, more even than the words, sent a shiver of sensation down Amaryllis' spine that had nothing to do with fear. Her heart was in her throat as she glanced down at the hand that had clamped around her upper arm and then up into the face of the man who'd detained her. Surprise went through her when she met Reese's pale blue gaze instead of Dante's deep sapphire eyes. She hadn't realized until that moment that his voice was almost identical to Dante's. Her mind went perfectly blank. "Talk?" she echoed.

She'd hardly gotten the word out when he snatched her into a room along the corridor, closing the door behind them. Instead of releasing her once he had, he corralled her in one corner, placing a palm against the bulkhead on either side of her and Amaryllis felt as breathless as if someone had punched her in the stomach. "I'll be missed," she said with an effort.

He frowned. "I'll escort you to the barracks myself."

Amaryllis blinked as that statement washed over her with equal parts fear and gladness. "No offense, but they already look at me like…."

Reese tilted his head questioningly when she didn't finish. "Like?"

Her mouth felt dry. Her lips stiff. She licked them, searching her mind for something that would put a safe barrier between them. "I'd just as soon they didn't suspect me of being a plant to watch them."

"Like I was?"

Hurt surged through her full fold. She gave him a look. "Except that now we know you never were one of us. It's a different sort of betrayal."

Anger glittered in his eyes. "I didn't betray you."

"No. You were just doing your job. That almost makes it worse. I … we idolized you, looked up to you, and you aren't even real."

Several emotions chased across his features, anger uppermost. "I *am* real," he growled, dipping his head to capture her lips. She evaded him, twisting her head to one side and lifting her palms to place them against his chest to hold him at bay. He caught her wrists, pushing them behind her so that she had to arch her back to relieve the pressure on her arms. His mouth, seeking flesh, settled along the side of her neck like a firebrand. She gasped as a rush of heated sensation washed through her, both seduced by the lure of his heat and infinitely wary of it.

"Don't!" she gasped as he wove a path downward and nuzzled his face between her breasts.

He hesitated and finally lifted his head to look at her. "Why? Because I'm not real? Or because you want me and you don't want to now that you know what I am?"

Amaryllis stared at him speechlessly, embarrassed that she'd been so transparent and he'd seen it. When she said nothing, he dipped his head once more. Making no attempt to kiss her lips, instead he nipped a string of kisses along her cheek, then traced the line of her jaw to her chin.

Sensation erupted through her, lifting the fine hairs all over her body to stinging life. He hesitated when he reached her mouth, waiting, his heated breath fanning against her lips, making them tingle with heightened sensation.

Amaryllis wasn't entirely certain of whether she closed the distance or Reese did, but the ability to formulate any sort of objection deserted her the moment his lips covered hers and his essence flooded her senses, intoxicating her with desire. She surrendered completely to the lure of pleasure, stroking her tongue sinuously along his as he explored her mouth with desperate thrusts. Lifting her hands, she skated her palms along the hard, bulging muscles of his chest, dug her fingers into the thick ridge of muscle along his shoulders, battling to retain her balance when weakness and dizziness swarmed around her.

Abruptly, he tore his mouth from hers and trailed his lips hungrily along her throat to the valley between her breasts. Cool air wafted across her nipples as he disgorged her breasts from the cups of her halter style top, causing her nipples to pucker and stand erect. She uttered a whimper of pleasure at the jolt that went through her as he covered one peak with his mouth, suckling the sensitive nub. The sound seemed to tear what little restraint from him that he'd held onto. He grasped her around the waist, lifting her up for better access and divided his attentions between her breasts, suckling and teasing first one throbbing nipple until she thought she would black out from lack of oxygen and then the other. She wasn't even aware of wrapping her thighs around his waist until she felt the ridge of his distended cock nestling along her cleft. He slid his hands from her waist to her buttocks, cupping them in his palms, massaging them, then slipped his fingers beneath the edge of her briefs and traced her damp cleft.

Amaryllis clung tightly to him, gasping for breath, her heart thundering so hard in her chest it felt as if it would explode. Moisture gathered in her sex, the walls of her channel clutching mindlessly for the feel of his hard flesh. She uttered a choked cry as his fingers found the ultra sensitive nub of flesh nestled in the valley of her cleft, rubbing it and sending jolts of electrifying sensation through her. Lifting his head, he covered her mouth with his own once more, thrusting his tongue in and out in a rhythm that made desperation climb over her to feel his cock thrusting inside of her. As if he'd read her mind, she felt him fumble briefly with his clothing and then the rounded head of his cock pressing against her, piercing her body's opening.

Gratified, she pressed down in counter to his thrust, trying to sheathe him within her body. Frustration surfaced when she found she could get no leverage to take him inside her.

Breaking the kiss, Reese glanced around the room and finally settled on the seat of a straight chair with her straddling his lap. He bore down on her hips, thrusting upward to meet her and Amaryllis groaned as she felt her body yielding reluctantly, clinging to his hard flesh.

A fine sheen of moisture broke from his pores. His muscles began to quiver with the effort of his restraint. Groaning, he lifted her up and thrust again. Sinking inside of her that time to the root of his cock, he went still, squeezing his eyes tightly shut, gasping hoarsely.

Amaryllis' eyes drifted closed as she leaned her forehead against his, willing her body to adjust to the almost painfully tight intrusion of hard flesh. She opened her eyes again when she felt his palms along her cheeks.

"Amy," he murmured huskily, brushing his lips lightly across hers before he covered her mouth and kissed her deeply. Her body quickened, clenching around his cock. Groaning, he tore his mouth from hers and began to move. Stroking his cock along the sensitive inner surfaces of her sex with each thrust and retreat, he lifted her hips upward, then pressed her down in counter to each hard thrust. With each stroke waves of electrifying, heated pleasure washed through her, building toward a crescendo. She clutched his shoulders, groaning almost incessantly as the tension built inside of her to a fever pitch, began to expand beyond containment.

His cock jerked as he reached his own crisis. Abruptly, ecstasy exploded inside of her, dragging a sharp cry from her throat. She buried her face against his neck, clutching him tightly as it rocked her with shock wave after shock wave of purest bliss as she felt his body erupt inside of her with his own culmination.

Every ounce of strength seemed to leave her. She collapsed weakly against him, gasping for breath, felt his arms surround her in a tight embrace as he struggled to regulate his own breathing. Warmth of a different sort filled her as he held her closely against his chest and began to stroke her back soothingly.

"I know you're afraid and confused, but we are not as different as you imagine," he murmured after he'd caught his breath. "And I would never allow harm to come to you."

It took an effort to lift her head and look at him. "You know."

"Yes."

"Dante?"

He shook his head. "I always knew. From the very moment I first saw you I knew that only nature could produce something so wonderfully, uniquely beautiful. I knew I shouldn't tear you from your own people, but I could no more resist doing so than I could self-terminate. I want you for my life mate. It's why I brought you."

Chapter Twelve

Awkward didn't begin to describe Amaryllis' feelings as she was thrust through the barracks door by the guard Reese had handed her over to when he'd bowed to her wish not to be seen returning her. However, it was only partly because she could feel dozens of interested gazes as she strode quickly through the barracks and into the latrine beyond. Most of it revolved around the things that Reese had said to her, her complete lack of self control, and her horror and confusion over the fact that she'd fucked both Reese and Dante with the same mindless enthusiasm and within a matter of days.

After all her internal wailing and breast beating over the fact that Dante had given no indication that the event between them was more than merely a desperate physical need.

Goosebumps erupted on her flesh as her mind instantly conjured images of her sitting astride Reese's lap, his cock buried so deeply inside of her that she couldn't think or feel beyond the exquisite pleasure of their joining. Before the image had even faded, the memory of her writhing in an agony of ecstasy beneath Dante arose within her mind's eye and her sex throbbed in reaction.

She didn't know how long she stood stock still, simply staring blindly at her own reflection in the mirror above the lavatory as if she'd never seen herself before, her mind a tumultuous wreck. Finally, physical discomfort penetrated her turmoil, however, and she looked down at herself. A sticky wetness had soaked her briefs.

Semen.

She reeked of sex and doubted anyone she'd passed had failed to notice even if they'd been too blind to see that her clothing was in disarray, her hair looked as if she'd been standing in a wind tunnel, her lips looked swollen and bruised and the skin of her neck and upper chest were reddened from Reese's caresses.

"Jesus Christ and all the saints!" she muttered the curse she'd so often heard her father use, wondering if it was merely seminal fluids or if it was 'loaded'.

She'd been too stunned by what had come afterward to give it any thought, but she realized now that Dante had ejaculated inside of her, as well--which was the reason, no doubt, that Reese had sent her into the shower, to wash the scent of Dante's possession from her.

And if the meds had worn off that kept her libido in check--which seemed indisputable--then her birth control was no longer working either.

She brushed the thought aside. She couldn't deal with that possibility at the moment. At any rate, regardless of what the cyborgs claimed, she simply couldn't accept that they were capable of reproduction.

She'd idolized Reese, thought he was quite possibly the most magnificent representation of mankind ever born--and she supposed, even though now she knew he hadn't been 'born' at all, subconsciously she still idolized him. Possibly that was why she was so susceptible to his attentions. But how could she possibly excuse her behavior with Dante? How could she excuse her complete break with the traditions of her upbringing by making love with both within so short a time--and there was no sense in trying to lie to herself about that. She might not know how either of them truly felt, but she knew herself. She wouldn't have felt passion so keenly if she hadn't felt more for both of them than mere lust.

She knew very well that no one on any of the 'civilized' worlds considered such archaic traditions worth a second thought. The idea of sex purely for recreation, and not as a part of a relationship, didn't particularly bother her for that matter.

What bothered her was that she'd felt such passion when neither of them was human in the strictest sense of the word, regardless of the fact that they weren't much, if any, more android than she was.

What disturbed her more, and totally confused her, was that she knew very well that it hadn't been anything as simple as purely recreational sex … with either Dante or Reese.

But what worried her the most was that she was very much afraid that no amount of reasoning was going to make her any less susceptible if she found herself in a similar situation again.

She discovered the following day when they filed into the rec room that she'd been relegated to invisible again. She wasn't particularly surprised. She wasn't even deeply regretful considering the state Violet had put her in the day before. She was a little disappointed, though, that Cain didn't make any attempt to approach her. It would've been nice to have someone to talk to occasionally even if she had to mind her tongue.

After weeks of travel, fear of discovery gave way to the misery of sheer boredom, which she missed when new anxieties reared their heads. Occasionally, she managed to get a deck of cards and play a few rounds of solitaire, but by and large she did nothing more than pace the room restlessly, as bored as she had been before they'd been allowed to spend a part of their days in the rec room.

The voyage began to seem interminable. She'd never taken such a prolonged space voyage and found it unnerving to think that the place where they were going was so distant from all that she knew. The possibility of escaping dimmed as time passed and was finally extinguished altogether.

She'd made it a point, at first, not to look up at the observation windows, but even when she finally decided a surreptitious peek now and then would probably go unnoticed, she saw no sign of Reese for nearly two weeks. It occurred to her to wonder if their tryst had been discovered and he'd been confined to the brig as Dante supposedly had, but she had no way of finding out. She wasn't even privy to the gossip circulating among the hunters since they had a disturbing way of falling silent whenever she passed near enough to overhear their conversations.

She caught glimpses of Dante often enough, but seeing him unsettled her almost as much as not seeing Reese.

Two weeks after her encounter with Reese, she was curled up on a couch, staring out of a porthole at the unending, and infinitely depressing night of deep space when Cain settled next to her. She glanced at him in surprise.

"I'm not at all certain that I'll ever be able to look at a night sky with any sort of admiration again," he said pensively.

The comment dragged a reluctant smile from her. "I was just thinking much the same thing."

He smiled faintly in return. "I'd claim to be extraordinarily perceptive except that I'm fairly certain everyone here is thinking much the same thing. You'll note, no one glances toward the portholes any longer."

Amaryllis chuckled wryly. "And here I thought they were simply avoiding the area for fear of contamination," she retorted dryly.

Lifting a dark brow, he glanced around the rec room and finally up at the observation windows. Curious, Amaryllis followed his gaze. Her heart jerked in her chest when she saw that both Reese and Dante were standing at the observation window above, scowling at the man who sat beside her.

"I expect you're at least partially right. It *is* for reasons of health, but I don't think it's fear of contamination."

Amaryllis resisted the urge to fan her heated cheeks. "I don't think I follow," she said stiffly.

A mixture of amusement and annoyance lit his green eyes. "I think you do, but if it disturbs your sense of modesty to speak of it, I completely understand."

Amaryllis sent him a sharp glance and reddened again. "They're afraid to speak to me because of … the rumors?"

she demanded with a mixture of indignation and disbelief.

Both of his dark brows rose this time. He tilted his head curiously. "*Is* it merely rumors? The cyborg twins seem to have a different perspective on the matter. One or both can generally be seen standing at the observation windows, usually wearing identical scowls if any of the hunters even start in your direction."

Amaryllis frowned thoughtfully, digesting the comments in silence and trying to decide whether there was any truth to it. She often had the sense that she was being watched, but she'd thought a good bit of that could be put down to hypersensitivity or plain, old fashioned paranoia. It was understandable given her situation, a combination of her fear that they would realize she was human and her certainty that her behavior was being judged as much because of her own sense of guilt as because of the snide comments two of the huntresses had made to her.

She *had* noticed that any time she glanced toward the observation windows, though, and either Dante or Reese was there, that they were looking directly at her. It was the main reason she avoided looking in that direction. She didn't want to encourage either of them to think she was interested when she didn't know how she felt about them.

That didn't necessarily mean that either Reese or Dante was warning others away from her, but it was possible their interest could've been interpreted that way.

"You think they're afraid of the cyborgs?"

He shrugged. "Under other circumstances, it would be more accurate to say 'respectful'. Under current circumstances…."

She could see his point. "If you think that, then why are you speaking to me?" she asked curiously.

He studied her in silence for several long moments and finally a grin dawned. "Either you are the most adorably obtuse female I've ever met, or, like every other huntress in this room you are far too deeply engrossed in sorting through your feelings on the matter to realize what's going on around you."

Amaryllis blinked at him, mildly offended by the comment despite the fact that he'd obviously not intended to be insulting.

"Men are actually pretty simple creatures … even if they happen to be cyborg men and not human men. In one fell swoop we've ceased to be an army and become colonists for a distant world. It, surely, can't have escaped your notice that, in this room alone, hunters outnumber huntresses roughly two to one. By my calculations--depending, of course upon just how many cyborgs await us on our new home world--those numbers are obliged to climb sharply. I'd thought, perhaps, your interest was engaged elsewhere. Since that still seems to be a matter of debate I see no reason not to pursue my own interests."

Amaryllis felt her jaw go slack with surprise. "You're … uh … you're … flirting with me?"

He grimaced. "Not very well apparently," he said wryly.

She frowned. "Because there aren't enough females to go around?"

A pained expression crossed his features. "In fact, very, very badly," he amended. He tilted his head at her speculatively. "I don't suppose you'd believe me if I said that it was love at first sight?"

"No."

He sighed. "I thought not."

Amaryllis couldn't help but chuckle. She decided he must be teasing. "You first saw me three years ago when I arrived for training."

"At first notice?" he suggested.

She repressed the urge to smile. "Which was when you finished counting heads, I suppose?"

His lips tipped up at one corner, capturing her attention. He was certainly not unfamiliar to her even though she'd never worked with him. Up until Reese had joined their group, though, she'd been inclined to think Cain was probably the most attractive of all the hunters. His features were sharp, too angular to really be considered 'beautiful', and there was nothing at all boyish about him, but there was something so thoroughly masculine about him that he was extraordinarily attractive in an indefinable way. He had been to her, anyway, but then she'd been starved for male attention and, she thought, inclined to fall for any attractive male that glanced in her direction without a look of revulsion crossing his features.

After the corrective surgery that had made her 'normal' the boys she'd known throughout her childhood had ceased to torment her and tried to engage her interest, but she hadn't trusted any of them enough to allow them to come near her.

And she'd still yearned to be courted as the other girls were and more than half hoped she would have the chance of some sort of relationship once she left the colony. It was born in upon her the moment she entered training that that wasn't going to be an option. Fraternizing wasn't allowed, at least not that sort of fraternizing, and the company took steps to ensure the temptation was minimized by lacing their contraceptives with drugs that inhibited sexual arousal … which only meant they weren't preoccupied with sex, not that they never thought about it.

It certainly hadn't kept her from noticing that she was surrounded by drop dead gorgeous, extremely well built men, but then none of them, including Cain, had seemed to notice her. Not that that had particularly bothered her. She'd spent her entire life admiring from afar without expectation of actually being noticed herself and found she was completely comfortable with it … far more so than getting up close and personal.

"To be perfectly accurate, it was when you arrived for training. I was the one who signed you up, but I'm not surprised you don't remember. I've never seen a volunteer look quite so terrified."

Amaryllis blushed to the roots of her hair. She remembered. She was surprised he did, though, but then again they didn't get that many recruits--in fact none, except her if she accepted what they'd been told. The others had all been programmed to 'volunteer' for service.

It flickered through her mind to wonder why they'd decided to induct her when she wasn't one of the soldiers they'd built, but she supposed after a moment that they'd feared unpleasant questions might have arisen if they'd refused her when she was supposedly bionically superior to the other recruits. "I wasn't."

His brows rose skeptically.

"All right, I was. But that was only because everything ... was so new to me," she finished lamely, erecting her guard with an effort, suddenly acutely self-conscious of the fact that her background didn't even begin to match the one common to the others.

His eyes narrowed speculatively. "I was surprised they accepted you. You didn't seem ... soldier material to me."

She gave him a look. "I was damned good at it, thank you. Good enough they considered me qualified to work solo."

"Until your 'accident'," he amended.

Admittedly, her performance hadn't been what it should have been, but faulty intelligence had played a part in the fiasco, as well. She'd been tracking one--a female cyborg-- she'd never been sent out to take down a male, and certainly not more than one at the time. She knew she should've been more careful, but the plain fact of the matter was that she'd trusted the intelligence she'd been given when she shouldn't have, and found herself outnumbered. "I was outnumbered four to one," she said finally.

"I'd always thought that seemed curious. In retrospect it seems less so."

"How is that?"

"I think the objective was to capture you--which is the reason I referred to it as your accident. Apparently the company thought so, too, and that's why they paired most of the huntresses with a hunter. I'd requested to be assigned as your partner, but your recovery seemed uncertain at the time and they assigned me to Violet instead."

Amaryllis was surprised both by his request to be assigned to her and the suggestion that the cyborgs had had plans for them far longer than she'd suspected. "So you're thinking Reese was assigned to protect me?"

"By The Company, yes."

She frowned. "But not by the cyborgs, who were really giving him his orders?"

His lips thinned. "I'd like to say yes, but, in all honesty, I doubt it. You are certainly of value to them ... but more so to some than others."

"Meaning?"

He smiled wryly. "I am not going to allow you to badger me into furthering his cause when I've more interest in my own."

"Which is…?"

He chuckled. "Pledging my undying devotion, of course, before it occurs to the cyborg twins that a woman wants to be wooed before she's…."

"Screwed?"

Laughter gleamed in his eyes. "Made love to."

The conversation was risqué, for her, to say the least, but she found that she was far more intrigued and entertained than offended or embarrassed.

"There's a difference?"

His eyes narrowed speculatively. After a moment, he shifted to face her, laying an arm along the back of the couch and then propping his cheek on his hand. "Worlds. I'd be more than happy to show you."

Amaryllis chuckled but shook her head. "You have to be in love for that ... not in lust."

"But I am," he protested.

"Which?"

"Both," he replied promptly.

"You always were such a tease, Cain. You were in lust with me last week!"

Chapter Thirteen

The teasing light vanished instantly from Cain's eyes. A look of annoyance took its place as he glanced up at Violet.

"Trying to work your way through the harem?" she added, gesturing to the room at large.

"I see I underestimated you … partner. Clever. Any rebuttal on my part will only make me look worse."

Violet shrugged. "She was never in any danger of taking you seriously. Were you, Amaryllis?"

Amaryllis glanced uncomfortably from Violet to Cain. He was angry, no matter how well he hid it, but the question was, angry because what Violet had said was the truth? Or because she was lying and he couldn't defend himself without looking as bad as she'd painted him? She managed a tight smile. "We're all bored and anxious, Violet, but I don't think trying to create trouble among ourselves is at all wise."

Surprise flickered across Violet's face, but anger quickly supplanted it. She leaned down until she was almost nose to nose with Amaryllis. "Then maybe you should consider who you dangle after," she said through gritted teeth.

Amaryllis' fist clenched reflexively. Before she could do anything she might have regretted later, however, she felt a warm hand cover hers in warning. She glanced down at the hand when Violet had straightened and stalked away and then up at Cain. Almost reluctantly, he withdrew his hand from hers.

"I can't woo you if you're in solitary for belting her in the mouth," he murmured, his tone teasing. "Not that I wasn't tempted myself," he added reflectively.

She gave him a look. "It was the 'in your face' thing," she said tightly.

He feigned a look of disappointment. "You're not

dangling after me, then?"

A snort of laughter escaped her. Amaryllis clapped a hand over her mouth. "You can laugh. It isn't you she wants to pound into a bloody pulp," she chided him.

He grimaced. "No. She has something equally horrible in mind for me, though. She seems to be laboring under the impression that we should make the partnership more permanent."

It wasn't exactly a revelation. "Really? She suggested she was interested in … one of the cyborgs."

He shrugged. "It's my considered opinion that we're all going to need a little reprogramming if we're to manage this mating thing the cyborgs have in mind. Frankly, we just don't have the skills for it. Look at how badly I'm faring and I've at least had a little practice … programming, at any rate."

Amaryllis looked as confused as she felt.

He frowned, all traces of amusement vanishing from his expression. "My programming scenario. It was my wife I lost. But then none of it actually happened, did it? The woman I thought I loved never really existed except in my mind."

It didn't really matter, though. The mind believed what it had been told. "They really are cold blooded bastards, aren't they?" Amaryllis said angrily. "How could they … why would they create such awful histories for everyone?"

He scrubbed a hand over his face. "So that we wouldn't turn out like the cyborgs."

"But … everyone has horrible memory implants. Isn't that as bad?"

"They couldn't leave us with anything we could track down and disprove. Maybe they thought the emotional wounds would make us harder, more dangerous. It's anybody's guess, but, for my part, I rather envy the cyborgs. At least they always knew. It isn't easy going to sleep a man and waking up a cyborg … enemy of the true people."

Amaryllis felt a pang of empathy. Impulsively, she

grasped his hand and gave it a sympathetic squeeze. She'd been so wrapped up in her own concerns it hadn't occurred to her that all the captives were as confused and anxious as she was. "You think it's as bad as that?"

His fingers tightened on hers. "I do. I hope you're not still considering going back. There *is* no going back, you know," he said gently.

She shrugged. "I will miss … what I left behind, but I realize the chances of making it back are less than nothing now. Unless they agree to take those of us back who don't want to stay, there's no way we'd ever manage it on our own."

He smiled faintly. "You're not precisely resigned to your fate then, are you?"

She forced a smile. "I don't give up on anything very easily."

* * * *

"You've been avoiding me. Now why, I wonder?"

Amaryllis had just settled against a broad column in a quiet corner of the rec room where she'd hoped to escape notice. She jumped at the voice near her ear and glanced up at Cain in surprise. She reddened guiltily. "I haven't been."

"You don't lie very well," he said wryly.

She sighed. "I thought it best to avoid … trouble."

He grinned, arching a dark brow. "Now I'm trouble?"

"Violet."

The teasing amusement vanished. His lips thinned. He glanced away from her, studying a group of hunters that were engaged in a game of pool at one of the tables across the room. "I thought as much. You believed her, then?"

Her gaze flickered over his handsome face searchingly. "I don't think you're like that … but you could be."

He glanced at her questioningly and she smiled faintly.

"You are very … persuasive."

"Am I?"

His grin was infectious. Amaryllis felt her own lips trembling on the verge of a smile. She nodded. "And I couldn't help but wonder…."

"Don't," he said implacably, then scrubbed a hand over his face. "This isn't a game to me, Amaryllis." He moved imperceptibly closer, until barely a foot separated them. "I'm in deadly earnest. If we didn't have cyborgs swarming all over us I'd show you just how serious I am."

His words as well as the promise in his eyes were as tangible as a caress and Amaryllis' breath left her in a rush. Sensation prickled along her skin. Heat pooled in her belly.

"If you keep looking at me like that I'm liable to do something really stupid," he growled warningly.

It scared her that she wanted him to. She swallowed with an effort and dragged her gaze away. It was more difficult to banish the images that rose in her mind. She cleared her throat. "I'm having a lot of trouble adjusting to … all of this. I don't know how I feel about anything except … it has helped more than I can say just to have someone to talk to." Not to feel so terribly alone and isolated.

He smiled wryly and shrugged. "I can live with that …for now."

She shook her head. "I'm not so sure this would be a good thing--for either of us. I don't want to cause you any trouble."

She didn't mention Violet, but they both knew Violet wasn't going to stop. Maybe she realized her interest in Cain was a lost cause, and maybe not, but even if she did she'd made it clear that she wasn't simply going to go away.

Reese had indicated that she was here because he'd seen to it that she was and, she suspected, he considered he had a prior claim on her. Beyond the fact that both Reese and Dante had the ability to drive her over the edge of reason with passion, she didn't know how she felt about either one of them, but she had a feeling neither of them would consider that they'd finished what they'd started. Once they arrived on the new world and were no longer segregated they might take violent exception to Cain, particularly if they decided that Cain was taunting them by taking advantage of the situation.

It wasn't that she suffered any doubts that Cain could hold his own. She simply didn't want him to have to.

For that matter, she didn't want to think that Reese or Dante might be hurt because of her.

"Is this to protect me, or them?"

Amaryllis reddened. "Maybe it's to protect me."

He studied her a moment and shook his head. "I'll give you my word I won't provoke a confrontation, but I'm not going to back down from one either. But if you think you can avoid it by refusing to have anything to do with me, you're wrong. They've been watching us together since I approached you and neither of them look the least pleased about it."

Amaryllis glanced up guiltily at that comment, more than half suspecting that Cain had only said it to gauge her reaction. She saw, however, that he'd stated nothing but the truth. Reese was standing at the observation window directly above them with murder in his eyes. Dante, standing slightly to one side of Reese, looked more angry, if possible.

A shiver of uneasiness went through her with the realization that she'd instigated just the sort of thing she was hoping to avoid. She glanced at Reese angrily. "You knew they were there!" she said accusingly.

He gave her an assessing look. "I told you I did," he said coolly.

"I mean when you stopped, when you … acted as if you were going to kiss me."

His lips quirked upward on one side. Devilment gleamed in his eyes. "I had a lot more than kissing on my mind."

Her heart fluttered in her chest, making her suck in a sharp breath. In the next moment, her eyes narrowed. "You're trying to provoke a fight!"

He gave her a look of innocence. "Not I."

"I don't like this … at all!" she snapped unhappily. "Am I supposed to be flattered?"

"Some women would be."

She poked him in the chest with her finger. "Well, I'm

not. And I'll tell you something else, the three of you can slug it out if you want to, but *I* will decide who I want to be with."

"In that case, you'll need a sample for comparison," he growled.

Amaryllis was still gaping at him in surprise when he grasped her waist, jerked her up against him, and bent down to cover her mouth in a kiss that was filled with both anger and passion and provoked a nearly instantaneous riot of sensations from her.

Chapter Fourteen

Taken completely off guard, Amaryllis was too stunned to think, much less to act. The heat and urgency of his mouth filtered through her senses first, warming her to an exquisite awareness of the hard body she rested against. The rough caress of his tongue along hers, the invasion of his unique scent and taste, made her heart quicken, stole the breath from her lungs. Waves of heat swept through her, leaving dizziness in its wake. A heaviness settled over her so that she leaned weakly against him, clutching at him for support.

Sensing her reaction, Cain's arms tightened around her, his kiss becoming an erotically thrilling imitation of the mating dance. Amaryllis' body reacted as if it he was making love to her in truth, the muscles low in her belly clenching almost painfully. Blackness swirled around her. Her knees went weak.

With obvious reluctance, he broke the kiss. Holding her tightly still, he rested his cheek against her head, struggling to catch his breath. "That didn't feel like indifference to me," he growled hoarsely next to her ear.

The comment was enough to penetrate the haze of passion he'd aroused in her and Amaryllis pushed away from him, locking her knees to keep from melting into an ignominious puddle on the floor. She was too stunned to find anger, however, could do nothing more than stare at him speechlessly, listening to her heart thundering in her ears.

Several moments passed before she realized the sound was more than her pounding heartbeat. It was the tramp of booted feet.

Unnerved, she moved away from Cain and peered around the column that blocked her view of the entrance to the rec room. A half dozen cyborgs had filed into the rec room and halted near the entrance.

One stepped forward. "By order of the commander, Reuel VH570, the ship is now open to you. So long as you do not abuse the privilege by straying into unauthorized zones, including the flight deck and launch bay, you may come and go as you please. Hereafter, you will take your meals in the mess with the crew. You will continue to quarter in the barracks."

When they departed once more, they left the door of the rec room standing wide.

Everyone in the room exchanged questioning glances with the people around them. Abruptly, the silence that had fallen over the room at the entrance of the cyborgs was broken by dozens of people speaking all at once.

Amaryllis exchanged a look with Cain. She saw that he was leaning against the column, his arms crossed over his chest, his lips curled in a rueful smile. "Looks like I might be spending the remainder of the trip in the brig after all."

Amaryllis frowned, still trying to grasp the implications of the announcement that had just been made. Cain's comment didn't even penetrate her mind until she followed the direction of his gaze.

Reese and Dante were advancing purposefully toward them. Four of the cyborgs that had entered the rec room to make the announcement rushed inside once more and intercepted them. Dante and Reese sized them up, exchanged a look and slugged the two men directly in front of them so hard they flew backward several feet, taking out three game tables and a half dozen chairs.

An alarm sounded. Four more cyborgs charged into the room. Around the room, every hunter tensed, as if restraining themselves from entering the fray with an effort. It wasn't their fight--as yet--but it was clear that the weeks of incarceration had them chafing for action. Amaryllis surged forward without any clear idea of exactly what she intended to do. Cain forestalled her by grasping her around the waist. She turned to glare at him.

"I don't think you need to get into the middle of that."

"You complete ass! You'll all end up in the brig."

He shrugged. "It was for a good cause."

Amaryllis looked at him blankly. "What cause?"

"Mine."

Irritation surged through her. "I hope it was worth it!" she said tightly.

A mixture of desire and amusement gleamed in his eyes. His lips curled up at one corner. "It was. It definitely was," he murmured huskily, lifting a hand and tracing his thumb lightly along her lower lip.

Amaryllis' belly clenched reflexively. Resolutely, she ignored the warmth his look and his touch engendered. Uttering a frustrated sound of impatience, she wrestled with the grip he had on her.

He released her, eyeing her warily, but after glaring at him indecisively for several moments, she merely turned and plowed her way through the crowd of onlookers.

They'd begun to shout encouragement--though for whom she hadn't a clue--as if the fight were for their entertainment.

They were like ... juveniles, she thought with some dudgeon, pausing to watch as Reese and Dante battled the cyborgs trying to bring order with only one goal in mind-- Cain. Cain watched their progress with interest, his arms crossed over his chest, one shoulder against the column where she'd been standing with him.

It dawned on her abruptly that, in a very real sense, she supposed they were juveniles.

They'd been conceived in a lab, attained awareness of the world at maturity. They might be bastardized human beings, but they were still human beings--super human--but still with many of the same weaknesses. They'd been programmed, but deprived of the natural learning processes of humans. The dam created by programming and drugs had burst and they were experiencing emotions they had no idea of how to deal with because they had no experiences to draw from, and the cyborgs were even more deprived than the hunters who'd at least been given a past, programmed childhood experiences. Nor had they been given social skills simply because they'd never been intended to be anything other than killing machines.

It was no doubt only because of their programming as soldiers that they'd managed any sort of order at all.

Despite the disgust she felt at their display of barbarism, empathy welled inside of her, as well, and for the first time she felt a true kinship with them rather than the sense of alienation she'd felt since her capture and the realization that she was the only natural born human being in a sea of bio-engineered beings. She'd experienced much of the same anger, frustration and--in truth--fear. She'd wanted to belong, to fit in, and didn't feel as if she did. She'd wanted love, passion, romance and had no idea of how to go after those things she wanted to experience so badly for herself or deal with those basic human needs.

She still didn't know how to deal with it.

Giving the growing melee in the center of the rec room a wide berth, she left the room and, after a little thought, headed for the barracks.

The barracks was deserted. She was relieved and at the same time unnerved by the absolute quiet in the huge room usually rustling with movement and whispers.

She wasn't altogether certain of why she'd returned to the barracks. All she'd had on her mind was putting as much distance between herself and the battle in the rec room as possible. She could've gone anywhere on the ship, but the barracks had come to represent a refuge as much as a prison. It wasn't much of a refuge anymore, not when everyone had the run of the ship.

The timing stank. Just when she'd started to think being imprisoned wasn't so bad if it meant she could avoid a confrontation with Reese and Dante, the commander decides to be generous and give them the run of the ship!

Just when Cain had decided to behave outrageously and kiss her right in front of both Reese and Dante!

It might almost have been funny except for the fact that

there'd been no time for tempers to cool and by now Reese, Dante, and Cain were most likely cooling their heels in the brig.

It was good enough for them!

How dare they fight over her anyway, as if it would make any difference at all. *If* she decided to stay *she* would be the one to decide whom she wanted to be with.

Who was she kidding? There wasn't going to be an 'if' to it. Cain was probably right about the rest of the hunters. If they tried to go back now, they'd be on The Company's hit list. She might find herself on it, for that matter, because of what she knew, but if she could avoid that pitfall, then she certainly didn't have to face the fear and hate that they would once it was known that they were cyborgs, as well. The hitch was that she doubted she would be allowed to return and she certainly wasn't going to make it back on her own. She wasn't a cyborg. She couldn't just download the information off of their data bases like the others could and she was no pilot.

If they didn't find out what she was, she might well be more accepted by the cyborgs than she had been by her own people, but that was another big 'if'. Reese knew. Dante knew. Even if they kept that information to themselves, how long before others figured it out? And, if and when they did, what then?

She massaged her aching temples.

Maybe the safest thing she could do was just to give in to the inevitable? Reese had said he wanted her for his mate. He would protect her secret.

Cyborg or not, she certainly couldn't claim to be repulsed by him.

She realized then that one of the things that was really bothering her was her reaction to all three men. Maybe she wasn't fit to contract with anyone? Her father had contracted twice before he'd contracted with her mother, her mother once before, but in her memory neither of them had even once considered terminating contract or breaching it by taking a lover outside their contract.

She'd been as interested in the opposite sex as any other healthy female, but, naturally enough, she'd only been able to wish from afar until she was full grown. By that time, she'd decided to join the militia, however, and she hadn't had much opportunity to experiment with her sexuality. Both of the times she'd tried sex it had been a complete disappointment, even though she'd considered both of them attractive at the time.

How could she have guessed that she would be insatiable?

She didn't know whether to put it down to some defect in her morals or chemical makeup, or if she'd always had the potential and it had just been stifled by the meds the company gave them.

She would've liked to think that, maybe, she'd reacted to Reese and Cain the way she had because she'd had a huge crush on both men, but then what excuse could she give herself for Dante?

Even if she wanted to contract, was she fit for it? Or would she find herself serving time for breach?

She frowned, trying to remember whether she'd ever had a reaction with anyone else even close to what she'd experienced with Reese, Dante, and Cain. She couldn't, but then three was bad enough, and she couldn't be certain that she wouldn't if the opportunity arose.

One thing was for certain, she didn't want to know badly enough to experiment and see. Everyone was off their meds and on the prowl now. She had enough trouble with what she'd already stirred up.

Almost as if on cue, she heard footsteps and looked up to see Violet striding toward her purposefully. Her belly clenched, but she'd known it was coming.

She surged to her feet.

Violet stopped near the foot of her bunk. "I hope you're satisfied! Cain's been taken to the brig for fighting."

Anger surged through Amaryllis. It wasn't as if she'd asked him to provoke Reese and Dante. She'd tried to avoid any sort of contact with him at all. "Not especially, but I guess they are. It's what men do, after all, and they really don't need an excuse when they're itching for a fight."

"If you hadn't led him on there wouldn't have been any reason for a fight."

Amaryllis gasped in outrage. "I didn't lead him on," she growled. "I didn't come on to him either."

"Right. Like you didn't with Reese or Dante?"

Amaryllis glared at her. "Don't start that holier than thou shit with me! I know damned well you've taken at least as many lovers as I have, probably more."

"I never incited any of my lovers to violence by trying to make them jealous."

She hadn't either, not intentionally anyway. "Because you couldn't?" she asked sweetly.

It was all the goading Violet needed. She launched herself at Amaryllis with a howl of rage. Expecting it, Amaryllis merely leapt out of her way. Unable to change directions or stop once she'd become airborne, Violet slammed into the bulkhead. The collision stunned her. Before she could recover and launch another attack, Amaryllis landed on her back, grasped both of her arms and twisted them behind her. "I know this is hard for you, Violet, but try not to be a complete moron. If you want Cain, this damned sure isn't the way to get him. What do you think you're going to do? Kill me and toss him over your shoulder like he's a prize? There are three males to every single female on this damned ship. And they're all pretty. Pick another one."

"Cain is mine!" Violet said through gritted teeth.

"That's his decision, not yours … and he obviously disagrees."

"He wanted me before he noticed you, and I want him!"

Amaryllis seriously doubted it. If he had, there would've been no reason to notice her. "And I want to go home! But we can't always have what we want, can we?"

Violet growled and tried to buck her off. Amaryllis tightened her knees around the other woman's middle, pushing up on her arms until Violet subsided, then shook her head in disgust. "This is really so completely crazy! I thought I was backwards when it came to relationships, but even I know someone either likes you or they don't. There's nothing you can do about it. It wouldn't matter if there wasn't another female within 10,000 light-years. He might settle for what he could get, but do you really want someone to settle for you only because they can't have what they want?"

"Meaning you?" Violet ground out.

Amaryllis rolled her eyes, but she realized she was wasting her time trying to reason with Violet. The problem was, she didn't know what to do with her if she couldn't. She couldn't just continue to sit on her and if she let her up she was more than likely to attack again. "Fine!" she said through gritted teeth. "If you think it's going to make you feel any better to get your ass kicked and then get thrown into the brig, suit yourself. But I'm sure as hell not going to let you kick my ass just because you're a fucking idiot!"

As she'd expected, the moment she climbed off of Violet, the woman scrambled to her feet and launched herself toward Amaryllis again. This time, instead of side-stepping, Amaryllis dropped back, catching herself with her hands, and kicked upward.

Violet was too close. Instead of catching her with both feet, Amaryllis caught the woman with one foot and one knee, launching her sideways rather than over her head as she'd intended. Before she could get to her feet, Violet recovered herself. Leaping forward, she caught Amaryllis around the waist. Her momentum carried both of them backward. They flipped over the foot of one of the bunks, hit the mattress and bounced off onto the floor.

Amaryllis landed on top. Even as she scrambled to regain her footing, however, she felt hard fingers digging into her hair. Fire flooded her scalp as she was dragged upward by her hair. She swung blindly at the new threat. Her arm was caught and twisted behind her back so hard she thought for several moments the joints would separate.

"Cease!"

The roared command jerked her out of the haze of battle. Gritting her teeth, Amaryllis subsided, dividing a glare between the two cyborgs that held her.

If she'd had any doubts about the barracks being watched, the guards surrounding both her and Violet dispelled them.

Without a word, the cyborgs marched her and Violet from the barracks and into the corridor.

The brig was in the bowels of the ship. Amayllis had thought the barracks was up until that point.

Not surprisingly, it was full. Embarrassment filled her as she was marched down the main corridor and finally shoved into a small cell. Violet was pushed into a cell opposite hers.

They glared at each other for several moments before Amaryllis finally turned and surveyed her accommodations.

It wasn't a hell of a lot worse than the barracks.

Shrugging, she plopped down on the narrow bunk and braced her back against the wall that separated her from the next cell.

"Are you injured?"

Amaryllis rolled her eyes. It was Reese's voice.

Just her shit house luck to be bunked right next to him. Apparently the gang was all here.

"I'm fine," she said through gritted teeth.

"What happened?"

She wasn't about to admit to anything so shameful as having been dragged into fighting over a man. "I had a difference of opinion with Violet--that dainty little flower sitting in the cell across from me."

He was silent for several moments and she had the uncomfortable feeling that he knew exactly why Violet had attacked her. "We need to talk."

Instantly visions of the last 'discussion' she'd had with Reese filled her mind. She covered her face with her hands, feeling a rush of both embarrassment and desire, but a hysterical urge to giggle swelled in her chest, as well. She'd spent years suffering agonies of envy of all the girls who'd had boyfriends, certain she never would, and now she had three bull headed, absolutely single minded cyborgs chasing after her like she was some sort of sex goddess or something. "I think it's going to be a little difficult to carry on a 'discussion' under present circumstances."

To her surprise, he immediately grasped the innuendo. From the tone of his voice, he wasn't particularly happy that she'd brought it up. "I meant talk," he said tightly.

"I don't particularly want to talk--to you or anyone else."

The silence lasted longer that time. "You've chosen Cain?"

The question and the inflexion of his voice spurred a riot of emotions, making her heart tighten painfully in her chest and she realized a number of very unpalatable facts all at once.

As appalled as she was to find herself lusting over Reese, Dante, and Cain all at the same time, she had far more to worry about than lust. She wasn't over her crush on Reese, not by a long shot, and she felt just as distressed over the idea of choosing Reese over Cain, or either one of them over Dante. She didn't want to do it. She didn't think she could. No matter which she chose, she would have a lot of regrets to live with, more than she wanted to face.

And she would have to. No matter whether there were hundreds, or thousands of cyborgs awaiting them on the cyborg planet, it would still be a small community and that meant she'd be running into one or the other of them all the time.

"I chose my life already when I decided to become a soldier. I'm not cut out for anything else. I don't want anything else," she lied. The truth was, she did. She wanted a life like her parents had had. She wanted to be 'normal'. It was all she'd ever really wanted and the one thing she could never have.

Maybe fate had dropped her right where she belonged, a misfit in the midst of other misfits, and yet even among them she didn't quite fit. The hunters differed from the cyborgs but they still shared the bond of being the same as each other. Despite their own varying physical attributes, the cyborgs shared the bond of having been created the same.

She was still different and, beyond her mixed feelings about considering forming a family unit, she was still afraid she would never truly fit in. Both Dante and Reese already knew she was different. How long before everyone else realized it, as well? And, once they had, even supposing they decided to allow her to live among them, they would know she was different and she would be able to feel them staring at her where ever she went and know she was being judged, hated for being different.

"We have a standing army. You needn't give that up if it's what you want. You would still be allowed to form a family unit."

Surprise flickered through Amaryllis briefly, but she wasn't particularly pleased by the information when she'd expected that to settle the matter. She decided to try a different tact.

"You would be more … content with someone who has more interest in forming a family unit than I."

"One of my own kind, you mean?" he asked in a harsh whisper.

Touchy. She hadn't realized he would be so touchy about it. The anger in his voice unsettled her and riled her own anger. "I don't know why you think you want me anyway. You've hardly spoken to me in all the time we've worked together. Why the sudden interest?"

He was silent so long she'd decided he couldn't come up with a convincing lie.

"I was … afraid."

The comment startled her. It also completely caught her attention. "Why?" she asked, genuinely confused.

He seemed to wrestle with himself for several moments. "Could we discuss this when we have no audience?"

He had a point. They didn't have any privacy, and yet she could hear the others who'd been confined talking. She couldn't think they had a great deal of interest in her conversation. Finally, she got up and moved to the front of the cell. "Why?" she demanded, pressing her face to the bars so that she could see him in the next cell.

He scrubbed a hand over his face. "It was forbidden."

Her lips flattened. "Sex was forbidden. We could've been friends."

"I do not want to be your friend," he said harshly. "And I could not take a chance that I would be tempted to do something that would make them suspicious of me. It seemed … safer to keep my distance."

Amaryllis frowned. "You were afraid you'd blow your cover? Or that they'd reprimand you with brig time so that you couldn't spy for the cyborgs?"

"I was afraid they would separate us so that I could not protect you," he growled irritably. "And…."

Amaryllis didn't know whether to be insulted or flattered. She supposed she was a little of both. She'd assumed Reese had been so protective because he'd been under orders to watch her closely and she'd resented it.

It was still insulting that he'd considered her incapable of taking care of herself. "And?"

He sighed. "I was … uncertain."

Amaryllis frowned. "Uncertain of what?"

He made a sound of impatience. "I was not programmed in the way to entice a female for the purpose of mating. I do not know how. I thought … I had planned to have that programming added," he finished uncomfortably.

Amaryllis bit her lip, torn between the urge to giggle and the desire to comfort. "You did … very well with the sex," she finally offered.

Instead of seeming pleased, he looked frustrated. "I could not have or you would have known that I was making love to you," he said stiffly. "And you would not have allowed that … *hunter* to touch you."

Chapter Fifteen

Guilt swamped Amaryllis. She resented feeling it. Nobody owned her. She wasn't bound by any oath, or any contract. She had a perfect right to enjoy sex, or flirtation, with anybody she wanted to.

She didn't want to hurt anyone, however, especially someone she cared for, and it sounded to her as if Reese was saying he was hurt by it.

Warmth spread through her, hopefulness that he actually felt something for her besides desire. Desire was good, and she wasn't unappreciative, even if it didn't necessarily follow that it was particularly personal. If he actually cared, though, and not merely in the sense that he believed he'd 'marked' his territory and had ownership rights….

There was something that didn't quite fit, though.

"You weren't jealous of Dante," she pointed out hesitantly, remembering almost the moment she questioned it that he'd actually seemed pretty pissed off when he'd found her in Dante's cabin, reeking of sex.

He seemed to wrestle with himself, but in the end he neither admitted nor denied the accusation. "He did not know that I wanted you for myself."

Amaryllis thought that over and realized he was trying to make excuses for his brother.

"Besides, if I had done what I wanted to, I would have been here, while you were there."

She hid a smile. It was as much of an admission as he was likely to make. He *was* jealous. He was still ruled more by logic than emotion, though, or he wouldn't have considered the consequences until *after* he'd made his peace with his brother.

That wasn't such a bad thing, was it?

There was a lot to be said for having enough self control

to think things through before acting.

She shook her head at the direction of her thoughts, realizing she was actually entertaining the thought of accepting Reese's offer. It was insane even to consider it and not because of any prejudice about him being a cyborg. He was right. He was as human as she was, however he'd been created.

The thing was, he was no more cut out for forming an alliance than she was. Whatever he wanted, or believed he wanted, he'd been designed strictly as a killing machine. Maybe he was right and it would take no more than additional programming to fix that little problem, but she had her doubts that anything could completely overcome his previous programming and it was out of the question even to think about complete reprogramming. He wouldn't be the same person and she adored the person he was.

"We will talk when we reach Gallen."

"Gallen?"

"Home."

The single word raised a plethora of feelings, but yearning was uppermost … for her own home, for her mother. She wished desperately that she could seek her mother's advice, but then it occurred to her that her mother would probably think she was a basket case even to consider having a serious relationship with a cyborg.

She wouldn't understand that Reese was a person, not a machine.

It was as well that Reese thought it best to hold the discussion until they reached the world the cyborgs called home. It would give her time to learn what if any options she had and to decide what she really wanted to do.

She didn't know whether to be relieved or sorry when she discovered she needn't worry that Reese would change his mind and try to press her for an answer. The guards arrived later that evening and moved him to another cell further along the corridor. Six dreary days later, she was released from lock up. The day after that, they landed.

Chapter Sixteen

Amaryllis was almost as terrified as she was excited at the prospect of being off ship after months in space.

No one else seemed to share her reservations. When the order came to disembark, the corridor flooded with eager 'colonists' of both the hunter and the cyborg variety, although Amaryllis supposed they were all cyborgs now.

Or maybe they'd decided to call themselves something else? She thought a little hysterically.

She was pregnant.

She figured that was reason enough to be battling hysteria even if she wasn't facing a world she was fairly certain she wasn't prepared for.

She was still in a state of shock over the realization, still unable to completely accept her suspicions.

She didn't have to look far for the source, but she still had a hard time accepting that she'd been impregnated by a cyborg.

How had they developed the capability? She knew damn well The Company would have made certain they couldn't reproduce, regardless of the other liberties they'd taken and despite the fact that they'd deliberately developed a human/robotic hybrid.

Did it matter now?

She'd been trying to deny it for weeks, ignoring all the changes in her body that told its own story. She'd almost managed to convince herself that it was pure imagination. After all, she'd never been pregnant before. It seemed more likely that her suspicions could be wrong than that she'd hit on just why she didn't feel quite as she should. Right? But she knew she could continue trying to deny it until the baby--or whatever it was--was born, and it wasn't going to change a damn thing. Denial wasn't going to stop it from happening.

It could've been either one of them.

It could've been both for all she knew.

She didn't care. All that mattered was that she was almost certain she had something growing inside of her and she didn't want it there.

She couldn't face producing a freak.

She wasn't about to bring something into the world to go through the hell she'd gone through.

Her parents had always said it was the radiation storms, that they'd had inadequate shielding at a critical time in her development. There'd been a time when she'd believed them, but that was before she'd been facing the possibility of producing some 'thing' herself.

And if that wasn't bad enough, she'd mated with a cyborg. They'd been engineered for excellence, but there had been no expectation that they would reproduce and therefore no concern that their genes could affect future generations. His genes could be as fucked up as her own probably were.

She wanted, desperately, to find a physician who could tell her just how bad it was and remove it if it was as she suspected. She knew that was impossible though. They'd know inside of five minutes that she wasn't one of them and who knew what would happen?

Her only hope, as far as she could see, was to get on an outbound ship as soon as possible and find help.

Reese and Dante were waiting for her when she finally made her way down the gangplank. If she hadn't been so distracted, she would've been looking for a way to avoid them. As it was, Reese had gripped her arm before she even realized he was there.

She glanced at him and then Dante.

"We have a home. You can stay with us until … until you decide what you want to do," Reese offered.

Amaryllis blinked at him in dismay. It took her several moments to realize he wasn't talking about her condition, couldn't be because he had no knowledge of it. It took her several moments longer to jog her brain into functioning.

"I'm going to stay at the barracks," she said finally, remembering the announcement that had been made shortly before they'd landed that accommodations for those who had not made other arrangements could be found at the barracks near the edge of town.

Reese and Dante exchanged a look.

"I will be staying at the house of a friend," Dante said coolly.

Amaryllis must have stared at him a full minute before she realized what he was saying. She glanced at Reese and then at Dante again. He was a medic. But would he have enough knowledge of medicine to know how to check her? Would he know what to look for? He could probably tell her, positively, whether she was or she was not pregnant, but she'd find that out in due time without having to be checked.

What she needed to know was whether the child was normal or if it was defective and, if it was defective, what course she should take.

She shook the thought off, horrified at the desperation that had spawned it. Dante might know her secret, but he might also have fathered the child. She couldn't let either one of them know.

Reese had spoken of contracting for a family unit. He wouldn't understand at all.

Finally, she shook her head. "My decision has nothing to do with you."

He reddened, turning to glare angrily at the distant horizon.

Amaryllis stared up at him in dismay. She hadn't spoken to him since she'd been discovered in his cabin. She was fairly certain that he hadn't turned her in as she'd first believed, but he'd avoided her since, and she didn't know whether it was because of Reese, or because he thought she hated him for betraying her trust. "I didn't mean that the way you obviously took it. I'm just…." She searched for something to say that would be palatable to both of them.

"...confused right now and I need time to adjust."

It was patently obvious that neither of them was happy about her decision, but they apparently thought argument would be useless. After exchanging another glance, as if they were communicating telepathically, they escorted her to the barracks.

Amaryllis would've preferred they hadn't and it had nothing to do with the fact that she saw Cain watching the three of them speculatively from the terminal. She was in no fit frame of mind to deal with him either.

It was a beautiful world. Dimly, she was aware of that even through her abstraction, aware of the pure sweetness of the air, the gentle caress of the breeze, the comforting warmth of the sun. Abundant vegetation covered the surrounding hills. Tiny flying creatures fluttered among the branches of strange trees and brush and soared overhead, singing strange songs through alien throats. The city, Gallen, nestled comfortably alongside the natural surroundings, the buildings as beautiful in their own way as the land the cyborgs had obviously taken great care to leave as undisturbed as possible.

It lightened her spirits, drew her from her self-absorption. "It's ... beautiful," she said, her voice tinged with surprise as she stopped short to study her surroundings. She didn't know what she'd expected, but this was certainly not it. She supposed she'd thought that it would look much like the planet of her childhood.

Typically, the terra farmers were sent to planets that would barely sustain life and it was up to them to create a planet more hospitable for the colonists that would come later. They had tried to make their personal habitats as 'homey' as possible, but the structure itself was utilitarian and painfully ugly. Beyond the habitat, vegetation was sparse, scraggly and often deadly, and so, too, were the few creatures to be found. The air was breathable, but no one went outside the dome without a suit and a respirator. They'd lived in almost perpetual gloom despite the bright artificial lighting because the atmosphere was so thick the sun barely penetrated it to brighten the ground, much less the glass dome that guarded their habitat.

The 'playground' was an area in the center of the dome that the colonists had set aside as safe enough for the children to play. But, although to the young child she'd been it had seemed a place filled with adventure she alone was excluded from finding, the truth was it was as horrible as the remainder of the habitat.

This world was one of such perfection it filled her with wonder, as if she'd slipped into a fantasy world where the sun never burned and the flora and fauna had evolved solely to give comfort and sustenance and pleasure. And, as if guided by their reverence of such beauty, the cyborgs had created a city equally beautiful, built of the pink and white veined stones that erupted from the earth here there, the roofs topped with tiles baked from the soil itself, and everywhere--on the pillars that supported the roofs and the walls--relief carvings that reflected the climbing vegetation and flowers and bird-like creatures surrounding it so that the city itself seemed a part of it all, rather than an intrusion.

"Is this--real?"

Reese, she saw, was smiling at her with obvious pride. "Yes. I'm glad our new home pleases you." He turned then and, from the rise where they stood, pointed out the buildings of importance in the city--the hall where the council members met; the education centers; the medical/research center; the center for laws; the fort for the militia.

Spiraling out from the city proper, Amaryllis could see glimpses of other buildings. "What are those?"

"The plantations already established. On that rise there is the home that Dante and I built together. It is small by comparison to many of the others, but we did not need much room to be comfortable. In any case, we wanted to wait until we had a family and build to suit our mates."

Amaryllis felt her face redden. After glancing uncomfortably at Dante, she began to move again, heading toward the barracks. Without a word, Reese and Dante fell into step beside her.

The barracks, she discovered as they approached it, was far more simple a structure than the others, but still surprisingly pleasing to the eye and as luxurious inside as an upper end apartment complex. She was assigned quarters at the main office and given supplies. To her relief, Reese and Dante excused themselves and departed once they'd walked her to the barracks.

Her heels echoed hollowly as she moved briskly along the virtually deserted corridor that bisected the barracks and finally found the door to her own quarters. It was sparsely furnished, more utilitarian, like the barracks she was accustomed to, but far larger, containing a private bath, a tiny, well stocked kitchen area and a combination living/sleeping area.

She didn't have much enthusiasm for exploring. Depression had settled over her from the moment Reese and Dante had departed, leaving her no reason to try even to appear hopeful about her situation. She plopped into the only comfortable chair the quarters boasted, fighting the tightness of pure misery in her chest.

There'd been only one ship at the landing--the ship they'd traveled on.

She wasn't getting off this planet and she had no idea what the hell she was going to do.

Chapter Seventeen

Amaryllis didn't even claim the most rudimentary cooking skills. What little she did know had been gained from watching her mother prepare meals, but, naturally enough, she had no actual experience in preparing food. After a while, though, she began to realize that at least a part of the hollowness in her belly was hunger and she dragged herself up and went to find something to fill the void. The meal she managed wasn't anything to brag about, but it satisfied her need for food.

Afterwards, bored and anxious, she decided to go out to test her freedom. To her surprise and relief, she was allowed to pass without question. She found herself heading directly toward the med center without even realizing that was the destination she'd had in mind. A great crowd was gathered in the streets, however, and, unnerved, she made an about face as soon as she saw that something had the cyborgs surprisingly stirred up and quickly put as much distance between herself and the crowd as possible.

She wandered the other, nearly deserted streets of the city for a time and finally, tired and more depressed than ever, returned to the barracks.

It was just as well she hadn't been able to get near the hospital or she might have been tempted to do something really stupid. She had no idea how the cyborgs might react if they discovered they had a human among them--they might merely send her packing but somehow she doubted it would transpire that their idea of a solution and hers coincided so well. They might decide to keep her since there seemed to be a rather shockingly uneven ratio of men to women, but she was very much afraid that she would never really be accepted even if they wanted her to stay.

And it could be far worse. They might decide to terminate her, or imprison her until they could deport her.

She was almost desperate enough to risk it just so she could have some peace of mind regarding her pregnancy. She *had* to know if it was normal. But how?

It occurred to her as she made her way along the main thoroughfare towards the barracks that she might have another option.

This planet was abundant with life and appeared to have been capable of sustaining life for thousands of years if not longer. There must have been intelligent life on the planet when the cyborgs arrived. It seemed ludicrous to think there wouldn't have been on such prime territory. The question was, how intelligent? Advanced enough to help? What were the chances that they would be willing to help even if they had the technology? Or had the cyborgs slain them when they'd claimed their world? Or driven them to some distant corner so that she might search for years without finding them?

It seemed a long shot, but she figured it couldn't hurt to look and see if there were any signs of other intelligent beings.

Reese met her at her door when she reached her quarters once more. Her belly instantly clenched with nerves at sight of him.

It wasn't altogether because she dreaded the 'talk' he'd put off until they landed.

He looked--absolutely divine. He'd shed the uniform they'd worn during the trip. Now he wore nothing more than what amounted to a loin cloth to cover his privates. Around his waist, he'd fastened a leather belt that secured an ornately handled sword and scabbard at his side. He'd pulled his long, blond hair into a queue at the base of his skull and tied it with a twisted length of leather.

The uniform conformed to the shape of his body in loving detail, and she'd known he was built well, but their coupling before had been so frantic they hadn't actually taken the time to undress and she hadn't had the opportunity to admire his body.

Nor did she think she'd ever properly appreciated his classical features as she did now for although she'd always considered him heartstoppingly handsome, she'd always been too overawed to do more than sneak peeks at him.

The scanty clothing that had been furnished for her own use made more sense to her now. Obviously, his clothing and the clothing they'd been given aboard ship were not only typical, but in common usage among the cyborgs because the planet's climate required nothing more.

For many minutes, she simply stopped and stared at him. Finally, however, she realized that he was giving her an equally thorough examination. Discomfort settled over her as his gaze swept over her belly and she jolted forward once more.

Yet another thing to worry about, she thought wryly as she punched in her code at the key lock of her quarters. The climate might be balmy enough to make clothing unnecessary, but that it also left her with very little to hide her condition. She had no clue of when it would become obvious that she was breeding, but she doubted it would be long.

"Make yourself comfortable," she offered a little stiltedly, gesturing in the general direction of the chair as she headed toward the bathroom. "I'm going to freshen up."

She didn't feel the need to wash up nearly as badly as she felt the need for just a few minutes to collect herself. On the other hand, she didn't want him to know she was stalling for time. She didn't linger.

Reese was pacing the floor when she returned to the living area.

Amaryllis studied him with a mixture of surprise and uneasiness. "You didn't want to sit down?"

He glanced at the chair distractedly and finally shook his head.

"Refreshment?"

"No. I thank you."

Amaryllis nodded, studied the chair a moment and finally

decided to leave it in case he changed his mind and sit on the bunk that served as a couch during the day. She didn't particularly want Reese towering over her, but he did even when she was standing. She figured she might as well get as comfortable as possible, particularly since her knees felt a little weak.

The moment she settled, Reese stopped pacing and knelt in front of her. "You have decided?"

Amaryllis frowned at the abruptness of the question. She hadn't expected him to come straight to the point and she wasn't particularly pleased that he had. "No."

He looked confused. "The hunter--the one called Cain--he is here. You are here."

"He's here?" she echoed, surprised.

"You did not know?"

"I didn't."

He looked somewhat relieved, but also confused. "You have decided not to contract with him?"

Amaryllis felt blood flood her cheeks. "He hasn't asked."

"You are waiting for him to ask?"

Indignation added to the color in her cheeks. "I'm not holding my breath, if that's what you mean," she snapped.

He frowned. "I do not understand."

"What don't you understand?"

"Why would you hold your breath?" he asked curiously.

Amaryllis bit her lip to keep from smiling. "It means I'm not waiting for Cain to ask, OK?"

He still looked confused but finally he took her hand. "I have come to ask if you will not decide yet. I have made an appointment for reprogramming."

He looked so earnest Amaryllis didn't know whether to laugh or cry. It was probably the sweetest thing any man had ever said to her and she would never have imagined Reese, whom she'd always thought of as practically a demi-god, would be so desperate for her approval as to consider such an 'improvement' necessary.

To her horror, tears filled her eyes.

Reese's reaction was far more violent. He released her

hand as if he'd suddenly discovered he was holding fire and leapt to his feet. "You are not pleased."

It was a statement, not a question. Amaryllis didn't trust herself to speak. She shook her head.

His face hardened. After a moment, he nodded sharply, turned and strode toward the door.

Amaryllis leapt to her feet. "Wait! Don't go!"

He halted and turned to look at her questioningly.

Moving toward him, she placed her palm on one of his hard cheeks, stroking it. "You don't need to do that. Not for me."

He nodded. "I understand. It would not make a difference."

All the doubts and fears Amaryllis had been harboring shattered. One thought emerged crystal clear. She couldn't just allow Reese to leave thinking that she cared less than nothing about him. It hurt her to see him trying to preserve an emotionless front when everything about him told her he felt pain.

Shaking her head, Amaryllis caught his hand and tugged on it until he reluctantly followed her back to the couch, then pushed on his chest until he sat down. When he'd settled, she placed a knee on either side of his hips and sat on his lap, facing him. "It *would* make a difference. It would change you and … and I love you just the way you are," she finished, leaning toward him and brushing a light kiss across his hard mouth.

She felt a jolt of surprise go through him, either at her words, or the kiss, or perhaps both. When she leaned back once more to study him, his expression was a mixture of desire and disbelief and confusion. She could see that he was reviewing every exchange between them, trying to understand how it might have happened that she would fall in love with him, but it wasn't something that could be analyzed. The first time she'd set eyes on him it had knocked the breath right out of her, as if she'd been body slammed by his pheromones. It would probably be more accurate to say that nothing he'd done or said since had knocked the sense into her, not even when she'd learned that he'd been sent to infiltrate them. She smiled faintly. "You'll never figure it out," she murmured, rubbing the tip of her nose against his.

He swallowed audibly. His hands were shaking slightly when he captured her face between them. "Amy," he said gustily, leaning forward to brush his lips lightly against hers.

Her lips tingled at his touch and she flicked her tongue out, tracing the shape of his lips. His breath left him in a rush. He hesitated and then covered her mouth with his own, thrusting his tongue into her mouth to caress the sensitive inner flesh.

The warm intoxication of desire flowed through her as his essence flooded her senses, bringing a flush of heightened sensation to her skin. It took an effort to lift her eyelids when he withdrew to study her once more. "Will you make contract with me?" he asked, his voice raw with his own needs.

A knot of misery gathered in her throat at his insistent question. She found she couldn't meet the look in his eyes. Instead, she studied the musculature of his broad chest, tracing the bulges and dips that defined each muscle mass with the tip of one finger.

She did love him. She didn't care what he was supposed to be, only what he was. She would've liked nothing better if she could've just closed her mind to all her doubts and jumped at the chance he offered her.

But she loved him. She might be carrying his baby, and she might not. She might be carrying some horrible deformed thing. She might never be able to bear a normal child and she knew that was what he wanted. A family. Not just her. A family.

It wouldn't be right and it wasn't something one did to a person they loved. She couldn't lie about something as important as the possibility that her genes were as defective as her body, not even a lie of omission. And she couldn't bring herself to tell him. Horror filled her even at the thought of doing so.

He might want her anyway.

Or he might look at her like everyone else had always looked at her. Even after she'd had all the surgeries that made her look normal, all they'd been able to see was what she'd been before.

She didn't think she could bear that look from him.

Instead of answering his question, she leaned down and followed the path her finger had traced with the tip of her tongue. He tensed, released a pent up breath that was like a groan.

"Amy," he said hoarsely.

She lifted her head to look at him.

He stroked her cheek. "I want to do this correctly."

Amaryllis frowned in confusion.

Frustration flickered in his eyes. "By your customs. But--I have need."

Relief flooded Amaryllis. She slipped her arms around his neck, sliding forward on his lap so that his engorged cock was nestled along her cleft and sending delicious tremors through her. "To hell with the customs. We'll make new ones," she muttered, grinding her cleft along the hard ridge of his cock. "I have needs too."

Leaning forward, she caught the lobe of his ear between her teeth, sucking it. "I'm wet for you," she whispered. "I want to feel you inside of me. It felt so good when you were inside of me before."

He caught her shoulders in his hands, hesitated, as if of half a mind to push her away. His fingers tightened, digging into her flesh. Abruptly, he relaxed his fingers, slipping his arms around her. Clutching a fistful of her hair, he tugged her head back and lowered his mouth to her throat, sucking open mouthed kisses along the sensitive flesh of her throat, the side of her neck. She closed her eyes, savoring the awakening of her body, the heat and tension that began coiling inside of her.

Again he paused, but this time it was to rid himself of the sword belted at his waist. Amaryllis heard it drop to the carpeted floor. Briefly, disorientation made her head swim as he twisted around, lowering both of them onto the bunk. Before her equilibrium had quite settled, she felt his mouth along her collarbone, felt his hands pushing her breasts from the cups of her halter. Her nipples, almost painfully sensitive with her pregnancy, sent twinges of discomfort through her as blood engorged them. She gasped when his mouth covered one distended tip, digging her fingertips into the hard flesh of his shoulders.

The heat and adhesion of his mouth, the teasing nudge of his tongue, intoxicated her, separated mind from body so that she couldn't think. She could only feel the pleasurable sensations bombarding her in waves that seemed to grow stronger and stronger until she was fighting for breath, until darkness swam around her and the urgency to feel him inside of her overwhelmed all other considerations.

She ran a hand between them, over his hard belly, delving the tips of her fingers beneath his loin cloth. She touched the head of his cock, explored it, shifted until she could almost wrap her fingers around his hard length. He jerked, surged upward until his cock filled her palm.

It was as delightfully hard, and thick and solid as he was and her belly clenched almost painfully in anticipation. Heat and moisture flooded her passage.

He reached down, fumbled briefly with the tie and released the cloth. Before she could try to wedge his cock past the leg of her briefs, he pulled away, grasped the straps on either side of her hips and jerked them down her thighs to her knees before settling over her again.

She uttered a sharp gasp as she felt the head of his cock delve her cleft, slip along it, nudging her clit.

She was bound, unable to spread her legs wide enough to accommodate him.

It took several moments for her heated brain to register the fact that her briefs were pinning her legs together, and many more than she wanted to devote to the effort of wriggling out of them.

A fine sheen of moisture covered them both by the time

they'd managed to engage their bodies, for despite the moisture that had gathered to ease his passage, her body resisted the girth of his cock. Reese made a sound that was half groan of frustration and half desperation, caught her around the waist and heaved upward. Amaryllis dug her heels in to counter her thrusts and then wrapped her legs tightly around his waist, panting as she felt him slipping more deeply inside of her, felt herself stretching.

Shaking now, he withdrew and thrust again and again until he'd sheathed himself fully inside of her. They paused to catch their breath, sharing a deep kiss that began with heat and ended with a conflagration. Gasping, he released her lips and began a desperate, driving rhythm. Amaryllis squeezed her eyes tightly together, luxuriating in the pure bliss of his fierce possession, feeling him right down to her soul as their warm, intimate flesh merged, caressed each other in a tight embrace. Delicious waves of excitement wafted through her, of electric pleasure, coiling tightly inside of her, building until her entire body felt as if it hummed with ecstatic energy. Abruptly, it ruptured, sending her flying over the edge of rapture into mind sundering bliss. The spasms of pleasure rocking her caught Reese, pitching him into his own shattering release. Shuddering, shaking, he thrust until his cock ceased to ejaculate and collapsed weakly on top of her, gasping for breath.

The weight of his body crushed the air from her lungs. Amaryllis had to struggle to catch her breath. He shifted after only a moment, however, easing the pressure as he nuzzled her neck and upper chest.

She was just beginning to thoroughly enjoy his affection when he murmured, "There is great rejoicing in the streets. The first child is born."

It took Amaryllis several moments to ascend the depths of satiated bliss to even partial cognition. "Wha…?"

"Reuel's woman has given birth." He chuckled lazily. "If we do much of this, we will have our own before the contract is signed."

Amaryllis shoved at him and sat up, feeling a surge of panic and the anger that walked hand and hand with it. "What? His woman? She isn't a person anymore? She's just 'Reuel's woman'? Anyway, it isn't possible. I saw her on the ship. She wasn't that far along."

Reese propped his head on his hand, frowning, confusion and dawning anger in his eyes. "Dalia has given birth. I didn't mean it the way you think. But it is true. I've only just come from the medical center. The child is strong and healthy and perfect." He frowned thoughtfully. "There was something said about the gestation period being shortened because of the ability we have for rapid cell regeneration."

Sheer terror replaced the panic and Amaryllis shoved him off of her abruptly, stalked from the room and slammed the bathroom door behind her. Leaning weakly against the door, she wasn't even aware of her surroundings for many minutes. She couldn't even think. Disjointed sentence fragments kept running through her mind like a chant-- shortened gestation period--rapid cell regeneration--strong, healthy, perfect baby--time--not much time.

The discomfort of a warm, sticky wetness oozing down her thigh finally brought her back to the present reality. She stared down at it for several moments as if it was a live thing crawling along her leg.

It was a live thing, full of live things.

Christ and all the saints! What had she been thinking? It wasn't like she could get pregnant, again. She was already pregnant, but wasn't that enough of a complication in her life, compounded as it already was with the fact that she didn't belong here at all?

She hadn't been thinking.

She'd only been feeling--allowing her emotions to overrule what little judgment she had.

She had to fight the urge to simply climb out of the tiny window set between the lavatory and the shower and run until she couldn't run anymore.

After a moment, she discarded the halter and climbed into the shower, bathing herself thoroughly.

Not that it mattered now.

She discovered when she got out that she didn't have anything to put on. Naked, she left the bathroom and crossed the room to the chest that held the clothing she'd been given.

Reese was watching her. She was aware of it without actually looking at him.

"Something is wrong."

An understatement. She sent him a questioning look, trying to keep her expression merely curious. "Why would you say that?"

Frowning, he got up and adjusted his clothing then reached down and scooped up his sword and fastened it at his waist. "You did not give me an answer."

"To what?" Amaryllis asked, playing dumb with an effort.

His lips tightened. "The contract?"

"Oh! I did. You just weren't listening. I don't know what I want to do. I told you I wasn't cut out for rearing a family. I really don't think I can do it."

"You have overcome much in your life, become an excellent soldier. You can do whatever you set your mind to do."

If that was supposed to be a pep talk, he should've left out the 'overcome much' because it only made her keenly aware of her shortcomings, only emphasized the fear that was gnawing at her like cancer and the growing desperation she felt to rid her body of the tragically malformed being that was no doubt growing there, unaware of the horrendous struggle life would be because of its deformities.

Anger surged through her abruptly. "Then maybe it's just a matter of wanting to and I'm not sure that I do."

Her anger provoked his. "Then what was this," he growled, gesturing toward the rumpled bed.

"Great sex?"

He looked so furious that for several moments she felt a touch of fear. He ground his teeth. "I am not a pleasure droid," he gritted out and stalked toward the door. He hesitated when he reached it, as if he had something more to say, or as if he was hoping that she would stop him. She didn't. Without another word, he stalked from the room and slammed the door behind him so hard she was a little surprised it didn't crack and fall into pieces.

Her shoulders slumped when the sound of his tread along the corridor outside faded. "It's just as well," she muttered to herself.

Chapter Eighteen

Amaryllis was torn between the need to seek comfort, somewhere, and the need to hide like a wounded animal. Her head ached incessantly from struggling to find a solution when there didn't appear to be one, and her chest ached from a tightness that gave her no relief even when she slept.

For two days, she wandered almost aimlessly around Gallen, until she noticed that, wherever she went, the male cyborgs she passed stopped to study her speculatively. She didn't know whether it was because she kept walking around and around the medical center, trying to get up her nerve to enter, trying to come up with some sort of plan of action if the search for help backfired on her, or if it was because every male cyborg on the frigging planet was in the grips of mate hunting, but their interest made her too nervous to consider continuing her routine.

She couldn't bear to stay penned up in her quarters, though, certain she would go completely mad. Finally, she decided that she would roam the countryside around Gallen and search for some sign of the native inhabitants. It seemed unlikely she would see any sign so close, even if there were an intelligent species on the planet, but it beat the hell out of doing nothing at all.

Notices had been posted calling for a town meeting, she saw when she left the barracks. She didn't know what it was about, and she didn't especially care until it occurred to her that it was probably about the hunters and what the cyborgs intended to do about their 'new recruits'.

Making a mental note of the time and place, she turned her steps toward the landing field instead of the city. She was half way to the field before she emerged from her self absorption enough to realize she was being followed. There was no way, of course, to see who it was without giving away the fact that she knew they were there and after a few moments she decided just to pretend she hadn't noticed. It might merely be someone who was walking in the same direction. It didn't necessarily follow that she was being shadowed just because they both happened to be going in the same direction on the same road.

She was so dismayed when she reached the field and discovered that the ship had vanished that she had to jog her instincts into action and duck out of sight.

Either he had seen her duck behind the pillar, he was expecting an attack, or she made some slight sound that gave her away. When she slung a fist at his jaw, he caught her wrist mid-air, jerking her from her hiding place and twisting so that she slammed back against his chest. She was too stunned for several moments to do much more than gasp, but in that split second flash before he'd thoroughly subdued her, she'd realized that it was Dante and her fear subsided. Briefly, she struggled to free herself, but his arms around her were like solid titanium bands.

"Why did you attack me?" he asked harshly, his head lowered so that his breath brushed her ear, sending shivers of sensation along the sensitive flesh there.

"Why did you follow me?" she gritted out.

He was silent for several moments. "To make certain you came to no harm."

"I can take care of myself," she snapped. The words were no sooner out of her mouth than it occurred to her that the statement didn't hold a lot of weight at the moment. "I realized it was you only a moment too late," she added, stretching the truth only a hair.

When he said nothing, she twisted her head to look back at him. Amusement was gleaming in his eyes. She glared at him.

"Anyway, I saw no danger … except the person following me."

"I made no attempt at stealth. If my intention had been to do you harm…."

She'd been too distracted to be on guard. If she'd still been on active duty, and he had been an enemy, she would be dead now and they both knew it. "I hadn't expected a threat so near the city. Is security so lax then?"

"There is always danger--anywhere--for the unwary."

Amaryllis let out a gusty sigh of exasperation. "Point taken. You can let go of me now--unless this is your idea of romance?"

His hold on her loosened and she pulled away and turned to look up at him. "Why did you really follow me?"

He studied her in silence for several moments. "Initially-- to talk. But your walk seemed more purposeful than not. Why did you come here?"

"Not to attempt escape, if that's what you're thinking," she said dryly. "I don't know how to pilot a ship and unlike you, I can't just jack in and download the programming."

He flushed slightly. She wasn't certain if it was because of her tone or the reference to his origins, but she regretted the comment almost at once. "What did you want to talk about?" she added quickly.

He looked uncomfortable. "I wanted you to know that I did not betray you."

She studied him piercingly for several moments and finally shrugged. "I realize that. At first, I thought I just didn't want to believe it. Later, I came to realize that it wasn't just wishful thinking."

He looked relieved, but also confused. "Reese told you?"

She frowned. "Told me what?"

His lips tightened. An expression of chagrin replaced his irritation. "I suppose I should have, but I did not realize that you were the one Reese had … chosen, not until … afterward."

Amaryllis stared at him a long moment, trying to decipher the undercurrents of that comment. It sounded very much like he was saying he regretted what had happened between them and, to her surprise, she also realized it hurt to think he might. However she felt about Reese, she'd wanted Dante. She'd formed a bond with him in that time she'd

spent with him secreted away from the others. "Sooo …
you're saying you wouldn't have fucked me senseless if
you'd known Reese had a prior claim?"

He shook his head slowly. Both desire and amusement
gleamed in his eyes. "You misunderstand. I do not regret
loving you. Each time I look at you I remember, and I can
almost feel the softness of your skin, taste you, hear your
sighs of pleasure, feel your heat surrounding me--and I
want you again."

Amaryllis swallowed with an effort, trying to banish the
images he'd conjured in her mind, trying to tamp the rising
tide of heat that flushed her skin with tingling sensation.

He moved closer, lifting a hand to trace his fingers lightly
over one cheek.

"I do not even particularly regret that Reese tried to take
my head off my shoulders, or that I spent nearly a month in
solitary for concealing you. I only regret that my need for
you clouded my judgment and led to your discovery," he
murmured, leaning down and capturing her lips beneath his
in a kiss filled with need.

Amaryllis' head swam as a heady rush of desire filled her,
her body instantly remembering and responding to the call
of his, as if the moments of intimacy they'd shared had
marked her as indelibly his just as surely as Reese had
when he'd laid siege to all her senses.

A confusion of emotions pierced her desire, bringing with
it an unwelcome dose of reality. Reluctantly, Amaryllis
withdrew before temptation could overwhelm her.

Dante drew in a shuddering breath and leaned his
forehead against hers, stroking the side of her neck with
one large hand. "Make contract with me, Amy. I want … I
want to have a family with you."

A sense of despair filled her. Couldn't she just look to
someone for comfort without having them want more than
she felt like she could give? she thought crossly. She'd
hoped to avert another situation like the one with Reese by
avoiding intimacy. She might just as well have let him
screw her brains out. At least then she would've found

some release from tension, if only briefly. "Don't call me that," she said angrily, pushing away from him. "I'm not Amy anymore. I haven't been Amy for a long time."

His hands dropped to his sides. He looked at her with a mixture of anger and confusion. "Reese calls you Amy," he said finally. "Is that it?"

Amaryllis glanced at him sharply. She saw then that he wasn't just angry. He was hurt. A sense of contrition filled her. "It's not that. It's … it reminds me of everyone and everything that I'll never see again." It struck her then with a finality she hadn't felt before. She couldn't go back. She could never go home again. Even if the cyborgs freed her and allowed it, even if she could somehow find a way to convince The Company that they didn't need to kill her to keep their secret safe, she had a baby growing inside of her that was only half human. Whether she terminated the pregnancy or not, she was never going to feel the same again. She was never going to *be* the same again. She'd had Reese and Dante inside of her, a part of her, and she'd loved every moment of it.

No one on any Earth colony would ever accept her again as being 'one of them'. And she wouldn't be able to bear listening to them discussing 'the machines', as if the cyborgs weren't human at all. She, at least, had had a choice. They hadn't.

It was ironic, really, that she'd become half cyborg only to be accepted as a whole human being by the rest of her race, and these people had been made half without their knowledge or consent and were considered nothing but machines.

"So you choose to be alone?" he asked angrily. "We are so different that you can not stomach the idea of sharing your life with one of us?"

Actually, they weren't really very different at all. They were about as fucked up as the rest of the human race, except that it had been with premeditation that The Company scientists had chosen to produce them this way. The goal, she supposed, was to give them the ability to think, and act, and follow orders like a human without having the undesirable conscience that so often made killing difficult or impossible and carried with it long range debilitation. "I do *wish* you'd stop throwing that in my face!" she snapped. "It's got nothing to do with you. It's me, alright! If it had been my ambition to be nothing more than a breeder--if I'd thought I would be any damned good at it--do you think I'd have chosen to be a soldier? You'll have a far better chance at having what you want if you choose one of the others."

He didn't believe her. She could tell by the way he was looking at her. "Why? Because we are the same?"

"Yes!" she snapped, poking him in the chest with her index finger. "Because they selected only the best, the most superior DNA to produce you, all of you. You wouldn't be taking the risks breeding with inferior genetics could produce."

She stared at his stunned expression for several moments and finally brushed past him and walked briskly away. Tension filled her as she rounded the terminal and paused at the road, trying to decide whether to head back to the barracks or continue her exploration. She finally decided on the latter, because it represented a refuge of sorts.

Dante didn't follow her. She didn't know whether to be relieved or hurt. Deep down, she knew she was right, but it would've been soothing to have him brush her logical considerations aside and tell her it didn't matter, that she was perfect in his eyes.

Even if it was a lie, it would have been nice.

Chapter Nineteen

Cain was leaning against the wall, his arms folded over his chest, when Amaryllis left her quarters the following day. She checked when she saw him, more than half tempted to retreat and lock the door.

He lifted one dark brow. "Coward," he murmured with amusement.

Amaryllis' lips tightened. Instead of retreating, she slammed the door and very pointedly turned and strode down the corridor. Cain fell into step beside her. After a few moments she gave up the effort to try to out-walk him. His legs were far longer than hers. She'd have to run to outdistance him.

She sent him a resentful glare.

"Where are we off to today?" he asked agreeably.

"*I'm* going for a walk--in the countryside--alone."

His dark brows rose. "Out for a lover's tryst?"

Amaryllis ground her teeth. "I said alone."

"You said you were going alone. You didn't specify that you intended to remain alone," he pointed out pleasantly.

She ignored that. "Where are you going?"

"By curious coincidence, I, too, am going for a walk in the countryside, alone."

Amaryllis didn't know whether to laugh or punch him. They'd exited the building by that time and had stopped by the road. "Which direction were you headed?"

He seemed to consider it for several moments. "Which direction were you headed?"

She pointed.

He looked pleased. "I was going that way myself. Perhaps we could walk together? I don't mind telling you, this place makes me uneasy. I'll feel better to walk with a military woman."

Amaryllis chuckled in spite of her irritation. "And you can't defend yourself, of course, having no similar training."

He shrugged. "I have no weapon."

Amaryllis plunked her hands on her hips. "Well, I'm not armed either."

"Au contraire! You have a sharp tongue and a rapier wit."

Her eyes narrowed. "If you're implying that I'm stupid…."

All traces of amusement left his face. "I would never imply anything of the sort. I'm merely pointing out that you have no more idea what roams the countryside than I do, no more training, and no weapon to defend yourself if you should meet with trouble. And there are beasts here in plenty that would just as soon drag you off and force you to accept them if they can't convince you to be willing."

"The cyborgs?"

"What else would you call them? They have been given nothing but the most rudimentary humanity and can not react with anything but animal instinct and the programming they were given--which doesn't leave a lot of room for finesse. They are barbarians, and until and unless that is corrected with additional programming, they will remain little more than that. At the moment, they happen to be in hunter mode. They are hunting mates. Thus far their military programming has kept a modicum of order, but there are none that are not aware that females are in limited supply. The more aggressive will make certain that they are not the ones left out in the cold with no mate and no hope of one unless they can kill off one who has a female and take her."

Put that way, the situation was far more frightening than she'd realized. Uneasiness drifted over her, causing the fine hairs on her body to lift as if sensing danger.

"But you have--finesse?"

His lips curled at one corner. "Artificial, but, yes. I'd be more than happy to demonstrate, if you like."

Amaryllis reddened as the suggestion sank in, but she felt

far more comfortable with this line of discussion. "Strictly in the interests of education, I suppose?"

His eyes gleamed with amusement. "Absolutely."

She shook her head and turned along the road, deciding it might be best to have company on her walk after all. He fell into step beside her. "Pardon my persistence, but is that a yes, or a no?"

She chuckled. "You weren't serious?"

"That depends."

She glanced up at him. "On what?"

"Whether that was a yes or a no," he replied promptly.

She laughed outright at that. "I never knew you were such a tease."

He smiled faintly. "You're certain I'm teasing?"

Instead of responding, she glanced up at him speculatively. "What happened to Violet?"

His lips flattened with annoyance. "I've no interest in Violet."

Amaryllis lifted her brows skeptically.

"Currently, she's being courted by no less than three cyborgs and appears to be very satisfied with herself."

Amaryllis declined to comment on that.

"And, no, it isn't sour grapes. I prefer my women a little less … abrasive."

Amaryllis' lips twitched. "Your women?"

He gave her an irritated glance, but finally sighed gustily, running a hand through his dark hair. "We've all lost everything and everyone we've ever known," he said tiredly. "It doesn't make it any easier to bear knowing that most of it was manufactured and never real to begin with."

A sense of both shame and empathy smote Amaryllis at the same time. She'd been so self-absorbed she hadn't taken the time to consider that she wasn't the only one suffering. "Everyone must be having trouble adjusting," she said thoughtfully.

He shrugged and finally smiled wryly. "Some more than others, I imagine. As it happens, I'd begun to suspect long before the cyborgs took it upon themselves to enlighten us.

It wasn't as much of a shock, or as hard to accept as it might have been."

She tilted her head at him questioningly. "What made you suspect?"

"Their creativity--or perhaps I should say their lack of imagination. I handled new 'recruits', remember. I saw all the backgrounds on everyone." He glanced down at her thoughtfully for several moments and Amaryllis felt a prickle of uneasiness. She looked away, and discovered to her surprise that they'd almost reached the landing field.

"Almost without exception, everyone had had a tragic life that left them alone in the world. At first, I didn't think that much about it. The policy was that the company had no interest in anyone with 'baggage', ostensibly because of the dangers in the work and the travel. Single men and women with no family wouldn't have their minds elsewhere when they were supposed to be concentrating on their job. Then you came along."

A coldness washed over Amaryllis. She should have known that Cain would have figured it out if Reese had.

Chapter Twenty

"I'd thought I would take the path just here," Amaryllis said, changing directions abruptly and leaving the road.

It occurred to her forcefully that the three males who'd shown the most interest in her just happened to be three who knew, or at least had guessed, that she was not a cyborg. She couldn't help but wonder if they would've been drawn to her anyway, or if their interest had been spurred by that knowledge.

It was a dampening thought.

She'd wondered how it was that she'd suddenly become so desirable. She should have known it had to be something like that.

"How far along are you?"

Amaryllis stopped as abruptly as if she'd hit a tree. "What?"

"My wife was pregnant when she died," he said pensively. "Of course, she wasn't my wife. I wonder if the memory was entirely computer generated or if she actually exists somewhere?"

It took an effort to continue walking. Amaryllis discovered her knees suddenly felt rubbery. Was it that noticeable? She wondered. *She* had noticed, but it was her body after all. Her waist had thickened until there was only a faint curve between midriff and hip. Her belly had begun to take on a roundness that hadn't been there before, but she hadn't thought the changes were that noticeable--so far.

"Does he know?"

Amaryllis reddened, but she didn't look at him. She kept her attention focused on her feet, watching the uneven ground for anything that might trip her up as she stalked rapidly along the path. "Who?"

"The father," he said tartly.

She glared at him. "Maybe, when I figure out who it is, I'll tell him," she snapped.

He caught her arm, dragging her to a stop. She balled her hand into a fist, resisting the urge to clock him with an effort.

"Go ahead if you think it'll make you feel any better."

There was sympathy in his eyes. It was almost her undoing. She looked away, blinking against the sting in her eyes, but she put up only the barest resistance when he pulled her into his embrace. Wrapping one arm around her, he stroked her head and back soothingly. It felt so good, just to be held and comforted that Amaryllis had to struggle even harder to keep from bursting into tears. "Tell me what's wrong, baby. Would you like for me to kill those nasty old cyborgs for you? Because I'd be delighted to if it'll make you feel better."

"Don't joke, not now," Amaryllis said in a voice muffled against his chest.

"Who's joking?"

She pulled away and looked up at him. One glimpse of the glitter in his eyes was enough to assure her he definitely wasn't just saying it to distract her. "No!" she said, horrified and struggling abruptly to push him away.

His arms tightened. "Shhh. I didn't say it to distress you."

She relaxed fractionally, allowing him to draw her close once more.

He was silent for several moments, stroking her as he had before. "Would it distress you if I only beat them *nearly* to death?" he asked pensively.

The question almost startled a chuckle out of her. "Yes," she said sternly.

He sighed. "I was afraid of that." After a while, he pulled away from her and caught her chin, tipping it up so that he could look at her face. "If you aren't harboring ill will toward the cyborg twins, then why have you sent them packing?"

Amaryllis' heart clenched. *Had* she run them off? Forever? She berated herself the moment the thoughts popped into her mind. She'd meant to, after all. It was a good thing if she had, and for the best, for everyone. It was patently obvious that neither of them would settle for what she felt comfortable giving--they wanted total commitment.

It would have been nice taking either or both as lovers. They stirred her senses to heights she'd never before even imagined she could scale and the affection they seemed to feel for her would have been a great comfort in the trials she faced.

God only knew why they were so determined to make her their mate. They should have been appalled at her genetics. If he'd studied her background as he claimed, Reese certainly knew, and Dante ought to. He'd done the med scan on her, after all. Surely, if they were acting on basic instincts alone as Cain said, they could *sense* she wasn't a good choice for mating and, if they couldn't, then they certainly had the grasp of logic needed to calculate such a risk.

She had no intention of discussing the reasons behind her behavior with Cain, however. Let him think whatever he liked. It probably wouldn't be nearly as bad as the truth. His question made her curious, though. Reese had said that Cain was staying in the barracks, and he'd certainly known which rooms were hers.

"Is that why you didn't come before? You were waiting to see if I meant to accept Dante or Reese?"

He smiled wryly. "Actually, I grew weary of waiting for you to come to me. Since it didn't appear that you were going to, I decided I'd have to make the first move."

Amaryllis' jaw went slack with surprise. Chuckling, he lowered his head and kissed her solidly on the mouth. As brief as the kiss was, it penetrated her surprise and stirred warmth to life.

She lifted her lids with an effort when he withdrew, giving him a reproachful look.

"More?"

She gave him a look and pulled away.

"I'm devastated."

"You sound devastated."

He chuckled. "I couldn't help but notice you didn't answer a single question."

"You are so observant."

"Ouch. Then maybe you'll tell me why we're wandering around in the woods?"

Amaryllis had spotted a small stream just a little ahead of them and wondered, if she followed it, if it would eventually lead her to the natives. They were bound to live near a source of water, weren't they? She threw him a look. "I'm ... just exploring."

"Ah. I noticed you explored the landing field yesterday."

Amaryllis had been on the point of moving closer to the stream for a better look. She stopped in her tracks and turned to look at him. "You saw me?"

He shrugged. "Contrary to what you seem to think, you're in no condition to fight your way out of an attack. I just thought I'd keep an eye on you. Dante beat me to it so I left you in his capable hands."

Amaryllis frowned. "I thought it was the cyborgs you were worried about."

"Not the cyborg twins--not that way. They're both besotted with you and wouldn't harm you. Are we looking for anything in particular? Because if you're thinking they might have concealed the ship here, I can't agree. The vegetation is far too thick."

The blush that had mounted her cheeks at his comment about Reese and Dante deepened. "I'm not looking for a ship," she said crossly, plunking her hands on her hips and looking around the area.

"What then?"

She sighed irritably. "Signs of civilization."

"It's in the other direction."

"You're so funny! I meant *other* civilization. Natives."

"The cyborgs cleared them out."

Amaryllis looked at him in surprise. "There are other intelligent beings here?"

"Now why are you so surprised when you just said you

were looking for them?"

Amaryllis gritted her teeth. "Christ and all the saints! You are the most irritating man! Will you be serious?"

His eyes glittered with speculation. "As you please. Why are you looking for them?" he asked coolly.

Amaryllis looked away. "Just curious," she lied.

"They are barbarians, dangerous savages. And, since I'm not allowed to wear a weapon as of yet, I'm thankful to say quite a distance from Gallen."

Disappointment flooded her, but she wasn't ready to give up yet. "You called the cyborgs barbarians, too, and they're civilized."

"Why are you looking for them, Amanda?"

Amaryllis glanced at him sharply. "I'm not Amanda anymore," she said tightly.

"Because the company gave you the designation Amaryllis, so you would fit in with all the rest of their 'flowers'? But you were born Amanda Maria Rios, weren't you?"

"Christ and all the saints! Does *everyone* know? Because if I've been quaking in my boots all this time when it's common frigging knowledge, I wish to hell someone had told me!"

His eyes widened. "The cyborg twins know?"

"I *wish* you'd quit calling them that! Yes! They know. Reese got into my file. He knew before we even started this mission. Dante discovered it after the crash. He was the medic that treated me."

Cain's eyes narrowed. "That's how Dante induced you to hide in his quarters?"

"He did it to protect me!"

"Did he? It looks to me as if he took advantage. I may have to kill him after all."

Amaryllis gaped at him in stunned surprise. Her teasing, often annoying, companion had vanished and in his place was the killing machine Cain had been designed to be. A shiver of dread scratched its way down her spine. "Don't! Please! I'll never forgive you!"

His eyes narrowed. "You're so certain I need your forgiveness?"

"He didn't do anything I didn't want him to," she said a little desperately. "I was scared to death. I needed … comforting."

His gaze moved pointedly to her belly. "It looks like he did a little more than comfort you," he retorted dryly.

When she said nothing more, merely looked at him reproachfully, he drew in an exasperated breath and expelled it slowly, raking his fingers through his hair as he struggled to regain control of his temper. "I don't understand you, Mandy. Are all females as completely contradictory as you? Or only the purely human variety? What are we doing out here? Why are you looking for the native inhabitants of this world?"

A knot formed in her throat, making it difficult to swallow. Relief was part of it, that she seemed to have averted a battle between Dante and Cain. Part of it was despair at seeing her last hope vanishing like a puff of smoke, but most of it was weariness from the fear and frustration that had been riding her for months now and was getting progressively worse instead of better. Her chin wobbled. "I'm scared. I just don't know what to do."

He caught her upper arms, giving her a slight shake, as if he could jog it from her. "Tell me, baby! It isn't just that you're afraid they'll find out about you, is it? I can't help you if I don't know what's wrong."

The words trembled on her lips, but she found she couldn't utter them. He wouldn't understand and he couldn't help her even if he did. He didn't have access to the med center, or knowledge of how to use any of the equipment. He would probably be more horrified and disgusted than helpful if he knew she wanted to abort the pregnancy to protect the child from having a life of pure hell. Even knowing what she did from her own experiences, she was as horrified at the necessity of what she had to do as she was determined to spare it from as much pain as possible. "I just … want to go home," she said lamely.

He didn't believe her. She could tell from his expression that he knew her desperation to go home wasn't just a yearning for faces and things familiar. After a moment, he pulled her close and hugged her tightly to him. "You know that's one thing I can't give you. I wouldn't even if I could. Whatever you think about this place, you're accepted here, as one of us, and no one would harm you even if they knew. Out there, your life wouldn't be worth one credit. The Company will have a price on our heads by now-- yours included. It would mean almost certain death even to try it, and to avoid death even for a time would mean being hunted and constantly on the run.

"I love you. Don't ask me to take you to your death, Mandy."

Chapter Twenty One

Amaryllis stiffened and pulled away to look up at Cain in stunned surprise.

He smiled wryly. "Isn't it enough that you've got three men who are crazy about you?"

It was too much, actually. On top of everything else, to be torn between her feelings for all three men was more than she could handle. She burst into tears and cried all over his chest.

It dismayed him. He stiffened, but he held her until she'd cried herself out. Finally, she pushed away from him, scrubbed the tears from her face with her hands and made her way to the tiny stream she'd spotted earlier. When she'd splashed cool water over her face until she felt better, she sat back on her heels and looked around a little desperately for something to dry with.

Cain had knelt beside her. He shrugged. "I'd give you my loin cloth, but I'm not at all certain seeing my dangling genitals is something you'd care for at the moment."

The comment drew a shaky chuckle from her. "I'm sure your genitals are as beautiful as the rest of you, but I'll use my skirt."

The sheer veil-like skirt was pretty much as useless as a towel as it was as a skirt, but she managed to wipe most of the moisture from her face. When she glanced shyly at Cain again, she saw that his color was slightly heightened, but he looked pleased with himself. "Men are not beautiful," he said, mock stern. "It offends the manhood."

A smile trembled on her lips. "You don't look offended."

"It's hard to be displeased by a compliment. Would you like to see if they're as beautiful as the rest of me?"

She bit her lip. "I might not be able to contain myself."

"All the better," he retorted, chuckling. He reached for her hand. "Come. I'll take you back to your quarters to rest. You must be weary after releasing such a tidal wave."

Amaryllis allowed him to pull her to her feet. "I'm sorry I cried all over you," she said self-consciously.

He tucked a finger beneath her chin and urged her to look up at him. "I didn't melt and it seems you needed the outlet. Feeling better?"

To her surprise, Amaryllis realized she did. Her head ached and her eyes were blurry, but she was tired, not tense as she had been. She nodded.

He leaned down and brushed a light kiss across her lips. "Good," he murmured against her lips.

It was dark by the time they reached the barracks once more. Amaryllis was still debating whether to invite Cain in and try to prepare a meal for the two of them when she discovered that Reese was waiting for them in the corridor.

She stopped abruptly and glanced up at Cain. "I don't want trouble."

His smile didn't reach his eyes. "I won't give you any."

"Promise me you won't start a fight!"

Cain glanced from her to Reese and back again. "Readily."

Reese didn't wait for them to reach him. He strode down the corridor to meet them. Uttering a low, animal growl when he was still some two yards away, he launched himself at Cain.

Amaryllis let out a squeak of surprise as the two men slammed into each other with a sound almost like a thunderclap. Reese's weight and momentum slammed Cain into the wall, shattering the thin layer of mortar that had been lathed on the wall as a finish. A fine, yellowish dust clouded the air.

With a growl, Cain slammed his head into Reese's, then thrust himself away from the wall and drove Reese across the corridor into the opposite wall.

"Reese! Cain! Stop it!" she yelled over the din the two of them were making as they used each other for a wrecking ball, first one and then the other slamming into the walls around them, cracking mortar and throwing more dust into the air.

Up and down the corridor, Amaryllis heard doors opening.

"They'll throw you both in jail for public disorderliness!" she cried when Reese tired of slamming Cain into the wall and wrapped his hands about the other man's throat. Catching hold of one of Reese's arms, she tried to pull him loose from Cain. He ignored her, tightening his grip on Cain's neck.

Someone grabbed her around the waist from behind, snatched her loose from Reese, and set her aside. The world spun dizzily. Amaryllis reached out blindly for the wall to support herself, gasping and coughing and blinking the dust from her eyes.

Dante, she saw, was trying to thrust himself between the two men to break them apart and she realized that it was he who'd pulled her from harm's way.

The dizziness didn't subside. It intensified until blackness surrounded her. Her body felt so heavy she couldn't seem to move. Her last thought was that she needed to sit down before she fell. She didn't even feel the floor when she hit it.

* * * *

"If you've hurt her, you son-of-a-bitch, I'm going to kill you."

Amaryllis frowned, trying to identify the voice.

"Silence! No one hit her. She fainted. She is coming around now."

It took more of an effort to open her eyes than she would've thought possible. Her eyelids felt as if they'd been glued shut. Darkness greeted her when she finally managed to open her eyes a crack, but it began to clear almost at once and she saw Dante was leaning over her. Reese and Cain, both coated with dust and as white as ghosts, stood on either side of him, peering down at her as Dante was.

Her head felt like it was going to explode. "What

happened?"

"You hit your head on the floor when you fell."

"I fell?" she asked blankly, lifting her hand with a great effort and trying to feel for the lump on her head.

"How many fingers am I holding up?"

Amaryllis stared at the huge hand that was shoved in front of her face. "Two," she said slowly.

"What day is it?"

"How the hell would I know that? I haven't seen a clock or a calendar since we landed," she snapped irritably.

Dante's lips flattened. "I should take you to the med center to make certain you don't have a concussion."

Amaryllis was instantly completely alert. "No! I don't have a concussion. I'm fine."

Dante rose to his full height and looked around and Amaryllis realized that she was lying on her bunk in her quarters. She frowned, but she couldn't remember getting from the corridor to the room. One of them must have carried her in after she'd blacked out.

"I'll stay with her and make certain she's alright," Dante announced.

Reese and Cain exchanged a challenging glance. "I'll stay, too," Cain said tightly.

Reese balled his hands into fists. "Over my dead body," he growled.

Cain's lips curled upward. "Gladly."

Amaryllis struggled up onto her elbows. "OUT! All of you! Don't you *dare* even think about starting again!"

"You could be hurt. I need to stay," Dante said tightly.

"Someone needs to stay anyway. The barbarian over there broke the door down," Cain pointed out accusingly.

"Fine!" Amaryllis growled. "The three of you stay. I'll leave."

Dante pushed her back against the bunk, holding her down. "Be reasonable. You need to rest."

"*Me*? Why should I be the only one that's reasonable?"

"You can't stay here alone. The door's broken," Cain snapped.

"I'll stay and guard the door--outside," Reese growled.

"And who'll guard the door when the MP's show up to haul the two of you off to jail?" Dante asked tightly.

Cain and Reese exchanged an uncomfortable glance. "I've got enough credits to pay the fine." He studied Amaryllis assessingly for a moment. "--For both of us," he added belatedly.

Amaryllis sighed. "I'm tired, but I'm not hurt. Just go away, please, all of you, before they come."

The three men exchanged silent communication and finally moved to the door. When they'd left, Amaryllis got off the bunk and shoved the chair across the floor, wedging it against the door. It wasn't likely to keep anyone out who wanted to come in, not if Reese could break the door down when it had been locked, but it would serve as a delay and an alarm if anyone tried to come in.

Not that she thought anyone would.

She found she was too exhausted to consider trying to fix something to eat. Instead, she grabbed a piece of fruit and nibbled on it on her way to the shower.

When she'd bathed, she felt even more drained, not rejuvenated. Instead of dressing once more, she climbed into the bunk and closed her eyes. Rest didn't come. Instead, she found herself idly stroking her rounded belly, wondering about the infant growing inside of her. There was no comfort in the fact that she hadn't miscarried. That only meant it wasn't too defective to live, not that it wasn't defective.

She was afraid to allow herself to think it might not be. If she convinced herself that it would be alright and carried it to term, then discovered it was horribly malformed, she wouldn't be able to live with herself. It was cruel to inflict that kind of suffering on an innocent when it need not suffer at all, but she was afraid she'd already passed the point where it could be terminated painlessly. It was no longer merely a collection of multiplying cells, without a developed nervous system and brain to register pain. She hadn't wanted to have to make the choice between giving it a life time of suffering or a quick death.

She was useless, powerless. She'd already failed the poor little thing and, one way or another, it was going to suffer for her incompetence.

Unable to come up with any solution or to bear thinking about it anymore when her head was aching fit to split from her endless quest for a solution, she turned her mind to trying to think what to do about Reese, Dante, and Cain. The competition between them had already erupted into violence several times. She didn't want their lives destroyed by it.

She had to convince them, somehow, to stop. Choosing one didn't seem a very good solution, even if she could, even if she didn't feel that it was wrong to allow them to think she could provide them with a family. Somehow, she didn't think that would end the fighting. Cain had suggested they could end up killing to get what they wanted and she didn't think it was at all farfetched that they might, especially after tonight.

Chapter Twenty Two

Hammering on the door woke Amaryllis late the following morning. She sat up groggily just as Dante shoved the chair out of the way and looked in at her. Glaring at him, she grabbed her pillow and flung it at his head.

He ducked it, but a faint smile curled his lips. "You are feeling better today, I see."

"I was," she said crossly. "Go away."

He frowned. "There is a town meeting today. You need to go. I will walk with you."

"I'm not going," Amaryllis muttered, falling back against the mattress and curling onto her side with her back to him.

Reese and Cain were standing in her living area when she came out of the shower sometime later. She checked, staring at them in outrage. Both men looked her over with keen interest.

"Is there a sign on that door that says 'come right in'?" she demanded, pointing at the broken door.

Cain and Reese exchanged a sheepish look.

"Did I *say* you could come in?" she demanded when neither man answered.

Reese's face hardened. "I came to escort you to the meeting."

"Well, you can leave again, because I'm not going."

"Everyone has to go," Cain said. "I will escort you."

"No, you won't. You can both leave."

They looked as if they wanted to argue the point, but after glaring back at her for several moments, both men stalked angrily from the room.

Amaryllis slammed the door and pushed the chair against it again. When she couldn't hear them any longer and was certain they'd both left, she got dressed, then paced the living area until she decided the meeting had probably already started.

For once, luck seemed to be on her side. The meeting hall was filled to overflowing. When she arrived, everyone seemed to be in the grips of almost hysterical excitement and no one noticed when she entered and found a place to stand and listen among those late comers standing in the back of the room.

She saw once things had quieted down once more that the reason for all the shouting and clapping seemed to be an infant. Reuel and Dalia were standing on the platform at the front of the room, proudly displaying the first child born to cyborg parents.

Amaryllis thought for several awful moments that she would burst into tears. She tamped the urge with an effort as the head of the council stood and began to speak.

He welcomed the hunters as full citizens. He told them they were free to come and go within the colony as they pleased and encouraged to become a part of it.

Amaryllis was waiting for the 'but'. It came. They would be expected to make an effort to join the colony. If, after a full year, they still wanted to return, they would be taken to one of the colonies of man and left.

A year.

She didn't have a year to spare. She didn't even have months.

She was still reeling from that news when the president made an announcement that was even more stunning. In order to try to keep peace among themselves, and because the males outnumbered the females by five or six to one, each female was expected to contract with at least two, and no more than four, males to form a family unit.

Amaryllis was so stunned she couldn't seem to take it in. Two? Four? What kind of family unit was he talking about for God's sake? The men would kill each other!

Minutes passed before Amaryllis realized the roaring in her ears wasn't the rush of blood pounding in her veins. The entire auditorium was in an uproar and rioting seemed imminent.

Unnerved, Amaryllis began trying to work her way toward the exit. She'd almost reached it when a hand clamped around either arm. She looked up to discover Reese and Dante standing on either side of her. Without a word, they plowed through the crowd and through a pair of double doors that led outside, ignoring Amaryllis' efforts to pull free.

They released her once they were outside.

"You said you weren't coming," Reese said tightly.

She glared at him sullenly. "I changed my mind."

"You should not have come alone. It is not safe, especially not now."

"And exactly how was I supposed to know they were going to make such an insane announcement?"

Reese and Dante exchanged a look. "No one knew. Nevertheless, it is the law. The situation has already been debated to exhaustion and no better plan was set forth. No one is completely satisfied, but they could not be, given the situation … and the law has merit."

"It has merit?" Amaryllis echoed, staring at Dante as if he'd lost his mind.

"There will be two to protect you."

"Three."

Everyone froze as Cain strolled up to the group.

"She need only choose two," Reese growled threateningly.

"But I've no intention of leaving her at your tender mercies," Reese retorted coldly.

Amaryllis felt a little faint as she stared up at the three men towering over her, all of them scowling at each other. Insanely, she remembered something her mother was prone to say. 'Be careful what you wish for.' She'd wavered between them, unable to decide which she cared for the most. She hadn't wanted to have to make a choice.

Now, she wouldn't have to, but it would not make things easier, for any of them, and it certainly wouldn't change the most important reason she had for not wishing to form a contract without anyone. "I can't," she said a little weakly.

That effectively claimed their attention and all three looked down at her assessingly. "You heard the proclamation. You do not have a choice," Dante pointed out. "We will not allow you to choose someone else."

Amaryllis tried to summon anger, but failed to ignite more than a spark. The truth was, she wasn't about to choose anyone else and she didn't particularly like the idea of appearing to be free for the taking. It was far more frightening to imagine what her life might become without them than with them. "This won't work," she said a little desperately. "You will do nothing but fight."

Reese, Dante, and Cain exchanged speculative looks. "We'll work it out," Cain said finally. "Right now, I think it'll be best just to get you away from here. The barracks is out. Neanderthal took that door out like it was made of cloth. Even if we barricaded it, you wouldn't be safe."

For several moments, Amaryllis thought a fight would erupt between Cain and Reese again. "You said you'd work it out," she said accusingly. "Quit calling him that."

Cain studied her a moment. "Fine. What's his name?"

She gave him a look. She didn't believe for a moment that he didn't know, or had forgotten.

"Reese," Reese growled. "We'll take her to our home. She'll be safe there."

"But who'll protect her from you? I'm coming, or she isn't going there."

"Nobody asked me!" Amaryllis said indignantly.

"Your vote doesn't count," Cain said coolly. "You'd demand to stay at the barracks and there are at least twenty unattached males living there. We can't protect you if we're going to have to stand guard over your door every night like we did last night."

No wonder they'd been so Johnny on the spot this morning, she thought, and lapsed into silence. Arguing with them obviously wasn't going to change anyone's mind.

Since that seemed to settle the matter, the four of them left the municipal building and turned north along the main thoroughfare. Gallen boasted very few motorized vehicles, their objective being to minimize pollution of the planet's atmosphere. Most walked wherever they went--no great hardship since the city wasn't huge--and Amaryllis wasn't surprised when they set out on foot. It was further than she'd anticipated however, for the plantation Reese and Dante had established was a goodly distance beyond the city, and she developed a hitch in her side long before they reached it.

She caught Dante assessing her when she massaged the ache, though, and tried thereafter to ignore it, but she was glad when they finally reached the tall gates that surrounded the property.

Despite her weariness and her uneasiness about her situation, the house was such a complete surprise that it dragged her from her abstraction. Reese had said it was small. She wondered what he'd used to measure it, because it looked enormous to her. She discovered once they were inside that it was certainly no illusion. Just beyond the double front doors was a spacious foyer. A wide winding stair led up from the foyer to the second floor. On the first floor, several doors led off the foyer on either side, but she caught no more than a glimpse of the rooms as Reese led her up the stairs.

At the top of the stairs, a wide hallway bisected the house. Five doors opened off of it, two on either side, and one at the end of the hallway opposite the stairs. Dante nudged Cain, pointed to the nearest door and headed down the stairs once more. Reese led her to the room at the end of the hall, opened the wide double doors and gestured for her to enter.

Amaryllis stopped on the threshold, staring around the room in wonder as the artificial lights winked on at Reese's command. The round bed, easily large enough to sleep a half a dozen people comfortably, dominated the center of the room. The comforter and pillows that covered it were thick, fluffy and of a deep, dusky rose color. Above the bed, yards of fabric in a like shade were gathered to form a canopy, draped through loops at what would have been the four corners of the bed if it had been rectangular and allowed to fall unhindered from there to pool on the carpeted dais on which the bed was perched.

Amaryllis took a couple of steps inside and looked around. The carpet beneath her feet was so thick she felt as if she were walking through water. It was patterned in a floral design, the dominating color slightly paler than the color of the bed cover and hangings.

Several comfortably padded chairs and tables were grouped to one side of the bed. On the other was a mirrored dressing table and tall chest with drawers. A wide, arched door stood open between the dressing table and chest. She moved closer and peered inside. Stone covered the floor and the walls of the huge bath. In the center, sunken into the floor, was a tub large enough to be called a pool.

"This must be your room," she said uncomfortably.

His brows rose, then descended, drawn together in a faint frown. "It is a duplication of one from a magazine. It is supposed to be a room pleasing to a woman. You do not like it?"

"It's … a little overwhelming," Amaryllis managed. "You didn't do this for yourself, then?"

"I did it for you. If you do not like it, you can change it to suit you."

Amaryllis' heart fluttered. Finally, she managed a smile. "It's beautiful. I don't know if I can get used to so much room. Our entire family quarters on the colony weren't this big and I've not even had that much room since."

He studied her doubtfully. "You can be happy here?"

Under other circumstances, she could've been deliriously happy here. She managed a tremulous smile, nodding. "Thank you, Reese, for your thoughtfulness."

He looked uncomfortable and merely nodded. "We share kitchen duties. It is Dante's night to cook. Tomorrow mine. You and Cain may choose the nights you wish to cook and then we will rotate."

Amaryllis bit her lip. "I can't cook."

"We have programming…." He stopped abruptly, flushing faintly when he suddenly recalled that she couldn't jack in and download. "We will teach you."

"That'll be fun for all," Amaryllis said dryly. "Is the kitchen fire proof?"

He looked at her questioningly.

"Never mind."

She remained where she was for some time after he'd left, her mind curiously blank. After a time, though, the shock began to wear off and, like a roaring tide, everything began to flood back with a vengeance.

Theoretically, she supposed the council members were correct and their idea was both practical, given the circumstances, and calculated to produce optimal harmony within the colony. A man sharing his woman might not be terribly happy, but five men alone, watching one man with, was a recipe for war.

How were the women supposed to *deal* with a house full of men though? How could she?

And what was she to do about her personal situation? With three virile males, even if she managed to find a way to terminate her pregnancy, she would be facing the same situation again.

Somehow, under the circumstances, she doubted there had been any interest in procuring birth control.

She might as well have been living in the dark ages.

Cain had been right. They *were* barbarians!

Chapter Twenty Three

By the time Amaryllis woke the following morning, she'd concluded protest was useless. Reese, Dante, and Cain had made up their minds and it wasn't likely she was going to change them, given the situation. As scary as the thought was of having to deal with all three, she wasn't even certain she would've wanted to if it hadn't been for her fears that she could make them happy by giving them the children they wanted and deserved. She was in love with Reese, but she cared very much for all three of them--it was impossible not to when they loved her--and if she'd had to choose, she wouldn't have been able to, not and be completely happy.

It was still nerve wracking to be escorted to the municipal building by all three. She might even have been embarrassed except that when they arrived, there were already several other groups waiting. Others arrived behind them.

The signing and ceremony were short once they were allowed to enter the chambers held by the council president.

A sense of unreality descended over Amaryllis as they left the building and paused at the main street to decide what to do next as it began to sink into her that she was contracted-- with all of them. After a little discussion, they followed Reese's suggestion to celebrate their contract by dining at the city's finest, and only, restaurant. Amaryllis didn't know whether to be relieved or not that their celebration dragged on through the remainder of the afternoon. On the one hand, it had been a very long, very nerve wracking day.

On the other, it was traditional to seal the family contractual agreement by devoting a full week to sharing their physical affection for one another and she wondered if they knew that. Reese had mentioned before that he wanted to follow her customs.

And did that mean a full week with all three? Or a full week devoted to each one? And, if each was to have a full week to himself, who was going to decide the order? And how was she going to survive it either way?

The prospect was almost as terrifying as it was exciting.

Twilight had settled over the land by the time they arrived back at the plantation that now, by contract, belonged to the four of them as a family unit.

Amaryllis' knees felt weak with nerves as they entered the house. She glanced from Reese to Dante, who were standing on either side of her, wondering how they would take a suggestion that they all simply while away the evening with a game of chance because she suddenly felt very shy about having sex with any of them.

She never managed to unglue her tongue from the roof of her mouth long enough to voice it, though. Dante and Reese each took one of her hands and led her up the stairs and down the long corridor to her room at the end.

She didn't know whether to be relieved or worried when Cain didn't follow, but she wasn't given a lot of time to consider that or anything else. As soon as they'd entered the room, Dante and Reese set about removing her garments and then removed their own.

They were almost frighteningly magnificent, their bodies sculpted perfection. Her doubts surfaced and she wavered briefly between a deep sense of her own imperfection and the sense of being feminine and desirable as she saw they way they looked at her.

Reese scooped her into his arms, carrying her to the bed and settling her in the center of it. Without hesitation, as if the two had discussed it and decided before hand, Dante settled beside her, as well. Like mismatched bookends, they rolled on their side, facing her, their heads propped in their hands.

Amaryllis glanced from one to the other, trying to decide whether she was more excited or unnerved by the prospect of making love to both--at the same time--in the same bed. The situation had a bizarre sense of unreality to it, but neither Dante nor Reese seemed the least uncomfortable.

"I love you, Amy," Reese murmured. Leaning down, he brushed his lips lightly over hers, evoking a tingle of sensation that warmed her to her depths. Her uneasiness vanished and she parted her lips on a sigh of pleasure, opening her mouth to his possession. He covered her mouth with his then, thrusting past her parted lips and possessing the exquisitely sensitive inner surfaces of her mouth with the rough caress of his tongue in a kiss of such hunger that her belly clenched painfully, desire literally exploding throughout her body. She felt the stroke of his large hands along her body. Sparking jolts of tingling awareness followed his touch, warming her, elevating sensation along her breasts and the flesh of her belly and hips and thighs.

A bolt of surprised pleasure went through her when warm lips that could only belong to Dante were pressed against her belly and nibbled a trail upwards, finally settling on the tender peak of one breast and suckling. She gasped into Reese's mouth as the flesh of her entire body leapt and prickled in a heated rush of dizzying sensation.

After that, she lost all ability to think, her mind clouding with the drugging euphoria of pleasure. Her body was under such enthralling assault that her mind couldn't focus beyond the sensations of warm hands and heated mouths.

She was gasping for breath when their lips at last parted and Reese wove a tortuous path with his mouth to her other breast, nipping at the engorged nipple before he covered it, sucking hard, nudging it with his tongue and sending tentacles of delight searing through her that seemed to draw at her sex. She dragged in a sobbing breath, writhing beneath Dante and Reese in nearly unbearable pleasure.

Heated desire coiled tightly within her. Within moments, her body was hovering near ultimate rapture and she began to struggle to hold onto the wondrous sensations just a few moments longer.

As if sensing her internal battle, Dante shifted his assault upward, claiming her lips as Reese released her other nipple and moved downward, sucking a heated trail of kisses along her belly.

When he reached her mound, he pushed her thighs wide, parted her nether lips and ran his tongue along her cleft. Amaryllis shuddered and moaned into Dante's mouth at the exquisite delight Reese's tongue imparted as he stroked her clit. She arched upward, seeking more, kissing Dante feverishly as she lost the battle to contain the pleasure and felt it expanding rapidly toward an explosive peak as Reese tormented her clit with the heat of his mouth and tongue.

She began to tremble as the first waves of ecstasy broke the dam of her resistance. Releasing her lips, Dante leaned down to capture a taut nipple in his mouth, sucking it hard. The jolt that went through her sent her over the edge into explosive culmination that dragged little whimpering cries of rapture from her.

When the last echoes of her climax faded, Reese slid up the bed. Giving each of her nipples a final, plucking caress with his lips, Dante pulled away, leaning back as Reese gathered her onto her side against his length, kissing her deeply and stroking her back in a slow caress.

Reluctantly, Reese lifted his head after only a moment and Dante slipped a hand around her waist. Dragging her back against his belly, he fitted her snugly against his body and slipped his hand from her waist to her breasts, nuzzling her neck, sucking at her ear lobe and then tracing the swirls with his tongue. A shiver of reaction skated through Amaryllis as she felt the heat of his breath against her ear. The fire that had only just been quenched, stirred to life once more. Heat curled in her belly.

She twisted her head around, seeking his lips as he nibbled a trail of kisses along her jaw. Releasing a heavy sigh, Dante settled his palm along her cheek, plucking at her lips with his and finally covering her mouth and thrusting his tongue between them, exploring her mouth. After a moment, his hand skated from her cheek to her breasts, lingered for several moments teasing her nipples and then moved on. Gripping her thigh, he urged her to lift it and when she did, he slid his cock along her cleft, gathering her body's moisture on the head of his cock.

Her eyes flew open when she felt him pushing his cock against her rectum. "What are you doing?" she whispered breathlessly.

He placed his palm on her cheek. "I would never hurt you. Trust me? Only tell me if I am hurting you and I will stop."

Amaryllis swallowed the knot of uneasiness in her throat and nodded fractionally. With great care, he pushed deeper, sliding his cock into her channel by tiny degrees. Amaryllis panted, trying to relax and allow him to claim her, but within a few moments the discomfort gave way to something entirely different as his cock stroked along something inside of her and quakes of intense delight echoed through her. She gasped in surprise and he went still.

"Am I hurting you, love?" he gasped hoarsely, holding himself still with an obvious effort.

Amaryllis shook her head. "It feels--so good."

A shudder went through him. After a moment, he continued, thrusting until he was seated deeply inside of her. He paused again, dragging in several shuddering breaths before he began to withdraw with equal care. Her body adjusted, accepting him, gratification building slowly inside of her with each lingering caress.

Moments passed and then he paused once more, holding himself perfectly still.

Reese slid closer and Amaryllis felt the head of his cock pressing against the mouth of her channel. She opened her eyes with an effort, watching his face as she felt him thrusting inside of her with great care, felt her body yielding slowly to his possession.

Prickles of heat erupted all over her, wild, dizzying jolts of pleasure rushing through her as he claimed her fully and she felt both Reese and Dante deeply inside of her. When they began to move in concert, both thrusting and retreating at once, she thought for several moments that she would pass out at the intensity of the ecstasy that shot through her. She groaned, clutching at Reese, lifting her leg higher to give them better access to her body, encouraging them to thrust deeper.

Her groans of pleasure seemed to push both of them beyond control. They began to move faster, pounding into her with the ferocity of their own desires. She felt Dante jerk, shuddering as his crisis caught him. In the next moment, Reese uttered a low growl of pleasure and began to tremble with his own release. The climax that burst upon her as she felt their hot seed spill inside of her was so sudden, so hard, it ripped a keening cry from her as her body began convulsing in rapture so powerful blackness swarmed over her, dragging her down into a dark abyss.

When she slowly became aware of her surroundings once more, she realized that she still lay sandwiched between them, her body impaled by theirs. She stirred, stroking Reese lovingly. Groaning, he lifted his head and kissed her, briefly, on the lips then rolled away.

Slipping from the bed, he padded into the bathroom and she heard the sound of running water. When Dante pulled away from her and lay back on the bed, she turned over, stroking a hand along his heaving chest. He swallowed with obvious effort, staring up at the ceiling. "It is--more difficult that I had thought it would be," he murmured thickly.

Amaryllis levered herself up so that she could look down at his face. "What, Dante?"

He looked away. "I see your love for Reese in your eyes when you look at him, and in the way you touch him." He turned his head to look at her. "I love you. I thought it would be enough to be able to have you even if I had to share you."

Amaryllis felt a painful knot tighten in her chest. "Believe me when I say I'm as torn in my own way as you are, but what I feel for you isn't diminished by my love for Reese.

If you will only look, you will see that I love you, too."

He glanced at her sharply, studying her face for several heartbeats. "It is only lust."

Amaryllis bit her lip to contain a smile. "You don't object to the lust?"

He reddened, a faint smile curling the corners of his mouth. "No."

She inched forward and kissed him briefly on the lips. "Then you should know that I couldn't possibly feel it so intensely for you if I didn't also love you. It just isn't possible for me to feel one without the other."

He gathered her tightly against him, kissing her hungrily. When he broke the kiss, his eyes were gleaming with both passion and amusement. "Reese is waiting for us in the pool. I gave my word tonight we would share to prove to you that we could do so without trying to cut each other's throat. But I will give you fair warning I want to have you all to myself."

Amaryllis smiled. "I hope this doesn't mean we won't be doing this again?"

He shook his head, but chuckled. "It could be that the three of us have bought more trouble than we bargained for," he admonished her, slapping one cheek of her ass playfully before he rolled from the bed with her and carried her into the bath.

Reese didn't look any too pleased at their delay in joining him, but he said nothing. Instead, when Amaryllis had stepped carefully into the pool, he pulled her close for a lingering kiss.

Dante caught her foot, tickling it with his fingers and she broke the kiss, uttering a choked laugh.

The two brothers exchanged a challenging glance. Amaryllis wisely ignored it, turning and settling in Reese's lap with her back against his chest. Taking a cloth from the side of the bathing pool, Dante lathered it, caught Amaryllis' foot once more and glided the cloth along her leg. Not to be outdone, Reese lathered a second cloth, soaping her breasts and belly and finally delving between her legs.

She gasped when his fingers found her clit, her eyes glazing as heat swarmed through her. Tilting her head back against Reese's shoulder, she exchanged a heated kiss with him, sliding the sole of her foot along Dante's as she did so.

He caught her foot. Lifting it free of the water, he nibbled her toes playfully before sucking one into his mouth. An electric current tickled along her senses at the feel of his mouth on her toes, leaving heat in its wake.

They bathed each other in a leisurely, sometimes playful manner, Reese and Dante teasing her as they bathed her, arousing the embers of the fire of desire. She returned the favor, bathing each of them in turn, caressing them with her mouth and hands.

When they emerged at last, Amaryllis' skin was wrinkled from the water. She was studying her fingertips wryly when Reese scooped her up and strode into the bedroom once more. She let out a squeal that was part fright and part delight as he landed in the center of the bed with her. Before the mattress had even ceased to bounce, she was writhing beneath his ravenous assault, on fire for him. Coming up on his knees, he grasped her legs. Lifting them straight up, he propped her legs on his shoulders and guided his cock into her, watching with intensity as her body engulfed him.

The feel of him delving inside of her, the passion on his face, ignited her senses. She moaned in pleasure, lifting to meet his first, tentative thrusts. Within moments the fever had gripped them both and sent them reeling out of control and he was pumping into her in quick, hard thrusts. Amaryllis cried out as ecstasy erupted inside of her, feeling joy fill her as Reese's hot seed bathed her womb as he too found his bliss. By the time she'd caught her breath, she was more than half asleep.

Someone--Dante, she thought--dragged her beneath the covers. She wiggled her butt against his genitals as he pulled her tightly against his length and he nipped at her shoulder and ear. In a few moments, Reese settled with his back to her and she drifted into unconsciousness.

She awoke sometime later to the warmth of a mouth suckling her breast, making heat curl in her belly. When she pried her eyelids open, she saw that it was Dante. Uttering a moan that was almost equal parts complaint and desire, she stroked his shoulders, opening herself to his caresses. He continued to caress and tease her until she was moving feverishly beneath him, encouraging him with whimpers of need to take her, and when at last he possessed her, he took her to shattering release within moments.

Chapter Twenty Four

It was well into the next day before Amaryllis swam upward from unconsciousness sufficiently to have any sort of awareness and it still took all she could do to pry even one eyelid open enough to look around and discover what the heavy weight was upon her. Dante, she saw, had his head pillowed on her breasts, his long, dark hair fanned out across her and tickling her chin. Turning her head slightly, she saw that Reese was sprawled on his belly beside her, and she thought it was probably his leg pinning hers to the bed.

Sighing, she closed her eye again, drifting, feeling little prickling aftershocks all over her body from the pleasure Dante and Reese had wrung from her over and over during the night.

Small wonder she was exhausted!

When she surfaced once more, she found herself alone in the bed. A delightful scent wafted past her nose and her stomach responded immediately with a growl of hunger. She had to lift her brows to crack her eyelids. Reese, she saw, was waving a succulent piece of meat back and forth in front of her face, a faint smile curling his lips.

Amaryllis felt a smile tug at her own lips in response. She licked her lips. "Food," she managed to say with an effort.

He chuckled. "I cooked for you. You want me to feed you, too?"

"Mmmm," Amaryllis murmured thoughtfully. "Maybe I'll just suck on that big piece of meat you gave me last night."

Desire flickered in his eyes. He tamped it with an effort. "This will give you more strength."

Chuckling, Amaryllis sat up, but she winced at the twinges of pain from strained muscles. Reese, she saw, was giving her a knowing look. He handed her the plate of food without a word, however, kissed her lightly on the lips and left again.

"Short honeymoon," she muttered, but dug into her food with a will, realizing she was starving. When she'd finished, she leaned over the side of the bed and placed the plate on the floor, wondering if she actually felt up to getting out of bed.

She had to hobble to the bathroom. By the time she'd soaked in the tub for a while, however, most of the aches and pains had subsided. She still felt very much like she'd engaged in a full scale battle with two cyborgs instead of making love to them all night, but she could at least move with relative ease.

When she'd dried herself, she dressed and went in search of the others. She found Dante, Reese, and Cain in the main living area on the ground floor playing a game of chance.

Dante looked up as she paused in the doorway suddenly feeling oddly shy and uncertain. His eyes lit with desire as his gaze flicked over her caressingly. When he met her gaze once more, he smiled, displaying a faint dimple in one cheek that she hadn't noticed before. Her heart executed a little flutter in response. Smiling tentatively at him, Amaryllis moved into the room.

She paused again once she'd reached the group, wondering if they would welcome another player or if she should find something else to occupy herself with. Reese glanced up from his game pieces, a slow smile of welcome lighting his face. "Would you like to join us?"

Cain flicked a glance in their direction before returning his attention to his pieces. "We're in the middle of a game," he said coolly.

The snub caught her completely off guard. She felt the blood rush from her face only to rush back with a vengeance. She managed a smile. "Actually, I never cared for the game," she said a little stiffly. "I think I'll take a walk."

That comment grabbed the attention of all three men.

They looked up at her with varying degrees of suspicion.

Her lips tightened. "In the garden--out back," she clarified.

"I will walk with you," Dante and Reese said almost in unison, then glared at one another.

Amaryllis couldn't help but notice Cain didn't offer or even look up for that matter.

She didn't believe for one moment that he was so engrossed in the game that he couldn't spare a few moments even to be civil.

She shook her head. "I don't want to interrupt the game."

"You already did," Cain muttered.

Amaryllis glared at the crown of his head. "Well, excuse me all to hell," she snapped, turning and stalking from the room.

The garden was beautiful, but Amaryllis wasn't currently in the mood to appreciate it. Instead of strolling down the neatly ordered walkways, she strode up and down them like a pacing tiger. She hadn't actually wanted to see the damn garden in the first place, but she was just as accustomed to being active as the men were and sitting around the house twiddling her thumbs held absolutely no appeal.

Obviously, she would not be allowed to leave the premises alone--possibly ever, certainly not until the dust had settled on the great mating race.

What was she to do with herself? She wondered suddenly. She'd been a soldier almost from the time she'd been released from physical therapy after the last of her operations. As often as not, it was a boring existence, but it was rare to have time on her hands and when she did that was generally filled with the search for entertainment.

Reese had said before that she could continue to be a soldier, but then he hadn't expected the situation to be as it was and she doubted seriously he would be as willing to allow it now.

Not that she intended to let him--or any of them--tell her what she could and couldn't do, but she was no fool. She wasn't going to put herself in a dangerously untenable position just to show them she'd do as she pleased.

In any case, from what she could see the military had very little to do beyond police the citizens of Gallen and patrol the area surrounding the city for possible threats--and she doubted there was even much need for that.

Reese and Dante were, she supposed, planters. She had no idea what it was that they produced, but they had a well established plantation. She'd seen the robots in the fields. She supposed Cain would find a place for himself on the plantation, as well.

What about her? She couldn't simply reprogram like they could. Even if she could find a niche she wanted to fill, she would have to learn new skills, and who would teach her?

Depression settled over her. She'd tried to tell them all that she wasn't suited to this sort of thing. She had NO skills beyond those she'd learned in the militia. Her childhood had been such a nightmare that she hadn't even learned the rudiments of homemaking--not that she could see much of a need for it. Dante, Reese, and Cain were completely self-reliant and efficient and they had house 'bots in any case.

She couldn't even cook. Unless they had no sense of taste, they were going to be vastly disappointed when it came her turn to prepare the meals.

She had severe reservations that she could even breed right.

She shook the thoughts off after a time, knowing that wasn't the real root of her current distress.

Cain was.

He was angry with her--unjustly so. She knew he was, no matter that he'd tried to pretend indifference and she knew it was because she'd been with Reese and Dante the night before, which she not only had a right to, but an obligation in the fulfillment of her contract. And she still felt guilty because he was angry. And she resented feeling guilty when she knew she hadn't done anything wrong.

She supposed it was harder for him to adjust because he'd

been created to think and respond to situations like a human and most worlds inhabited by humans still practiced monogamous unions, for the simple reason that humans were territorial by nature, especially human males. He'd even told her that he had been married before. It didn't matter that it had never really happened. In his mind, it had. In his mind he'd had a 'normal' union.

That thought sparked a less palatable one.

She knew it was completely unreasonable of her to expect him to love her--and really she didn't--but it was lowering to think he might feel no affection for her at all, because that certainly wasn't the case with her.

Had she completely misinterpreted his behavior only because she was hurt by it? What if he wasn't angry at all, but truly indifferent? Or, perhaps, he wasn't angry in the sense that he was jealous as she'd been thinking, but resentful because he hadn't gotten his turn?

He had such a droll way of putting things that she rarely took anything he said very seriously, but he'd said things to her several times that had suggested that he was merely shopping for a mate because he did not care to be one of the unfortunates who had to do without--which certainly seemed to imply that his main interest was in the sexual aspects of a union.

Of course he'd also said that he was in love with her, more than once, but she knew he was teasing then and she couldn't take that seriously. She'd thought he must care at least a little, though, or he would not have insisted that he would contract to 'protect' her from Reese and Dante.

Perhaps he was only angry because he could see how much she loved Dante and Reese and he thought she wouldn't honor her commitment to him? Or perhaps that she wouldn't do so with the enthusiasm that she'd shown them?

Should she try to talk to him, she wondered, to see if he would tell her what, if anything, was wrong?

He hadn't seemed very receptive to talking, though, and she'd never been one for approaching the unapproachable.

She had a hard enough time holding up her end of a conversation when the other person was actually friendly.

She shook her head, realizing she simply didn't understand Cain. He was far more complicated than either Dante or Reese, or he seemed so.

Maybe she was just being paranoid and he was only preoccupied and it had nothing to do with her at all?

When a full week passed and Cain not only failed to come to her room at night, even once, but was conspicuous by his absence during the day, Amaryllis was completely at a loss. She loved Dante and Reese and thoroughly enjoyed their time together, but she felt like she'd somehow failed Cain.

Chapter Twenty Five

Amaryllis didn't know whether to be more amused, or more annoyed when, precisely one week after the contract signing, Reese and Dante resumed their routine of before. Obviously, Reese *had* researched the customs of her home world as he'd claimed. Just as obviously, unlike his human counterparts, he was no slave to his passions.

Not that she had any room for complaint whatsoever, but it was more than a little disconcerting to discover that he, and Dante she had to suppose, had been so attentive simply because it was the 'custom'. They were no less passionate or affectionate afterwards when they were around, but they were rarely around. They'd dedicated the customary week, and then returned to their own interests.

Dante, contrary to what she'd believed, had no interest in the plantation. He had sought additional programming as a physician and researcher and spent most of his day at the med center, practicing the techniques he'd downloaded in real time when he wasn't working on a research project.

Reese's primary interest was in designing and building service droids and he was perfectly happy to turn over the running of the plantation to Cain when he discovered that Cain's interests lay in that direction.

Cain was involved in research and development himself-- research and development of marketable plants beyond those used for food and landscaping.

Amaryllis' personal demons came back to haunt her as soon as she found herself alone and she began a frantic search for something to keep herself occupied and her thoughts directed away from her insurmountable problem. But she knew there was little point in trying to decide on an occupation until she'd had time to research Gallen and see what they had need of, and that option wasn't open to her at the moment. Aside from the fact that Reese and Dante had both been very vocal about her leaving the plantation without escort, the government had posted warnings suggesting much the same--that women were strongly cautioned not to roam the streets of Gallen without the escort of the males of their household.

The inactivity was boring, but she didn't particularly want the sort of action she was liable to see if she defied the warnings.

She spent days exploring the plantation itself and came up with no ideas.

Finally, she decided that she could at least try her hand at learning to cook. She hadn't needed the expressions on Reese and Dante's faces the one time she'd tried it to tell her that she was very bad at it.

Since then, she'd been discontinued from the roster of cooks.

The service 'bot that kept the household running hadn't been designed to teach, but it had the ability to speak and respond to speech. Deciding it was worth a try, she summoned it to the kitchen and ordered it to explain the workings of the equipment. Once she thought she had a fair grasp of how each appliance worked, she demanded a list of the dishes the 'bot had been programmed with and immediately hit a snag. Apparently, the men did *all* of the cooking.

She paced the kitchen, thinking that over. "Can you jack in and download the additional programming?"

"Affirmative. I am capable of jacking in and downloading. Limitations. I have only 150 meg available."

Amaryllis chewed her lip, but she couldn't imagine that cooking programs would take up a lot of storage space. "Then do it."

"Parameters?"

Amaryllis stared at the 'bot for several moments, feeling perfectly blank. If she said 'everything' the 'bot would simply download until it ran out of storage and it could be downloading anything at all, including a number of dishes that she either couldn't handle or wouldn't be able to find the ingredients for. "Quick and simple main courses. Quick and simple side dishes using ingredients readily available in Gallen."

"Affirmative."

She followed the 'bot from the kitchen and down the main hallway to the room Reese had referred to as 'the study'. She stopped dead in her tracks when she entered the room behind the 'bot and discovered that Cain was seated at the desk, leaning back in the chair with his long legs propped on the desk top.

He turned to stare at her when she stopped, but otherwise gave no indication that he even realized it was she who'd stopped on the threshold. A full second passed. Slowly, he blinked, as if coming out of deep thought. Reaching up, he removed the jack he'd been using to download--something.

One dark brow rose questioningly and Amaryllis felt color flood her cheeks. "Sorry. I didn't realize you were here."

Something flickered in his eyes. Instead of commenting, however, he asked, "You needed something?"

Amaryllis sucked her lower lip self-consciously. She hadn't precisely wanted to surprise everyone with a new found ability to cook. It was more that she was embarrassed that she didn't know how, and didn't have the ability that they had to simply download it. That was just the sort of thing guaranteed to make her appear incompetent and inferior in the eyes of the cyborgs.

"Permission to download information requested by the mistress," the 'bot volunteered promptly.

Amaryllis glared at the 'bot, resisting the urge to kick it with an effort.

Cain's feet came down from the desk. "What sort of information?" he asked sharply.

"Instructions for preparing 'quick and easy main courses' and 'quick and easy side dishes'."

Amaryllis felt like her face had caught fire. "Never mind," she managed to say through gritted teeth. "It isn't important. I can do this another time."

Amusement entered Cain's eyes. "I would imagine the level of importance would depend upon who is to eat the 'quick and easy' dishes."

As *if* she wasn't embarrassed enough! As *if* she didn't know her skills in the kitchen were pretty much non-existent! Without another word, she turned and stalked from the room, slamming the door behind her.

He caught up with her in the foyer, grasping her arm and jerking her to a stop. She turned and gave him a 'drop dead' look. "You have an ungovernable temper," he said flatly.

"And I suppose you think you don't!" Amaryllis shot back at him.

Something flickered in his eyes. "I generally manage to control mine--not allow it to control me."

"No, you're just mean and nasty and insulting. You don't have to lose your temper when you're pissed off. You make everyone else lose theirs and still get the fight you wanted to provoke in the first place!"

He studied her in tightlipped silence for several moments, but finally the anger in his eyes was replaced with wry amusement. "I'll be a far better teacher than the 'bot," he said finally.

It took Amaryllis several moments to realize he was suggesting that he teach her how to cook. "Thanks, but no thanks!" she said nastily.

His brows rose. "You have someone else offering to instruct you? Something of far greater importance pressing?"

Amaryllis glared at him. What she really wanted to do was to go off somewhere and sulk and go over every single little snub he'd given her over the past couple of weeks, real and imagined, so she could really get herself worked up. It was pure *hell* being a human being and having to live with a race of beings that never allowed emotion to overrule logic and reason!

"You were busy," she said sulkily. "I don't want to

interrupt you." Her eyes narrowed when she made the last comment. In vain, she waited for the snide remark he'd made to her before when she'd interrupted their game-- 'you already did'.

His lips twitched, as if he knew exactly what she was fishing for. Releasing his grip on her arm, he held his hands wide. "As you see, I'm at your disposal."

The temptation was so great to slug him right in the jaw that Amaryllis felt a wave of nausea wash over her when she tamped it. She really, really didn't want to go into the kitchen with him, but she was just as reluctant to bear up his low opinion of her. "Fine!" she said tightly, turning and stalking to the kitchen.

He followed her at a leisurely pace. She was tapping her foot on the tile floor impatiently when he arrived. Ignoring the obvious signs of temper, he began by instructing her on the equipment.

"I got that already from the 'bot."

He ignored that, too, continuing until he'd demonstrated each appliance. When he'd finished, he turned to look at her. "Now. We'll start with something simple. Can you boil water?"

Her temper was already on slow boil. She gave him a narrow eyed look. "You put water in a pot and set it over the heat, right?" she said sarcastically.

He nodded and crossed his arms. She stared back at him for several moments, but she could see he wasn't going to say anything else until she'd shown him. Snatching a pot from the rack, she filled it with water and slammed it down on the cooking top. When she'd switched it on, she stood over the pot, staring down at the water. It didn't seem to be doing much of anything. "How do you know when it's boiling?" she asked finally.

"You could always stick your finger in it to test the temperature."

"Very funny."

He moved to the refrigerating unit and removed a tray of eggs. "When it's bubbling and churning."

It was a rocky start to say the least and Amaryllis was convinced he was just trying--and succeeding really well--to make her feel stupid and useless. The lecture became more interesting, however, when he began placing the eggs in the pot and explaining the different dishes she could make with cooked eggs.

She did so well with the first couple of recipes she tried she decided she was pretty darned good at it. She threw a grin at Cain. "This wasn't too hard."

His lips twitched. Lifting one finger, he flicked a crumb of egg yolk off one cheek. "Aside from the kitchen looking like a battle zone, you seem to catch on quickly."

Amaryllis glanced around self-consciously and saw that he hadn't exaggerated a great deal. "Guess I'll have to work on the technique," she said wryly.

He picked up a stuffed egg and held it up to her. "The real test is here--the taste."

Amaryllis studied it doubtfully but finally took a bite. Relief flooded her. "It's good!" she said happily. "It really is. Teach me something else. Something--grander. Really impressive. Dante and Reese are going to be so surprised when…."

It was unnerving to see how quickly he transformed from amusing companion to frozen wasteland. He smiled thinly. "Another day, perhaps. I need to get back to my study."

Amaryllis felt her jaw go slack in stunned surprise. As he turned and strode away, she called out to him. "Cain?"

He stopped at the door, turning to look at her questioningly, but his expression wasn't at all welcoming and she found she couldn't gather up the nerve to ask him what she really wanted to ask. She forced a smile. "Thank you."

When he'd gone, she stared absently at the food on the counter for a while and finally put it into containers and set it inside the refrigerating unit. The encounter left her feeling uneasy and guilty, vaguely angry and confused.

She missed having him to talk to, having him tease her. It had nothing to do with being lonely, or having no one to talk to now, though. It was Cain she missed and she couldn't figure out how to get through that stone wall he was steadily building between them.

She couldn't think it was because he wanted sex and needed that outlet. If he had, he had only to ask, and he knew it. For that matter, he didn't actually have to ask. He could have come to her room.

She'd wanted spontaneity but had realized being completely spontaneous could create problems. Reese was fighting a running battle with possessiveness. If she'd left things completely up in the air, Reese would have planted himself firmly in her bed and challenged anyone that wanted to take his place.

She'd told both Reese and Dante that, since Gallen had an eight day week, three nights of the week were hers. Period. She could spend them alone, or, if she wanted to spend the night with one of them, she'd do the choosing. She'd given each of them a special night that would be theirs alone and the remaining two nights were up for grabs--for spontaneity.

She had never quite gotten up the nerve to tell Cain which night was his, but she knew the three of them had discussed it. She'd heard them.

But Cain hadn't come to claim his nights yet.

Irritated, Amaryllis concentrated on cleaning up the worst of the mess she'd made, summoned the 'bot to clean the rest, and went up to her room to bathe. Dante and Reese would be back soon. She might not have anything special to offer them, but she figured edible was pretty special considering her last couple of attempts to feed the crew.

She mulled over the problem with Cain while she soaked. She wasn't much for subtlety. She far preferred just to go straight for the root of a problem and make a hole. Unfortunately, she just hadn't been able to bring herself to force a confrontation on Cain.

Indifference? Or jealousy? That was the real question.

She decided if she couldn't find the spine to demand to know point blank, then there had to be a way to find out which of the two it was--short of provoking a fight.

Seduction. But how the hell was she supposed to do that? She'd never taken on the role of aggressor before, not in this sort of situation. Her lack of self-confidence hadn't been a problem with either Reese or Dante. She'd only had to say 'yes'. Cain obviously wasn't going to ask and she had a feeling if she tried to ask him, he'd give her one of his withering looks and she'd--wither.

The only woman she'd actually seen 'in action' was her mother, but it took a lot of hard thinking to remember anything at all useful. Even when she did remember, she wasn't certain how useful it would be.

Perfume, clothes, special smiles and come hither glances.

She had perfume.

She didn't think she could master the come hither glance in this century.

He'd been ignoring her smiles.

She walked around the next thing to naked now, and there wasn't a huge variation in the clothing. Except for the colors, one outfit pretty much looked like the next.

She felt like weeping when she left the tub and went to examine herself in the mirror. Her belly looked HUGE! She stared at it in dismay, realizing she was really going to have to take the time to actually look at herself once in a while to avoid future shocks.

No wonder he wasn't interested.

The amazing thing was that neither Dante nor Reese had commented on it.

Maybe they had a stronger sense of self-preservation than she'd thought?

Maybe *hiding* herself a little better would help? She thought glumly.

A thorough search of the wardrobe she'd been provided with revealed that she had nothing even close to what she'd been thinking about. Even her uniform would've been better than simply walking around bare bellied when her belly was so--round.

She moved back to the mirror and examined the side

view. After some deliberation, she finally decided that it didn't look quite as big as she'd first thought. There was a very definite roundness that hadn't been there before, but if she could find something a little more concealing....

The skirts that she generally tied at her waist were virtually transparent, but she discovered when she tried tying it at her shoulders instead, that it seemed to have the effect she was looking for. It was open at the sides, however, and she had no belt to tie it with. After trying several variations, she finally chose two colors that seemed to go well together and used one as a top and the other as it was intended at her waist. The ties at the waist held the two sides of the skirt she was using as a top together, but allowed a peek of bare flesh on her sides.

Concealing, but not enticing. Her lips twisted wryly as she studied the effect.

She sighed, staring at herself critically. Finally, she stripped and pulled the skirts on again minus the top and briefs she usually wore.

The sheer fabric had a muting effect that was far more flattering to her mind than outright nudity, but she could still clearly see her breasts and the curly thatch of hair that covered her mound.

Her eyes narrowed.

If Cain didn't notice her in this, she would know he just plain wasn't interested and it had to be something else.

She'd heard both Dante and Reese return while she'd been experimenting with her clothing, listened as they'd mounted the stairs and gone to their rooms. After a time, they'd left again and gone back downstairs. Most likely, the three of them were gathered in the living room, talking or deciding on entertainment for the evening--which was usually some board or card game, although they occasionally watched digi-enactments on the hologram pad in the center of the living room.

Girding herself, she left her room and headed downstairs. Stopping by the kitchen, she collected her egg dishes first, deciding to arrange the food on a tray so that she wouldn't have to try to balance four different containers on her trip to the living room. She was nervous enough; she was bound to drop something.

Without allowing herself time for second thoughts, she strode down the hall to the living room, pushed the door open and headed for the nearest table to set the tray down. "I made food," she said brightly as she settled the tray and turned to look at the men.

She discovered when she turned that she had their attention. Unfortunately, she couldn't read much into their stunned expressions. Her smile fell. "You don't like it?"

Reese blinked, slowly, as if surfacing from a deep trance. Dante swallowed audibly. Cain simply continued to stare at the curly thatch between her thighs, his eyes glazed, his complexion slowly darkening.

A blush rose in her own cheeks in response. Maybe, she thought, unnerved, this was a mistake. Maybe she looked as ridiculous as she suddenly felt and they were just too surprised by her silly 'fashion statement' to think of anything to say.

"What?" Cain finally said, his voice sounding hoarse with disuse.

She curled her lips in a forced smile. She wasn't about to mention the outfit and force them to comment on it. "The food. Cain helped me. It's actually quite good."

She moved to the couch and flopped down on it because her knees felt weak and she had to do something before she turned tail and fled.

Their gazes followed her, zeroing in on her breasts as the abrupt movement caused them to jiggle and sway beneath the sheer fabric.

Dante got up jerkily and took one of the eggs, gulping it down almost whole. His brows lifted. "It is good," he said, swallowing convulsively again as he turned to her.

His gaze didn't meet hers, however. It zoomed in on her breasts and stayed there.

Amaryllis shifted. Sitting forward, she smoothed the fabric over her thighs. His gaze followed the movement and moved with her when she sat back again.

Maybe she'd misinterpreted their reaction? She thought a little hopefully. Maybe they were just surprised, not horrified, or embarrassed for her.

Neither Reese nor Cain had so much as moved. When she glanced at Reese, he blinked again, slowly, frowned and looked around as if he was trying to figure out where he was.

Cain very casually crossed his legs, but not before she noticed the hard ridge lifting his loincloth.

Smiling inwardly, she relaxed fractionally. "I should have gotten everyone drinks. I'll be right back."

When she returned, the three had pulled up a table and were half-heartedly attempting to sort through a game. They were still behaving strangely, but she saw when she met Reese's gaze that the thoughts running through his mind were all carnal.

Pleased with herself, she set the drinks out for everyone and settled on the couch once more, crossing her legs and lightly swinging the upper one.

When they'd cleaned the tray of eggs, the game got underway at last. Amaryllis didn't have much interest in that particular game, however. The looks they'd been giving her had fired her blood and she was far more interested in seeing how long it would take them to act on the desire she could see boiling inside of them--all three of them.

They were paying far more attention to the movement of her leg and the sway of her breasts caused by the movement than they were the cards. When it came her turn to discard, she leaned forward and tossed down two cards. Sitting back again, she uncrossed her legs and set her feet on the edge of the table, fanning her knees instead. The third time she parted her thighs, Cain shot to his feet so abruptly, his chair screeched as it slid across the floor.

Reese came to his feet almost simultaneously. The two men exchanged a look. More slowly, Dante rose. Abruptly, Cain muttered that he was going for a walk and strode from the room. Without a word, Reese crossed to her. Leaning down, he scooped her from the couch. Amaryllis let out a gurgling laugh. "What are you doing?"

His lips curled up at one corner. "I will show you."

Dante followed. Reese paused at the foot of the stairs. The brothers exchanged a look and then the three of them proceeded up the stairs.

Chapter Twenty Six

Amaryllis felt positively decadent when she woke halfway through the morning the following day. Ordinarily, she would've bounded out of the bed guiltily as soon as she realized she'd slept so late, but she realized she felt very little guilt over it. She had not, in point of fact, done that much sleeping.

She smiled dreamily at the memory. It had been the first time the three of them had played together since that first night and she realized she'd almost forgotten how good it felt to have both them at the same time.

The only fly in her soup was the fact that Cain hadn't seemed interested in joining them.

He'd definitely been interested, though. She was certain she hadn't been mistaken about that. She wasn't as certain that it was her in particular that he wanted, but at least she did know that he wasn't immune to her.

She frowned thoughtfully, but she was fairly certain that neither Dante nor Reese would have warned him away from her--and just as certain that, even if they'd tried it, Cain would've ignored it. In fact, it seemed that something like that would've made him more determined to have her.

She pondered over the possibilities for a while but finally decided that that was a dead end. He wouldn't talk to her and she didn't know him well enough to figure it out without some input from him.

He was needy, though. She was positive about that, and just as certain that he was unlikely to find it outside his contract. He simply didn't strike her as the type to willfully breach--besides which all the females were spoken for-- several times over.

She was just going to have to keep battering at him until he caved in. That was all there was to it. Maybe, once he'd had a little relief, whatever it was that was eating him would go away, and even if it didn't, he would surely be more open with her and they'd be able to work it out.

The best way to start, she decided, would be to put him in the position of not being able to avoid her. As long as he could avoid her, he would, and whatever was bothering him would only fester and get worse.

Throwing the covers off, she rolled out of bed and went to bathe. She debated briefly over what to wear but finally decided to go with the typical dress. A glimpse now and then of the veils would keep all of them more interested than seeing it all the time.

That thought led to an epiphany. Maybe she should try her hand at designing clothing? She didn't know how to make them, but if she *could* come up with ideas, she could ask Reese to design 'bots for her to do the actual labor of making them. As far as she'd seen, there was no one on the planet to fill that particular niche, and with a quarter of the population female, there would almost certainly be a demand for it.

Cain, she discovered when she'd searched the house thoroughly, had made himself scarce. "Coward," she muttered, plunking her hands on her hips irritably.

Balked of that possibility, she decided to try her hand at her idea and went into the study. She couldn't jack in, of course, which was a real pain in the ass and made for slow going since she had to depend upon voice response and visual. The computer did have access to design programming, but, not surprisingly, none of it dealt with fashion.

Unfazed, since she really hadn't expected it to anyway, she set to work streamlining a program that would. She was still working on it when Cain came in.

He stopped as abruptly as if he'd encountered a force field. If he hadn't, Amaryllis wasn't certain she would even have noticed him, she was so deeply into what she was doing. As it was, she *had* completely forgotten what had brought her downstairs to begin with. She glanced at him absently. "You needed the computer?"

He studied her for a long moment, apparently debating whether to go or stay, and finally crossed to the desk. Propping a hip on the edge, he studied what she was doing for several moments in silence.

"Designing?"

"Mmm," Amaryllis said absently. Ordering the computer to save and close, she got up and stretched her cramped muscles.

"What is this sudden interest in clothing?"

Amaryllis looked at him in surprise. "I need something to occupy my time."

His eyes narrowed, then moved pointedly to her rounded belly. "Forgive me for being blunt, but from what I've observed you don't seem to be having a lot of trouble finding something to occupy yourself with--and you may have more than you can handle when that little seed comes to fruition."

Amaryllis stared at him for a full minute while outrage slowly poured through her, finally erupting. "Seed? It's not a seed, damn you! It's a child--a part of this family unit-- just as you're supposed to be. Is that what this is all about?" she asked tightly. "The child? Or is it because I welcome my partners?"

"This what?" he responded coolly.

Amaryllis narrowed her eyes at him. Striding up to him, she poked the center of his chest with one index finger. "The cold shoulder you've been giving me, because if it is, let me tell you, you can stuff it! I didn't have any decision in any of this--not in coming here in the first place and not in contracting. Nobody forced you in to it. Nobody begged you. You *demanded* to take part--and I'm doing my best to cope, which isn't at all easy by damn, whatever the hell you seem to think. And, *yes*, I do enjoy sex with my partners and I'm sure as hell not going to apologize for it! Because I care for Reese, and Dante … and you! But if that isn't good enough for you, then I'll tell Reese and Dante you've changed your mind and want out of the arrangement."

He caught her as she moved to go around him, pulling her flush against his body. She looked up at him angrily.

"All that passion--for me alone?"

Amaryllis made a growling sound. "Don't tempt me, Cain."

He stared at her a long moment. "But you don't mind tempting me, do you, baby?"

The question knocked the wind out of her. "I don't know what you mean," she said evasively.

"I think you do. I think that little display last night was to see what buttons you needed to push."

He was so perceptive sometimes it was downright scary.

Or maybe she was just that damned transparent? Embarrassing thought.

She thought it over for several moments. "Did I push the right one?" she asked sweetly.

Amusement entered his eyes. "I'd suggest a little more subtlety and a little less bite, but that was a good effort at sarcasm--you did want to, then?"

Amaryllis blinked, mentally grinding her teeth. He'd been on a fishing expedition and she'd landed right in his net. She should have known. Tricky bastard!

She pulled free. "Actually, I netted what I wanted," she said haughtily, and stalked from the room. He caught up with her in the hallway, caught her totally off guard, swinging her off her feet. By the time her world had stopped spinning, he was halfway up the stairs.

"Exactly what do you call yourself doing?" she demanded indignantly.

He gave her a look. "Consummating our agreement."

Considering his mood, that was a rather unnerving thought.

She remembered suddenly something her mother had said to her--'Be careful what you wish for'.

She hadn't wanted it to be like this, though, she realized with perfect clarity. She'd wanted him to make love to her, not have sex with her.

She had no grounds to object, unfortunately, particularly

since she'd goaded him into it--threatened to terminate the agreement.

When he dropped her on her bed, she eyed him warily as he stripped the loincloth from his body, placed a knee upon the mattress and crawled toward her like a cat stalking its prey. Her heart was beating so frantically it felt as if it was trying to achieve light speed.

She jerked nervously when he slipped the straps of her top from her shoulders so that her breasts spilled into his hands. He hesitated, his gaze moving from her breasts to her eyes. After a long moment, he dropped onto the bed beside her. Scooping her up, he gathered her close, stroking her back. She heard him swallow. "You were right. I have a nasty temper."

Amaryllis lifted her head to look at him. "You're not angry anymore?"

He sighed tiredly. "No."

She dipped her head and kissed her way up his throat to his lips, brushing hers lightly across his hard mouth. "Then--make love to me," she whispered.

He rolled, carrying her with him and covering her mouth hungrily. Excitement shot through her as his tongue skated along hers, dueled, teasing the sensitive inner surfaces as his taste and scent filled her mouth, invading her mind like a heady drug. She'd known, she thought dreamily, that his kiss would be this good.

His hands, as he stroked her body, exploring every inch of her flesh and touching off flutters of eagerness in her, were gentle, loving, and exquisitely stirring all at once. She was already burning with need when he lifted his lips from hers at last and worshipped her body with them, nipping at her skin, lathing her with his tongue. A shuddering sigh escaped her as he burned a path along the center of her body to her belly, paused to strip her briefs from her and meandered upward again. Sucking one distended nipple into his mouth, he unfastened her top and caught the opposite breast in the palm of his hand, massaging it. Fire erupted along every nerve ending, sizzling, sparking and she moaned as her belly tightened with anticipation.

When he'd so thoroughly tormented each nipple in turn that she could scarcely catch her breath, she pushed at him, sprawling on top of him when he rolled to his back and lavishing her own brand of appreciation on his body. He jerked, jackknifing upright when she reached his belly and opened her mouth over the head of his cock, sucking the sensitive tip. Planting her hand in the center of his chest, she pushed him back. After a moment, he settled again, his hands gripping the sheets on either side of him tightly. He began to shake with the effort to remain still. A groan escaped him. Abruptly, he speared his fingers in her hair and tugged. When she released him, he dragged her back up the bed and kissed her deeply, feverishly, moving from her mouth, along her throat to her breasts. She gasped, moaned, parting her thighs and arching against him. "Ohh, Cain! Now! Please!"

For several moments, she thought he either hadn't heard her or he'd chosen to ignore her plea. Finally, he released her nipple and covered her mouth once more, pressing the head of his cock against the mouth of her sex. She gasped into his mouth as he pushed inside of her, forcing her body to yield to him. Tearing her mouth from his, she arched her head into the pillow, pushing up to meet him. Her body tensed, pleasure coiling tightly inside of her as his turgid flesh slowly invaded, stroking the sensitive inner flesh and touching off waves of exhilaration.

Wrapping her arms around him, she moved her hands along his back, stroked his dark head as he set a pace that spiraled her higher and higher until her moans of appreciation became sharper, keener cries that bordered on screams until, suddenly, her culmination burst upon her in a blinding flash of ecstasy. He shuddered, began to thrust more quickly, bringing his own crisis thundering down upon him.

They lay locked together for some time afterwards, each reluctant to sever their joining. Finally, Cain lifted slightly away from her, moving his cock slowly in and out of her almost playfully. Amaryllis opened her eyes a fraction to look up at him, her lips curling. "It feels sooo good to have you inside of me," she murmured lazily. "I would just as soon you stay."

His features went taut and Amaryllis felt him filling her, his cock growing hard. Her eyes widened as his thrusts became more purposeful. The heat that hadn't even completely dissipated began to rise inside her, as well. Within moments, she found her body hovering once more on the edge of the precipice. When she came again, it was harder, more explosive, longer than the first time and dragged a keening cry from her throat.

She was so sated afterwards, she was barely conscious when he rolled off of her and gathered her against his chest. She drifted lazily for a time, half asleep, half awake. She had no idea of how long, but the room grew dim as the day waned.

She stirred after a while, hearing footsteps in the hallway. Cain's arm tightened around her as the door opened. There was a significant pause and then the door closed again.

Smiling, she pressed a kiss against Cain's chest, whereupon he rolled her onto her back and made love to her again, teasing her endlessly until she could no longer keep it inside of her and cried out in rapture.

Reese was no less attentive to her needs when he came to her the following night. Nor did Dante stint on displaying his affection. After nearly a week and half, Amaryllis was so exhausted from her lovers' eager attention that she didn't even go down on the evenings that were hers for fear one or the other might take it as an invitation.

It was merely by chance, therefore, that she discovered the rivalry between her men had been taken onto an entirely different field--hers. She didn't know whether to be more amused or irritated to discover that they were vying to see who could make her 'sing' the loudest and the longest. She also didn't know how they finally determined a winner, but she was obliged to consider herself the primary winner in the contest.

Whatever the case, a tentative bond formed between them and if Reese and Cain continued to occasionally butt heads, those occasions were fewer and further between and fairly mild compared to some of their earlier disputes.

Somehow, though, true contentment continued to elude her and she was finally forced to face the demons she'd been trying so hard to keep at bay, the demons Reese, and Dante, and Cain had helped her banish to the furthest reaches of her subconscious by their demands upon her and their loving attention to her needs.

Cain had woken her fears on the day they'd argued and it was he who brought her whole world crashing down around her once more the night he felt the child stir beneath his palm.

They'd made love until the wee hours and Amaryllis was more than nine tenths asleep when he sat up abruptly and stared down at her belly.

"I felt it."

"Mmm?" she asked drowsily.

"The child. I felt it move."

Amaryllis was instantly as wide awake as if he'd tossed a pail of cold water over her. She didn't react or respond in any way. She was too frozen with shock even to think for several moments. Finally, she'd merely rolled onto her side and pretended sleep and after a while he'd lain down again.

She was more glad than she would ever have imagined when she finally woke from an exhausted sleep some time later to discover that Cain had gone. Feeling vaguely ill, she'd climbed from the bed and moved to the mirror to study herself, but she couldn't tell that her belly was any bigger than it had been the last time she'd noticed.

She covered her face with her hands, realizing she'd been lying to herself so long that she simply couldn't face the truth. No solution was going to come to her whether she worried it over in her mind constantly, or tried to ignore the problem by pushing it to the back of her mind as she'd been doing for weeks now. There *was* no out. She could feel the child move.

She didn't remember nearly as much about her mother's later pregnancies as she needed to know, but she did know that she was well beyond termination. Whatever she did now, she would be risking her own life as well as the child's.

But didn't she owe it to the child to do her best for it? Why should it have to suffer because she was a coward? Her own life was certainly no more valuable than the child's.

She cupped a hand over her belly when she felt a slight flutter, as if the child had heard her thoughts and was responding. What would the cyborgs do if it wasn't normal? Would they be as repelled as her own kind were? More repelled? Despite their human side, logic ruled them. Would they decide it was best to terminate it on the spot?

What would the child want? Would it want life anyway? Or would it spend much of its life hating--hating itself for being malformed; hating her for bringing it into world; hating everyone else for the horror it saw in their eyes whenever they looked at it?

She hadn't. There had been times when she'd thought she did. There'd been times when she'd felt like she hated the whole universe, but her parents had loved her, and her brothers and sisters had accepted her and loved her.

She moved back to the bed after a while and sat down to try to think calmly. Was she just being paranoid? Was she just frightening herself because of what had happened to her, or was the possibility real?

Her parents had always blamed what had happened to her on defective shields. The doctors had refused to be cornered one way or the other, but did that mean they didn't know? Or that they didn't agree? Or that they *did* know that it was the shields, but were afraid to say so because of The Company? And if it actually was the shields, did that mean it wasn't something she could pass to her offspring? Or had the radiation damaged her chromosomes?

She wished that she could see the child. If she could just

look at it, assure herself that it was developing normally, she wouldn't be driving herself crazy worrying about it.

There was no hope of that, of course. The cyborgs had made great strides in building this place, but they hadn't anticipated that they would have families. From what she'd heard it wasn't until they'd discovered Dalia had conceived that they realized they were evolving to a point where they would be able to bear young. Rumor had it that they'd been disastrously unprepared for Dalia's labor and delivery and they were still collating and gathering information. They were certainly not advanced enough in that area to have what she needed.

It plagued her mind throughout the day like an aching tooth, impossible to banish once more to a safe distance no matter how hard she tried. Time seemed to hang on her hands, but she found herself moving restlessly about the house, unable to concentrate on anything long enough to accomplish it.

It wasn't until she heard the scrape of feet in the foyer that she managed to compose herself even a little, but she was more relieved than sorry when she realized that it was her free night--she could spend the evening alone in her room worrying herself sick.

By the time they'd eaten, she was exhausted from her anxiety. Feeling somewhat hopeful that she might at least escape her worries for a little while, she excused herself and went up to bed. When she woke, the house was as dark and silent as deep space.

Chapter Twenty Seven

Amaryllis lay listening for a time to the tiny creaks and
groans of the settling house. Slowly, it dawned upon her
that everyone was asleep ... unless someone was standing
guard. It also occurred to her that this might be her only
opportunity to try to find out what she could about the
baby, to find out positively one way or the other so that she
could make an informed decision instead of one driven
solely by her fears.

Since she now knew there were native inhabitants, most
likely a guard was posted about the city around the clock,
but she doubted very much that anyone would be in the
med center. The cyborgs had so little need for such a thing
she'd actually been surprised to see one at all, but she
supposed it was probably geared more toward research
anyway.

If she could get in, she could at least find out what they
had. She could operate a scanner if they had one. She
doubted she'd be able to make heads or tails of a lot of the
information, but she only needed to find out one thing--was
it normal.

She'd fallen asleep in the clothes she was wearing so she
had no need to stumble around in the dark looking for
something to wear.

She just wished she had her uniform. As lightweight as it
was, it was made out of a material that was surprisingly
protective. There was no hope for it, of course. She hadn't
seen her uniform since she'd been captured. She removed
the skirting from her clothes, however. It wasn't any sort of
protection, but it could hamper her movements and she
needed to be prepared to defend herself, or run.

Which brought her mind to weapons.

She didn't have one and didn't know where to find one.

The cyborgs primarily carried swords. She didn't know why they seemed to prefer to carry swords instead of lasers, but they did, which meant it was highly unlikely she'd find a laser even if she took the time to look, and even swords weren't readily available. Until and unless the cyborgs began to trust, hunters weren't allowed to arm themselves at all, and she had a strong feeling that Dante and Reese kept their own weapons close to hand.

She was desperate or she wouldn't even have considered going out unarmed.

She'd just have to be careful she didn't get caught.

After very little consideration, she decided not to try to leave by way of the stairs. She wasn't that familiar with the structure and it was made of natural materials. Cyborg hearing was acute. One creaking timber and she'd have some explaining to do.

Moving from window to window, she checked the perimeter carefully. The moon had just cleared the tops of the trees and brightened the rear landscape, casting deep shadows in the lee of the stonework and plants, but she couldn't see any movement that indicated anyone was about. There was nothing below any of the windows to use to climb down, but no obstacles to clear either.

Calculating the distance, she decided she could make the jump without damaging her bionics and slipped the window open. She hovered on the sill for several moments, trying to decide what to do about the window, but finally realized she would either make it there and back without being caught, or not. If her mission was successful, then she would still need to get back into the house undetected. If they checked on her, it wouldn't matter whether the window was open or not. They'd immediately notice that she was missing.

Balancing herself, she pushed off of the sill, landing in the soft soil of the lawn in a half crouch. She held her breath, listening intently, but she could hear no movement that indicated she'd been heard.

Getting her bearings, she decided to take the most direct

route. A roundabout route wouldn't help that she could see and it would take more time.

She jogged until she neared the edge of the city. Slowing, she drifted into the shadows and kept to them as much as possible, stopping from time to time to listen and study her surroundings. The streets were deserted. Here and there, light spilled out of the window of a building, but she could see no movement inside.

She almost ran smack into a pair of cyborg guards on patrol, but managed to squeeze herself into a tiny corner and waited until they'd passed out of sight before she moved again.

More cautious now, she moved from one hiding place to another, scanning for some sort of cover each time before she moved on. There were a few lights on in the med center. For security? She wondered. Or was someone working the night shift?

She circumnavigated the building before she found an unlocked window that she could reach. Pushing it open as far as she could, she hoisted herself up and over the sill, then dropped into the room, catching herself with her hands.

Light from the corridor outside filtered into the room. Glancing around, she saw that it looked like an examination room. It seemed doubtful that she would have chanced on a room with a scanner, but she looked anyway, pausing from time to time to listen. As she'd expected, she turned up nothing.

Moving to the door, she pressed her ear to it to listen. When she heard nothing, she eased the door open and glanced up and down the corridor. The heels of her boots clicked on the tile floor when she stepped out of the room and she froze, listening once more. When she was certain she hadn't alerted security, she moved quickly down the corridor to the next examination room and ducked inside.

To her great relief, she found a scanner in the fourth cabinet she checked. Moving to the gurney in the center of the room, she lay back on it, switched the scanner on and moved it slowly over her abdomen. She sat up again when the light blinked, indicating the scan was complete.

The scrape of a heel on the tile floor startled her so badly she almost dropped the scanner from suddenly nerveless fingers. She managed to recover it just in time and clutched it against her frantically pounding heart, trying to determine whether the footsteps were coming in her direction or not.

A door, fairly close by creaked as it was pushed open.

They were checking the rooms!

Amaryllis glanced down at the scanner. The readout glowed in the dim light, but it was scrolling across the screen far too quickly for her to read it. One line seemed to leap right out at her, however.

Unknown life form.

"Oh God!" she whispered, clamping a hand to her mouth an instant too late to still the horrified exclamation.

There was a furtive movement, closer this time. Dropping the scanner to the gurney, Amaryllis abandoned any attempt at silence, dashing for the window. She'd barely landed on the ground outside when she heard the door of the examination room she'd just left crash open and slam against the wall.

Leaping to her feet, she charged down the side of the building until she reached the point nearest the next building, then followed that building until she reached an alley. Behind her, she heard the sound of pounding feet and the order to halt.

She ran faster, zigzagging down a street, then veering into an alley. Along the way, she collected two more guards.

Pain blossomed in her side. She ignored it. There was no place to hide and she was of no mind to chance being trapped even if she'd spied a likely looking spot.

She'd almost reached the edge of the forest when she ran headlong into a guard. The impact stunned both of them, but Amaryllis' momentum not only bowled him over, it propelled her several yards further and through a hedgerow. Disoriented, she scrambled to her feet as soon as she stopped rolling, staggered a couple of steps and finally found her equilibrium.

The woods were dark, however, with the trees blocking the little light filtering down from the moon, and she didn't have the advantage of night vision that the cyborgs did. Twenty feet more and the ground dropped from beneath her unexpectedly. She rolled part of the way down and skidded on one hip the remainder, landing in a trickling brook of icy water. It snatched the breath from her lungs, but the shock cleared her head.

Shivering, she realized she'd stumbled on a bit of luck. The cold water would make it harder, if not impossible, for the cyborgs to track her with heat vision. Sucking in a few breaths of air, she dropped down and half swam half crawled through the shallow water until the sounds of pursuit faded into the distance.

When she was certain the search had turned away from her, she climbed out of the water and sat on the bank for several moments, trying to catch her breath and figure out where she was.

She couldn't see the moon anymore and without that she had no idea which direction was north, south, east or west. The stars in the sky were unfamiliar to her, giving her no heavenly landmark at all, and she couldn't see even a glimpse of the city.

She couldn't stay where she was, however. The night was mild, but she was still cold from being in the frigid water so long.

In any case, she had to figure out some way to get back before she was discovered missing. Getting to her feet, she struggled up the embankment and looked around hopefully. At first, she saw nothing at all, but then, just as despair was beginning to descend upon her, she saw a wink of light in the distance. Her heart leapt. She couldn't tell whether it was the moon, or light from a structure, but it didn't matter. Either way, if she followed it, she was bound to find some sort of landmark that would tell her where she was.

She hoped.

A flutter of movement in her belly brought her focus to the baby.

The unknown life form.

A wave of nausea washed through her. What the hell did that mean?

The machine didn't have the data to interpret its findings, which meant the data was pretty useless.

Tears stung her eyes abruptly and she blinked to clear her vision.

She just couldn't think about it right now. Later, when she found her way, she'd try to figure out what it meant.

She'd been stumbling through the dark for nearly an hour before she realized she hadn't seen the wink of light not once since that first time.

She could be following some sort of phosphorescent weather condition, or animal, or even a plant.

She was so tired she felt like dropping where she stood.

And it had all been for nothing.

The authorities were going to be looking for whoever it was that had broken into the med center.

She stopped again, searching in vain for anything that might look familiar. When she saw nothing, she prodded her tired brain, trying to retrace her movements. The med center was practically in the center of Gallen. She'd headed roughly north, she thought, when she'd run from the patrol and Reese and Dante's plantation was north of town.

But how roughly north? And what direction had she taken after her collision with the guard? East, she finally decided.

So she was now headed the wrong way.

She thought.

The stream could have taken her in another direction entirely.

Abruptly, she remembered the little stream she'd found when she'd gone exploring with Cain. It must be the same stream, and if it was, then it wound around Gallen and would take her near the landing field, hopefully near enough she would be able to see the security lights.

Unfortunately, she'd left the stream almost an hour

before. Sighing, she turned and began to retrace her steps. After walking a little more than twenty minutes by her calculations, she heard the sound of gushing water. Hopefulness surged through her and she hurried onward. She'd just reached what she thought was the embankment when a cold, clammy, very hairy arm snaked out of the darkness and caught her around the waist, jerking her back tightly against an equally hairy chest. Almost at the same moment, a large hand clamped over her nose and mouth, cutting off her air supply.

Panicked when she couldn't drag in a breath of air, Amaryllis' fighting instincts kicked in sluggishly. She swung her arm reflexively toward her captor, connecting with a bony, hairy shoulder hard enough the creature let out a howl of rage. It didn't release her however, and within a few moments the darkness was no longer merely around her, it was clutching at her, sucking her down into nothingness. In vain, she clawed at the hand that was suffocating her, her efforts becoming weaker and more futile by the moment. Her last thought before she lost consciousness was that she'd killed Reese's baby and herself in the process.

* * * *

Reese wasn't certain what woke him, but he was instantly wide awake. He sat up, listening, but heard no sound that seemed to indicate a threat. Slipping silently from the bed, he pulled his sword from its scabbard and crossed the room, easing the door open. All was quiet, but he found he couldn't shake the sense that something wasn't right.

Leaving his room, he made his way down the stairs and checked the first floor, room by room. He met up with Dante when he reached the stairs once more.

"What is it?"

Frowning, Reese glanced around the foyer, looking for anything that seemed out of place. "Something woke me."

Dante nodded. "You take the front. I'll take the back."

When Reese reached the rear of the house, he found Dante studying the ground beneath Amaryllis' window.

His heart seemed to seize in his chest as he glanced up at the house and saw that her window was open. Cain was leaning out, his expression grim.

"She went out here," he said when both men looked up at him.

Reese looked down at the impressions in the soil. "She was alone," he said neutrally.

Cain landed on the ground behind Reese and Dante. "When she left, at any rate. I've got a feeling none of us are going to be too happy when we find out what our darling mate has been up to."

Reese sent him a sharp look. "Do you know what this is about?"

"I could guess, but it would only be a guess. I don't know anymore than you do."

"The child?" Dante hazarded.

Cain glanced at him in surprise. Reese looked as if he'd been pole axed.

"She told you?" Cain asked.

Dante shook his head. "She was … deeply disturbed, but she would not trust me enough to speak to me. It is only a suspicion I had."

"She is breeding?" Reese asked hoarsely, glancing around the area as if he thought she might magically reappear. He didn't wait for either of the others to respond. After glancing at the footprints again, he lifted his head, gauged the direction and took off at a run. Dante and Cain fell in behind him.

Dante glanced over at Cain. "You have no weapon. If we run into trouble, you will be the least useful. You should return to the house to watch over her if she comes back."

Cain's lips tightened. "It's nearly dawn. She would have returned by now if she could. I'm thinking she'll have more need of me wherever she's at."

The trail they followed led them to the med center. When they arrived, city security was still investigating a break in. The three retreated a short distance to consider the situation. It seemed indisputable that Amaryllis was the one they sought, and that she'd eluded them. The question was, where had she gone when she'd escaped?

Deciding Dante would be the least suspicious to ask questions, he was sent to see what he could discover. He returned a few minutes later.

"This way," he said, setting off at a jog.

Reese and Cain caught up to him. "What did you find out?"

"She was chased beyond the city perimeter. They lost her in the woods. They're combing the area now with scanners."

Reese's lips tightened. "Her heat signature won't be the same."

"The hunter's signature isn't, but hers will not be the same as a hunter's either."

"The variation is only slight. It might not arouse suspicions," Dante pointed out, but they all knew they couldn't afford to take the chance. Even if not for the fact that she was human, she'd broken into the med center. It didn't matter why, if she'd taken anything or not, she would still be punished if she were caught.

When they arrived at the area where Amaryllis had disappeared into the forest, they saw that the guards were walking the city perimeter, having decided, apparently, that their culprit would have re-entered the city at some point. The three exchanged a look.

"This explains why she hasn't returned. She wouldn't risk leading them back."

Cain surveyed the forest and frowned. "She was curious about the natives. Is there any possibility, do you think, that she found them? Possibly made friends?"

"No," Reese and Dante said almost simultaneously.

Cain's brows rose.

"They are cannibals," Reese said tightly. "We drove them from this place."

Cain felt his gut clench. "They're humanoid?"

Reese shrugged. "Two legged beasts, at any rate. They stalk a lone victim and attack in packs, like wild dogs. Two of our number were slain, their heads taken as prizes, before we discovered there were hostiles nearby." He turned to look at Cain for the first time. "I do not believe that they would come near, but if they have taken our Amy, she has not found friends."

Chapter Twenty Eight

When they had followed the signs of her passing to the stream, they surveyed a wide circle around it, looking for any sign of where she'd emerged. Finding nothing, they decided they would have to split up. Reese would go north. Dante and Cain would go south.

Cain glanced at Dante several times as they jogged along the streambed, scanning the embankment on either side. "Reese thinks she went the other way."

"Yes."

"But you didn't argue."

"Thinking is not knowing. We can not afford to lose time by all going the wrong way."

Cain shrugged, unable to argue with the logic of that statement. "There is one little problem, however."

"What?"

"If Reese finds sign first, we'll have no way of knowing it. By the time we realize we've gone the wrong way, it could be too late for both of them."

"I will know," Dante said simply. "And Reese will know if we find anything. This is the reason we took different directions instead of the same. So that each of us would know which direction she has gone without losing time."

Cain frowned. "Telepathy?"

Dante shrugged. "Perhaps, of a sort. It is more like I know what he wishes me to know and he knows what I wish him to know than speech of any sort. It is what led us to one another to begin with."

He stopped abruptly, turning, lifting his head as if he was listening to something Cain couldn't hear. "She is taken," he growled, heading back the way they'd come at a run.

Cain caught up to him after a few moments. "He's found her?"

"Her heat signature. A faint trace only, but she cannot be far or he would not have seen that."

* * * *

The first thing that Amaryllis became aware of was that her head felt as if it would explode. The pain in her ribcage was the second sensation her mind interpreted and fear followed that, the knee jerk fear that something had happened to the baby. A split second before she moved to avoid the discomfort, she realized her ribs were aching because of the bony shoulder digging into it. The realization saved her from giving herself away.

As her mind cleared, she became aware of a nearly overwhelming stench.

It took her several moments to realize the stench was coming from the creature that was carrying her and those that surrounded her. Pushing her discomfort to the back of her mind, she expanded her senses to detect what she could without giving herself away.

She decided there were about a dozen of the creatures around her. Close by, one was whining, or perhaps humming, beneath his breath. Two near the outer edge of the group appeared to be arguing, or muttering complaints. One moved with an uneven gait. She could hear one foot scraping with each step, as if he was dragging it.

It took a while to single out the sounds she thought indicated each individual, but she tallied it carefully and finally arrived at what she considered a fair guess.

Twelve to one and she was weaponless.

They were bound to become suspicious of her prolonged unconsciousness soon … unless they thought she was dead?

She decided to risk a peek through her eyelashes.

The first sight that greeted her eyes was a pair of hairy buttocks. A filthy thong divided the flaccid cheeks. The skin beneath the hair was somewhere between a pale blue and gray, but that might have been because the creature was so dirty.

There was enough light to see, but she had no idea of how

near dawn it had been when the thing had grabbed her and nearly suffocated her, so no clue of how long she'd been unconscious or how far they might have traveled.

The sun peering through the trees glinted off of something metallic, catching her attention and she realized that the creature had a sword strapped to his side. Excitement pumped through her. She closed her eyes, mentally surveying the state of her body.

She'd been hanging over the thing's shoulder long enough her entire body felt stiff and unresponsive. Sluggish circulation made it difficult to determine whether her hands were bound or not and she didn't dare try to move them to find out, or look.

She decided she'd have to assume they'd bound her wrists, but her arms were hanging over her head. The thought had barely registered when a hand tangled in her hair and jerked her head up.

She didn't have time to formulate a plan. The moment the fingers grasped her hair, she went for the sword. Snatching it from the scabbard with both hands, she swung it upward, gutting the creature that had grabbed her.

All hell broke loose then.

* * * *

Slowed by the need to look carefully to detect the faint signs, Reese had been tracking the progress of Amaryllis' captors for nearly twenty minutes when an inhuman scream split the still morning air of the forest. It took him two seconds to triangulate the direction of the sound's origin. He broke into a run then, his heart hammering with unaccustomed fear.

The ground had been steadily climbing since he'd left the stream behind, the soil becoming rockier and the vegetation thinning, making progress easier but detection of their passing more difficult. Until he'd heard the scream, he'd begun to worry that he would lose all traces of their trail and that anxiety nagged at him as he raced up the hill along with the fear that the forest and rocks had deceived him with the direction of the sound he'd heard. Within a few minutes, however, he began to hear the sounds of a battle; the clang of steel against steel; growls and grunts of exertion; howls of pain; the meaty sound of something hard connecting with flesh.

A flash of metal through the trees snagged his attention and he veered toward it. He could see nothing of Amaryllis when at last he caught sight of the excited natives on a wide outcropping of rock some fifteen feet above him, but he didn't doubt for a moment that she was the object of their frenzied interest. Uttering a howl of rage, he bounded onto a large boulder beneath the ledge and then launched himself upward.

The rock beneath his feet split as he landed on the edge of the outcropping. He teetered for a moment and then caught his balance. A half dozen natives, attracted by the sound of Reese's booted feet impacting with stone, whirled to face him, let out yells of surprise and excitement and charged him. Bending his knees, Reese launched himself over their heads, cleaving one of the creatures nearly in half as he flew over him.

He landed between the group that had charged him and the group that was still occupied with trying to disarm Amaryllis … or kill her. Two died before they even realized there was a threat behind them and, hacking to his left and right with his sword, Reese cleared a path through them and worked his way between Amaryllis and her attackers.

She threw him a look that was part relief, part apology.

"Stay behind me," he growled, turning to face the savages.

"You can't take them all," Amaryllis said, gasping for breath.

"I won't have to."

She wasn't certain what he meant by that. She didn't see anyone else, but she was too tired to argue with him at the moment. She knew no more than fifteen or twenty minutes had passed since she'd engaged the natives in battle, but she'd already been worn out from her escape the night before from the patrol. Moreover, she was bleeding from a half a dozen cuts since it was impossible to fend off every strike without taking a hit occasionally and felt vaguely dizzy.

She guarded his back, anyway, but discovered fairly quickly that Reese was backing both of them into a corner. "We'll be boxed in!" she shouted warningly.

He ignored the warning, forcing her back until he was taking the full brunt of the attack and she no longer had enough room to maneuver to try to help. All she could do was try to stay out of his way and not hamper his efforts at defending them.

The natives might have been startled by Reese's arrival. They might even have been intelligent enough to know fear when the raging blond giant landed in their midst, but their overwhelming superiority of numbers gave them courage and they showed no sign of flagging, or giving up. Within a few minutes, Reese was beginning to look as bad or worse than she did as they came at him by three's and four's and managed to break through his guard again and again, nicking his chest, his thighs, and his arms. The sword in Reese's hand was moving so fast it was little more than a blur of motion. Each time he was attacked from a new direction, he managed to block and parry, but there were too many of them and they were crowding too close for Reese to do more than defend their position. Amaryllis had begun to fear that the two of them would be completely overwhelmed when she heard the hunter's battle cry. Her heart leapt with relief.

Despite the heat of battle, the natives heard it, too. The moment those in the rear ceased to press forward to take the place of those who'd been injured or tired from wielding their swords against Reese, he launched an offense, cutting down three of the natives in quick succession.

Dante and Cain landed on the ledge behind the group like two great, wingless birds of war. Cain dodged two that launched themselves at him, leaping over them, landing in a dive and roll and scooping up a sword from the hand of one of the fallen along the way. When he came to his feet once more, a smile of grim pleasure curled his lips. Dante grabbed the first three that rushed him and tossed them over the ledge. Amaryllis heard one scream and then the meaty thuds as three bodies slammed into the rocks below in quick succession.

Within moments of their arrival, a half dozen warriors lay dead or dying and the ledge was so slick with blood that the battle became a *macabre* waltz of death as the fighters slipped and skidded with each step they took. When the few remaining natives finally realized that their numbers had dwindled drastically and they no longer had even the advantage of superior odds, they made a belated attempt to escape.

Reese and Cain cut them down as they ran. Sheathing his sword, Dante crossed the ledge and knelt to examine Amaryllis' injuries. "There are none that are serious," she said quickly.

Dante paused, his gaze meeting hers. His face was tight with both anger and anxiety. "You are more fortunate than wise then."

Amaryllis felt blood flood her cheeks, but she could hardly argue the point. It had been a stupid, careless thing to do and it might have cost both her and her baby their lives--the unknown life form. Tears filled her eyes. Her chin wobbled. "I didn't know," she said in her defense.

Some of the anger left him. "A mission without proper reconnaissance is always unwise, particularly when there was no good reason for it in the first place and one very good reason not to."

Amaryllis glanced toward Cain accusingly. Unfortunately, he had his back to her and missed the look.

"Do not blame Cain. Your condition is far too noticeable now to be anything but what it is. I had suspected weeks ago, but thought it could not be. Otherwise, you would have told me."

Amaryllis bit her lip, but she somehow doubted that he

wanted to hear her explanation.

Reese and Cain, having checked each of the fallen warriors to make certain none were a threat any longer, moved toward them. Reese studied her for several moments and turned to look at Dante. "She is alright?"

"Minor cuts. They will heal soon. I will need to examine her more carefully, but we must get her home first."

Reese nodded. "The … infant?"

"I can not tell without a scan, but I do not believe it has come to harm either."

Amaryllis couldn't help but notice he refused to look at her, or speak directly to her after that first accusing glance. He leaned down when Dante moved away, scooping her into his arms. "I can walk," she said stiffly.

He ignored her, tightening his grip on her when she began to struggle to be released. She subsided, sulking.

Silence reigned during the long trek home. Amaryllis had time to experience the full range of emotions attached to her situation--several times. She didn't have time to wonder what would happen if the authorities discovered it was her that had broken into the med center. She was too worried about what Dante, Cain, and Reese intended as punishment.

All three were totally pissed off at her, though, and she expected to catch hell as soon as they were certain she was alright and they had the time and privacy to give her a taste of their tempers.

She didn't know whether to be relieved or sorry when they arrived at the plantation and Dante merely escorted her to her room and left again. The lock clicked audibly, and rather ominously, as he closed the door. She sat on the edge of the bed for a while, waiting to see if any of them meant to come back.

Reese and Cain did, but not directly. They arrived at her bedroom windows and, after a great deal of hammering, secured bars in place.

She pointedly ignored them.

When they'd gone away again, she trudged into the

bathroom and soaked until it took all she could do to drag herself from the tub again. Wrapping a towel around her, she went back into the bedroom, collapsed on the bed and, in the middle of worrying what they would do next, lost consciousness.

Chapter Twenty Nine

Amaryllis was totally disoriented when she woke. Her brain was sluggish anyway, as if she'd been drugged, and she simply stared at the feeble light outside her windows for some time, trying to figure out why it looked like dawn when it had been around midday when they'd arrived at the plantation.

She finally decided that it was either evening, or she'd slept throughout the afternoon and night.

She felt like she could sleep another ten or twelve hours and wondered what had awakened her. Almost on top of the thought, she heard a scraping sound in the corridor outside her room and the tread of booted feet. Someone was moving something. That must be what had awakened her, she decided.

Slipping from the bed, she padded over to the door and grasped the doorknob. It took her several minutes to figure out that the reason it wasn't opening was because it was locked.

She'd forgotten she'd been locked in.

She stared at the door for a few moments, trying to summon anger and found she couldn't. Turning, she stared at the bed listlessly for a minute and finally staggered back to the bed and climbed in again, this time pulling the covers over herself. Despite her sluggishness, though, she discovered she simply couldn't summon sleep once more no matter how hard she tried. The longer she lay in the bed, the wider awake she became, particularly since the noise outside her room continued unabated.

Finally, she heard footsteps approaching her door and the click of the lock. She debated pretending she was still asleep on the off chance that she might be allowed to avoid a confrontation a little longer, but when the door opened, she sat up, eyeing her visitor warily.

It was Cain. His gaze dropped to her bare breasts, lingered there for several moments and returned to her face. "Did you sleep well?"

It seemed an innocuous enough question, but Amaryllis was wary of where it might lead. She nodded.

After several uncomfortable moments, he moved across the room and sat down on the edge of the bed. He rubbed his hands over his face tiredly. "Why did you do it? Where did you think you would go?"

Amaryllis was on the point of trying to explain why such a stupid decision had seemed like a very sound one at the time when his last question sank in. "What?"

His lips tightened. "Where were you running to? I know we didn't give you any choice in this, but we all agreed to try to make it work."

"You think I was running away? Is that what Reese and Dante think, too?"

He shrugged. "I don't have their ability. I don't know what they think. You're saying you weren't?"

Impulsively, she moved closer, caressing his cheek lightly with her fingers. He stiffened, but he didn't pull away. "As crazy as it might sound, I love you. I love all of you. I wasn't running away. At least, I suppose in a sense I have been, but not the way you think. It's…." Her face crumpled. "…the baby. I think there's something wrong with it. I just … I just wanted to know and I couldn't think of any way to find out except to try to get my hands on a scanner. You know I can't go to the med center. They'd know immediately that I'm … not the same as everyone else.

"It's just been driving me crazy, trying to decide what would be the best thing to do for it. And then, after I did the scan and everything else happened--all I could think about when I was fighting those horrible creatures was that the baby couldn't live without me, that it depended on me to keep it safe and give it life and I'd failed it. I think I'm just too selfish to do the right thing for the baby. I love it. I can't terminate it, even if it's so bad its life is a misery to it, I just can't do it."

"But I was afraid that you would all hate me for producing such a defective child and I didn't think I could face that either."

Cain studied her for several moments after she burst into tears and finally pulled her into his arms, holding her tightly.

Amaryllis wrapped her arms around his neck. "I'm so sorry, Cain. So sorry! I tried to tell you I was wrong for you. I tried to tell Reese and Dante, too."

He soothed her until she'd cried herself out and then went to get her a washcloth for her ravaged face.

"I hope this isn't going to become a habit," Cain said pensively.

Amaryllis mopped her face and peered at him. "What?"

"Crying all over me."

Her chin wobbled and he pinched it. "No more of that," he said sternly. "I don't mind a little watering now and then, but I enjoy your smiles and laughter much better."

She sighed. "I'm sorry. I don't really know what's wrong with me lately. Ordinarily, I handle problems much better."

"This isn't a problem," he said, patting her belly. "It's a gift, and one we would all have rejoiced in even more if you'd shared it with us."

"Everyone's really mad with me."

"Yes. You scared the hell out of us."

"It wasn't intentional."

"Which is why we've decided after a lot of consideration only to punish you for a week."

Amaryllis blinked at him. "Punish?" she said slowly. "You mean locking me in?"

"I mean no sex."

Amaryllis bit her lip. "You're not serious."

He sighed. "Alas, yes. I voted in favor of fucking you senseless, but Reese and Dante assured me that pleasuring you wasn't the sort of punishment that would teach you the right lesson, that it might have the adverse effect of encouraging you instead."

"You are serious?"

"Unfortunately," he said glumly.

Amaryllis was more than a little inclined to think he must be teasing her, but he certainly seemed serious. "For a week."

"Reese was inclined to make it more, but I pointed out that that would create an undue hardship on the disciplinarians."

Amaryllis shook her head. "I can never tell when you're joking."

His eyes narrowed. "I'm dead serious, baby. I adore you. We all do. But if you ever do anything that … dangerous again, you won't come away from it unscathed. I will make sure you deeply regret it. Now come. Dante and Reese are waiting."

Amaryllis stared at him distrustfully. "For what?"

"Dante has set up a monitoring station in the next room. As you pointed out, you can't go to the med center. We brought the med center to you. It's fully equipped. A little antiquated, I'm afraid, because for some reason the cyborgs hadn't gotten around to preparing for parenthood--possibly because that wasn't supposed to be an option for us, but fortunately for us Dante is not only fully qualified as a medic, he is also into research and development."

Amaryllis studied him uneasily, but she knew he was perfectly capable of carrying her, willing or not. She decided her dignity would suffer less if she went on her own steam.

Reese and Dante were both stone faced when she arrived in the examination room with Cain. If she'd been in any doubt that they were still furious with her, that cinched it, but she felt more like she was climbing onto an autopsy table than an examination table. When she'd settled, Dante moved the tray of instruments closer and began by checking her vitals. Her belly clenched when he picked up the scanner and slowly moved it over her.

He was silent for so long after he'd finished, studying the

read out, that she couldn't stand it any more. "It says unknown life form, doesn't it?" she said shakily.

He glanced at her then. "The one you used at the med center did because it was calibrated for cyborgs."

Amaryllis thought that over for several moments. "You mean … it's because you … or … uh … Reese fathered it?"

"Reese fathered the child," Dante said without inflection.

Amaryllis' gaze darted to Reese. If possible, his face was more stony than before, but it was the look in his eyes that made it impossible for her to maintain her own gaze. "But … it's normal?"

Dante gave her a look. "So far as I can see. Why would you think otherwise?"

Amaryllis didn't know whether to be relieved or not, but she could see Dante thought she was referring to them. "Because I wasn't born normal," she said stiffly, ashamed to admit it, but unwilling to allow Reese to think that she'd expected it because of what he was. "It's why I have the cybernetic limbs, not because of an accident."

Something flickered in his eyes. Relief? Uncertainty? After a moment, he turned away, moving to the table along the wall. When he returned, he was holding a strange looking object attached to a tiny portable computer. "What is it?"

He shrugged. "A prototype, and a crude one at that. But I think it will serve well enough for our purposes."

Amaryllis was horrified when she discovered that the strange looking probe was supposed to be inserted in her vagina. Reluctantly, she lay back and allowed him to carefully push it inside. He set the tiny computer on her belly and flipped a switch. Amaryllis stared at the screen for a full minute before she realized that the shadowy object she was looking at was the child inside of her. As grainy and blurred as the image was, wonder filled her and so much relief she thought for several moments that she would burst into tears again. She could see two tiny arms and legs. "It's … it's the baby!" she said, uttering a sound midway between a sob and a chuckle. "It looks … perfect!"

Dimly, she was aware that Reese and Cain had moved closer, peering over her head at the image on the screen as it moved its arms and legs, kicking, twisting around.

Abruptly, her heart seemed to stop in her chest. Her mind went blank as she saw an appendage she *knew* shouldn't be there. "What's that?"

Dante frowned. "What?"

"That … that thing. There."

There was a gleam of amusement in Dante's eyes when he looked at her again. "A penis."

"Oh my God!" Amaryllis exclaimed, dismayed. "She's got a penis?"

Cain and Dante burst out laughing and even Reese chuckled. "No, but *he* does," Cain said.

Chapter Thirty

They were *never* going to let her live that down, Amaryllis thought darkly. The first words out of Cain's mouth after the baby's birth were, "My God! She has a penis!"

Naturally, Dante and Reese had thought it was hilarious. She would've hit him with something if she hadn't been so overjoyed to see that the baby was, in fact, absolutely, perfectly beautiful. There was also the fact that she'd been too tired to look for something to throw at him and they all needed a good hit over the head and she certainly didn't feel up to that.

There was a definite advantage to having three doting fathers around, however. Except for feeding the baby and cuddling him from time to time, she rested while they fought over who had to change his diapers.

Despite the fact that Dante was adamant that he could pinpoint the exact moment of the baby's conception, he arrived earlier than expected … and later. He didn't conform to the development of either the human gestation period or the accepted cyborg gestation, which was considerably shorter due to the fact that cyborgs had been developed with rapid cell regeneration to accelerate maturity. By the time Amaryllis' secret was out, however, he'd reached the stage in development for rapid growth. Within a month he'd doubled in size. In the following month, he doubled again, coming into the world at a whopping eight pounds.

Reese was inclined to take full credit for his son's perfection. He was modest enough and thoughtful enough to credit her with it, but she could tell, deep down, he really thought it was all his doing.

They'd been angry with her for weeks after her escapade

that had nearly gotten her killed. Cain hadn't been joking about 'the punishment' and, in fact, it had been far worse than she would ever have thought it would be.

It wasn't just the 'no sex'. She pretty much got the cold shoulder from all three of them, and that went on for weeks, not just 'a week'. She'd begun to think that she could stroll naked in front of them, and wave it at them, and they would ignore it.

By the time they'd begun to unbend a little, Amaryllis had finally realized something important. They truly loved her. They didn't just think they did. They felt it and that was why they were hurt and angry that she hadn't trusted them enough to talk to them about her fears. They couldn't look at her afterwards for weeks without wondering if what she'd told them was true and she really hadn't intended to run away, and they couldn't look at her without remembering how badly she'd scared them when they'd thought they wouldn't be able to save her from her folly.

Convincing them that she loved them just as much in turn was a long, tiring, and thoroughly enjoyable experience for all concerned.

It was a good lesson, and one that made her realize that she *was* home.

The End

Printed in the United States
64641LVS00001B/91-93